CHAPTER ONE

Early 30's lady looking for a relationship. Looking for the following;

1) *Loves socialising*
2) *Funny*
3) *Kind*
4) *Enjoys holidays*

So there, that's my list. That's my dating profile. Keep it simple my mates say. It's easy for them to say when they are all settled down. Well except for Greg, but he's another story that can wait till later.

So, I'm sat at my friend's house, babysitting their children whilst they are out having a nice romantic meal and then no doubt having a few beers after at a local pub. Sounds like my ideal Saturday night to be honest. Don't get me wrong, I love looking after Natalie and Adam's kids, but once I've packed them off to bed it's just me, the TV and a bottle of wine. OK, so it may roll into two bottles, especially if Natalie still feels like a drink and a catch up when she comes back from her night out.

Hey, don't judge me on drinking whilst working! The kids, Tilley (short for Matilda) aged 10 and Flo (short for Florence) aged 12 are great kids. They usually want to spend the night in their rooms playing on their computer or on their phones. But reluctantly, when 'Auntie Emily' comes round, I insist on playing a board game or 2 or baking cakes.

Tilley and Flo are a joy to be around, we have great fun playing Jenga….and I even played fairly and didn't let them win….ok, lets be honest, I was trying my hardest to win. I've actually realised how competitive I am and had to back-down a little when I realised I was doing the 'loser' sign a little too much to Tilley, who at one point I swear I saw a few tears in her eyes when I was prancing around the room with my winning dance parade.

After a few games, when I let Tilley get her own back on her winning victory, I could see they were getting fidgety. So I get them to put their pj's on, brush their teeth and off to bed they went to watch a DVD they had picked. Then it's back to just me.

So let me tell you a little about myself. I'm Emily, early 30's (a true lady never reveals her age). I'm a part-time events manager at a hotel.

The hotel, Elliott Manor is a modest hotel based in Warwickshire, this is where I live. Only 20 minutes' drive, or 30 minutes with the annoying school traffic. 'The Elliott' is a 16th century building with 38 bedrooms and 4 rooms which hosts an array of events. There is also a bar/sitting area which provides meals/food snacks and is mainly used by the guests staying at the hotel.

So, one minute my job can entail organising a baby-shower or an end-of-life celebration to a wedding. No day is ever the same and I absolutely love my job. The hours can be quite stressful, often working non-sociable hours, but at least it gets me out of my house and luckily I have a great team of on-hand babysitters for my daughter, Anna.

Confidential

Its currently January, which is the quietest of months regarding work. With Christmas and New Years celebrations over, everyone wants to hibernate and save some money. The next 3 months are usually quite quiet, but I am grateful of a rest as I worked all over December.

In the summer months I rarely get a Saturday night off. Sometimes I do some work in the day for potential sales, but that's off and on. So it's great to spend time with Tilley and Flo although secretly I would love to be out (but we don't tell Nat this).

So, Anna, daughter, she is 6 years old with an attitude of a 16-year-old. She's the love of my life. Her wild curly brown hair that never seems to look tidy, and her cute dimples on her cheeks makes her the most beautiful little girl (well I am biased). She seems to have settled well in school, with a few friends which seem to change daily. No mention of boyfriends yet – but there's still time. She's just taken up dancing, which she seems to love. Mum here is not so happy. I sit in the kitchen with a group of other dance mums, don't get me wrong, I am certainly not one of these dance mums you see on TV. The way I see it, I welcome that she's off learning how to 'petit-jete' is a bonus. It's unbelievable how many work emails/phone calls I can do within that short window.

So, I just don't have time to sit and be sociable with these mums, they clearly haven't spoken to anyone all day and want to engage in mind-numbing chat about 'who has the best kid'. It's not my kid. I'm not afraid to admit she has her faults, she isn't perfect, but she grew up in my tummy for 8.5 months (the bugger was early), and I love her...faults and all.

Anyway, more importantly let's get back to me. So, I've been single 2 years or so now since separating from Anna's dad, Rob. We share custody of Anna, so Rob will have her most Friday to Sunday nights to allow me to work, and alternative mid-week one night (at his choice). I realise how lucky I am to have every weekend 'off' from Anna, but equally I do tend to work most of the weekend. Rob is more than happy to care for her at the weekends. He moved on fairly quickly and is dating a lovely young lady. His girlfriend, Sarah, has a 2-year-old, Tia who is not involved with her dad. So, Rob seems to be happy to spend his weekend with both the children. He seems very happy with his new life, and I am genuinely very happy for him.

My mad nights of my 20s have slowed down. My mates and I have got older, and my friends are settling down and having kids. Don't get me wrong, I still love to get together with my girls and let our hair down, we just don't roll in at stupid O clock anymore and do a full shift the next day with mascara trails still down our faces !!!

So here's me. Saturday night. Kids in bed. Sipping wine, scanning channels on the TV. Trying not to me feel sorry for myself. And according to Facebook everyone seems to be out.

'Ping'.........ohhhhh how exciting. A POF message. Now it's currently 11.30pm so this could mean 3 things.

1) It's someone who is out on a Saturday evening and is trying their luck
2) It's someone who is at home, kids tucked up in bed and now having some down-time
3) It's someone who has been out on a nice social evening with friends, a few beers and now home alone and catching up on their social profiles

Dating profile named 'Hot-guy' appears with a message simply saying

'Hey, you doing?'

Now, from this message you can assume its number 1, either that or they are a huge Friends fan.......I mean, who calls himself 'hot-guy' and in there profile says they are looking to settle down? Who is seriously that vulnerable to fall for that?

I scroll through 'hot-guys' pictures, and with the look of his six-pack and very limited facial pictures I can guess he probably has the face of a pig (how judgemental am I?), but with that hot body many people would stick some sunglasses on him, lie back and think of England.

I hear the front door opening. Natalie and Adam are back. Natalie comes bursting into the room, full of energy with a bit of a wobble on.

'Hey you, how's the kids?'. (need she ask, of course they are now fast asleep since the last time I looked in on them).

'They're great, fast asleep. How was your night out?'.

Confidential

Whilst Natalie proceeds on telling me about her night out and who she saw, she kicks off her shoes, and plonks herself on the sofa next to me. I can hear Adam clinking in the kitchen (I'm hoping he's happy I've done the washing up for them). Adam appears with a bottle of wine and a glass. So, I'm guessing Natalie is up for another hour of gossip.

'Hey Emily, I'm off to bed. Hope the kids behaved and see you in the morning'. And with that Adam trots off to bed.

Actually, I don't know why I've said 'trots'. Who actually trots anywhere? Isn't that what horses do? I could just imagine me doing the school run, trotting up to the school gates with all the 'school mums' gawping at me. Although thinking about it, isn't there a game where people use those wooden horses you used to have as kids and pretend they are a jockey?. Right, so I've just googled it and it's called 'hobby horsing'…..anyway, without judging, Adam definitely did not trot off to bed with his hobby horse !!!!

Let me tell you about my friendship with Natalie. Nat is my friend since school. I met her at our first year at secondary school and have been friends ever since. She is the complete opposite to looks than me. Whilst I'm fairly short with a few (ok more than a few) additional rolls around the waist, Nat is very tall with zero rolls. I like to think that us curvy ladies have those bubbly personalities to match, but Nat has one of these senses of humours that has me belly laughing and a few wee dribbles after a few too many wines. Nat works as a customer service advisor in a large supermarket, choosing to work part-time so she can ferry the children around on their endless school runs and after-school activities.

Confidential

That's another one 'ferry the children around'. Where does the term 'ferry' come from? It's not like Nat has a boat in her back garden and drags it out for the school runs !! She didn't win Bullseye back in the day and they presented her with a boat that she just drags out to take the kids Brownies along the canal !!

Anyway, Nat met Adam during a social event at her work when she was 20. Adam is head of security at the supermarket. I would love to say their eyes met across a tin of beans, but in reality, I think they were both plonked on the singles table at the work-do and the next thing you know they were exchanging numbers and sweet nothings.

Adam is the opposite to Nat. Don't get me wrong, he can have his humorous moments, but he tends to let Nat take charge and is the laid-back one in the relationship.

'So, now Adam's buggered off, what's the latest with you?' Nat asks.

It appears, that as most of my friends have settled down, they like to live there 'single' life through me. Don't get me wrong, they are all happy being in long-term relationships, but according to them, their life is more 'life numbing, and mine is much more exciting' – if only they knew that what they have is what I really want. Not just want, what I really, really want (admit it, you sang it?)

'Oh I've just had 'hot-guy' message me'. I reply, and with that, Nat steals my phone and proceeds to stroll through his profile. With a few 'mmmmms' I can see she is impressed by the 6-pack, but has she actually noticed his face yet? – I'm guessing that's not what she's concentrating her efforts on.

'Go on Nat, send him a message…..', but before I manage to respond she sends him a 'Hi gorgeous'

Whilst we sit there chewing the fat (oh my god, I'm on a roll – we weren't actually chewing anything, especially not fat), we have a look at the new profiles on the dating site.

'nope, too posh'

'nope, doesn't sound very interesting'

'nope, far too hot (I know my limits)

'nope, has a weird face'

'ping' – message from hot guy.

Nat and I squeal (far too many wines), I open the message, and we squeal even louder and I throw the phone on the floor. And there it was. The famous 'dick-pic'

Delete, delete, delete

CHAPTER TWO

Early 30's lady looking for a relationship. Looking for the following;

1) *Loves socialising*
2) *Funny*
3) *Kind*
4) *Enjoys holidays*
5) *No d---pics*

Waking up from Nat and Adams (I very often sleep over at their house when I'm babysitting or after a few wines), I look around the room. I'm in Tilley's bed, as Tilley and Flo share a bunk bed when I stop round. It's a proper girl's room, pink unicorn bed sheets. Teddy bears thrown all over the floor after it took me 5 minutes to get into bed last night due to the bear collection.

On the one of the walls is bright unicorn wallpaper and theirs a mini chalk board in the corner of the room with scribbles all over it. This room makes me feel all cosy and I'm contemplating staying here for another hour or so, deep in my own thoughts when I hear the kids giggling in the other room. I look round for my jumper to put on over my pjs as its far too early to put on a bra and no-one, especially Adam, does not want to be facing my boobs dangling to my knees first thing in the morning. I grab my jumper and head downstairs and make myself the first, and the best, cuppa of the day.

I scroll through my phone hoping to find the latest cohort of singular men ready to mingle, but it seems to be the same kind of blokes, looking for one thing. I click off and sigh heavily. I know my time will come to finally meet that 'one person', but today it doesn't look like it's going to happen.

I hang around for some toast, a quick catch up with Nat before getting ready for work. Today is one of my favourite events at the hotel, a baby shower. I love it how excited the parents and friends are, with all the interesting games they have spent hours scrolling on the internet for ideas on how to make their baby shower the most fun.

On my way to work I phone my events assistant, Greg to check the balloons have arrived and everything is going as planned.

'Hey Greg, how are you and how's is it going over there?'

'Oh Emily, we have a disaster' Greg is on one I can tell

'The balloons have turned up and there the wrong colour. We didn't want pink, we need blue. One of the caterers has called in sick, probably hungover from the football last night, and I'm running round like a headless chicken, trying to find the catering trays. I'm not sure how I managed to get myself into this job, I'm so over it. I'm quitting. Why does no one know how to present sausage rolls correctly on a plate?. And who the hell decided to order a trifle? A trifle is for Christmas, and Christmas alone. I'm trying to find out if there's sherry in the trifle because I do not want to be giving this to the pregnant lady and be sued. Then I'll lose my job, my flat and my cat. I'll have to live on the streets, and my cat

Confidential

will disown me, and take refugee with the neighbour, who I already know is secretly trying to entice Betty all to herself by giving her little bits of chicken. Don't think I don't know what she doing"

Oh bless him, Greg does tend to exaggerate somewhat.

Meet Greg, my 26-year-old colleague. Although he is my assistant, I do class him more of a friend since he started working with me. Fresh from college at 18, the first day I met him he came bounding into the hotel, dressed in somewhat very bright colours from head to toe with his head held high and an enormous grin and even larger aspirations.

'Pleased to meet you Emily, can I call you Em, or Emmy…no wait, what do your friends call you? I can't wait to start working together and I already know we are going to besties. But before I divulge in all my secrets, I want to set the record straight. I'm a straight talker, I don't mince my words, I'm doing this job for experience. I won't be staying long, as my dream is to become an events manager in the Savoy. But whilst you've got me, I'll work really hard and have a great laugh at the same time'

8 years later and Greg is still here, and his aspirations of working in the Savoy seems to have vanished.

Greg is very tall, with a slim physique. He shaves his hair (although I'm not sure if that's because he's hiding the fact he's receding and doesn't want to admit it). His flamboyant clothes make him standout in a crowd. Although he was devasted when he couldn't wear his favourite pink and orange stripey jacket to work. Unfortunately for Greg, we

Confidential

wear a very dull navy uniform suit. Doesn't do anything for any of our figures, but hey, it saves me spending money on work clothes, and I don't spend ages each day thinking about what I am going to wear. Much to Greg's disgust, he actually looks really smart in his navy suit. However, when out of work Greg seems to make up for the dull-mundane uniform by wearing the most outrageous outfits he can find. He honestly looks like he's constantly going to a fancy dress party. When Greg is not helping me with events he is either working behind the bar, or waiting – whatever he can find to do at the hotel. He's a hard worker and I love working with him.

Once after an end-of-life celebration, we needed cheering up, so we arranged to meet up with Greg and a few other work friends at his local pub. I turned up at the pub and there was Greg, wearing long black and white flared trousers, a blue and yellow waistcoat with a distinctive red shirt underneath. Honestly, with his height and tall legs he looked like he'd just come from the circus. He could have easily passed off as the Stilt performer. I admired his flare and confidence.

'Right Greg, calm down. Its 9.30, the shower isn't until 12.00 we have plenty of time. I'll nip to Celebrations and get the balloons sorted. Whilst I'm there I'll pick up some more catering trays. I'll be there in about an hour. In the meantime, do what you can to help with the catering.

"And Greg" I add "Don't panic – Betty is going nowhere'

I turn off my phone (thank God for Bluetooth in my car) and turn around to head for Celebrations to pick up the balloons and catering trays. Thank God they open on a Sunday morning, I think it's just for emergencies like this.

Celebrations is more of a warehouse, full of anything you need for a party, from decorations, hospitality to fancy dress costumes. I've often thought that if there was a lockdown for 24 hours then this is the place I'd be. Obviously not on my own, but with my mates, and of course a few bottles of wine, it would be so much fun. I can imagine it would be like that film Mannequin when she's stuck in the large store. Or it would be like pretty women, trying on all the outfits, except it would be fancy dress outfits. I remember a while ago, when there was a craze where people used to stay in Ikea overnight. They'd hide in the wardrobes (or somewhere) until security went home. Not sure who came up with that idea, but mine would definitely be stopping overnight in Celebrations.

Next to the warehouse is an entrance to a side shop which only opens at the weekends to the public. The business is family owned and is largely dependent on company orders as opposed to the public shop. I use them quite often as I like to use local suppliers and plus they are great when it comes to emergencies, just like this one.

I enter the shop, and no-one is at the counter (probably slacking – it is a Sunday after all). So I head out and through the warehouse door. Usually this is not allowed, but as I'm a regular I guessed it would be ok (and it was an emergency after all – we don't want to lose Betty to the neighbour).

In the warehouse I can hear a distant sound of some music playing and forklift trucks being operated but I can see no-one around. I start walking towards the stairs that leads to the warehouse offices when Sam appears.

'Hey Emily, let me guess – there's an emergency at the Elliott and Greg is threatening to leave again?'

Sam knows Greg so well. I smile. Sam is the manager of Celebrations. Inherited from his grandparents to his parents and now Sam is taking the reins. He's in his early 30s, average height with a few rolls around the midriff (he has the same problem as me). He has wild curly brown hair that looks like it's never seen a good hairdresser let alone any styling gel.

'Yep, you guessed it. We have the wrong colour balloons for a baby shower we're organising today. Can you help please? We need some to create an arch, then about 6 bunches to go around the room'

Sam immediately sets off to get the balloons. 'Blue ones' I shout, before I end up buying the wrong colour again. Whilst Sam starts blowing up the balloons (not literally, he has a special machine) I head back to the shop and grab some hospitality trays. I also check my phone for any other emergencies Greg may have. I notice I have a POF message from someone called Tim.

I check out his profile;

"Hey, my names Tim. Recently divorced, but looking for someone to settle down with" – tick

"I enjoy socialising" – tick

Confidential

"Going the gym" – tick

"And have a 1 child who is my world" – tick

I look at his photos, a couple of him on holiday at various destinations, the pyramids in Egypt, the Tower of Pisa and a few lovely beaches. He's obviously cut out someone on his photos but all the same – tick

I like the fact he doesn't put pictures of his child – tick

I don't understand why people do that on dating websites. Yes, I know you love you child and want to show them off. But unfortunately, due to the world we currently live in it's a big turn-off for me.

I quickly check out his message;

'Hey, I'm Tim. I thought I would drop you a message as I liked your profile and thought it would be great to have a conversation to see if we have a spark'

Nice message, nothing too seedy – tick.

I decide to reply later – I don't tend to message whilst I'm working – too many distractions.

I suddenly realise that my Mini Cooper may not fit all the balloons in my car. I look panic stricken, but I think Sam has read my mind

'Don't worry Emily, I'll bring them up to you in van. No extra charge, it's part of being a loyal customer'.

Confidential

CHAPTER THREE

Early 30's lady looking for a relationship. Looking for the following;

1) *Loves socialising*
2) *Funny*
3) *Kind*
4) *Enjoys holidays*
5) *No d---pics*
6) *No pictures of your kids on your dating profile*
7) *Drives a car bigger than a mini*

I arrive at the baby shower in plenty of time. The pink balloons hidden in our other room; the new blue balloons put into place curtesy of Sam.

I find Greg sneaking a few sausage rolls in his mouth in the kitchen whilst attempting to butter some bread for sandwiches. He's put his hair net on, even though he has no hair, but I like the effort.

Whilst I'm busy running around doing the last-minute touches, ensuring the gifts and table names are set I think back about when I was pregnant.

I had a great pregnancy, grew extremely round and was really lucky I didn't have any problems. I thought not drinking would be a big test for me, but seeing my tummy grow and then feeling the baby grow inside of me made me not want a single drop. I used to enjoy going out to social events, with Rob and take pleasure ordering a zero-alcohol free beer or cider. I was surprised at how similar they tasted. I loved being able to socialise, rubbing my tummy with pride. I used to think I was the only person pregnant and would be gutted if everyone else turned up to the event pregnant. I wanted to be the special one.

I never had a baby shower; I had a few friends over for some food and a general catch up (I even let them drink wine). There were certainly no presents. Today, the baby showers seem to have gone crazy. And it seems the new thing is the baby reveal. Something which I'm looking into hosting here at the Elliott. This reminds me, I must have a look at different baby reveal items – balloons, poppers (not the illegal ones), cakes etc.

The only grievance I had about being pregnant was that I had no cravings. I was really hoping I'd have a craving for a Macd's and test Rob to see whether he'd go and get me a big mac and nuggets at silly o clock in the morning. I couldn't even pretend I had cravings as I felt too guilty.

At 11.30am the parents and close friends arrive to bring the last-minute games and put a few last-minute pictures up on a poster they'd created. I must admit, the room looks great, and Greg seems to have finally calmed down.

At 12.00pm the guests start arriving including the 'mummy' who looks outstanding in her cream overtight long dress to show off her ever-growing bump. She looks about ready to burst but is radiant and loving the attention.

I greet all the guests and show them the seating plan. There are some overly excited friends, who clearly make the most of the bottles of Prosecco placed on their tables. A few

Confidential

speeches are made, by the mum and her best friend, which are quite touching, and I have a little tear in my eye (I'm a soppy sausage).

Then the games begin, it's the standard, guess the smell on the baby's nappy, pin the safety pin on the baby's nappy, whose the daddy pictures. Clearly someone has googled the standard baby shower games to play.

There's a few of the older relatives who are clearly there for the Buffett, so Greg and I start preparing for the Buffett to be ready. Before even Greg finishes the sentence 'the buffet is open', Auntie Mabel has already grabbed two sandwiches and a slice of quiche.

At around 3.00pm, the elderly relatives (clearly full from the Buffett) start leaving. The friends are searching for any leftover Prosecco on the other tables and are clearly having a great time and not ready to leave.

I let Greg go, as apparently he has a 'hot date' with some guy he met on Tinder last night and has to go and get 'the Buffett smell' off him. I tell him to text me if he needs me, or more importantly to text me to let me know all the gossip.

I manage a 10-minute break whilst the girls are now singing to 'Dancing queen' and sneak out to the kitchen and check my phone.

'Hey Tim. Thank you for your message. I liked your profile, and your holiday pictures look like you have visited some amazing places. I hope you have had a good day so far'

By 5.00pm I am starting to flag, the baby mum has been gone an hour ago, but luckily the friends are now starting the flag as well after singing 'All the single ladies' for the 3rd time. I ring them a taxi, and after many hugs (apparently I am now their new best friend and 'I must' go out for a drink with them), I bundle them into a taxi and off they go.

At 7.00pm I've finally finished cleaning up and checking my calendar for the next few days. It's always quiet in January, with a few parties thrown in and a big wedding planned in February which is taking up a lot of time. I decide the throw in the towel and head home. Again, what exactly does 'throw in the towel mean?' – I'm guessing I should make some elaborate gesture and dramatically throw a towel in the reception area before leaving !!

I head off home, happy in the knowledge that another great party was a success (wow, that sounds like a quote from 'blur')….let me re-sentence….

I head off home, happy in the knowledge that another great party was a success – park life.

I check my dating messages. Nothing from Tim. But I have received a new message from Evan.

'Hey Emily, loving your pictures, loving your profile. I hope you have had a great day even for a Sunday'.

Upon checking out his profile, it seems mediocre, nothing jumping out of me to scream 'avoid, avoid', but equally nothing to say 'message, message, message'. Just seems like a normal person (if there's such a thing anymore).

Evan's profile reads;

'Hey I'm Evan. Looking for someone that I have a general connection with. I work as an accountant which keeps me very busy during the week. In my spare time I enjoy rock climbing, big fan of rock music and I love my 2 cats'

Oh no, not another cat lover I think to myself.

I message back, nothing too sinister, just a general 'Hi, how are you?' that kind of thing and go for a shower to rub that 'Buffett' smell off me

After the full moisturising regime, I make pour myself a glass of wine (the joys of not working on Monday) and look for something easy watching on the TV.

I check my phone again and nothing from Tim or Evan - what it is with these guys who message but then don't message you back? But I do have a new message from Harry who seems pretty interesting from his profile. I respond with the usual chit-chat, and after an hour or so he suggests a call. I've had a few glasses of wine by now (don't judge me, it's my weekend), and so I agree – but no video call

Harry seems ok, we start with the pleasantries, but that's already boring me and making me lose interest (I'm actually polishing whilst we talk) when he suddenly asks;

'Do you believe in Zombies?'

Now suddenly the conversation sparks my interest. Don't get me wrong, I'm no nerdy geek, I just like inquisitive questions that makes me use my mind a bit.

'I can't say I completely rule it out. I've watched loads of zombie programmes. I like to think that if I was snuck in that scenario I would know what to do. What about you?' I ask back.

'Oh, I have a bunker made in my garden shed for that very scenario. Its equipped with canned food, torches, lots of batteries. I have even made weapons should I need to attack'

Oh my word !!!!!!!!!!!!!!!!!!!!

I spit my wine out all over my dining room table I am currently polishing. What the hell do I respond to that ????? Where do we go from here? Do I suddenly pretend that I've got bad signal and make that crackling noise, so it sounds like I'm losing connection? Do I hang up and pretend my phone has gone dead?

So, I decide to do the big yawn trick and tell him that I need to go to bed, something about getting up really early in the morning for my morning swim (I don't swim) and hang up.

Don't get me wrong, I'm all for being prepared. But seriously, I'm surprised he hasn't got ready for WWIII and started making bunkers in his garden. I wonder if you google mapped his location, there would be a moat built around his house.

Confidential

CHAPTER FOUR

Early 30's lady looking for a relationship. Looking for the following;

1) Loves socialising
2) Funny
3) Kind
4) Enjoys holidays
5) No d---pics
6) No pictures of your kids
7) Drives a car bigger than a mini
8) Doesn't believe in Zombies

Monday morning, time to get prepared to have Anna for the week and a busy work schedule. I lie in bed for a good hour more than I should, watching funny videos on my phone of dogs doing funny faces and people burping after drinking too much lemonade.

I drag myself out of my warm cosy bed and start getting ready. It's a comfy day, so I grab some leggings and a hoodie, put on minimal make-up and shove my hair into a ponytail (it's good to have a non-hair-straightener day).

Whilst awaiting for the kettle to boil I check my work emails for any event enquiries that have come in on Sunday. Just an enquiry about a 18th birthday party and a potential visit for a wedding in 2 years' time. I respond whilst making some toast for myself.

Mondays always seem like a weird day for me. Whilst everyone on a Sunday night has the Sunday night blues, I'm usually up for a night out (or dates). Although I keep saying I don't work Mondays I still send the few odd emails, or if we are extra busy I will work……so I always feel a bit lost.

Monday is probably the worst day to have off in terms of booking things, as no-where is open. Limited takeaways when you can't be bothered to cook, no beauty places if you fancied a sneaky sunbed, massage or having your nails done. Actually, scrap this. There's no-where open to indulge yourself, although I do appreciate these businesses do deserve to close on a Monday, these professions work over the weekend – so why not treat themselves to a day off?

I do the most laborious chores of changing my bed sheets, go food shopping for the week, then go to collect Anna from school. She skips out of school, hair all over the place, bag dragging down by her side, but I get a massive hug from her. Then we both skip out of the gates and to my (cannot hold many balloons) car.

I make a lovely dinner of cottage pie, broccoli, peas and gravy followed by some bananas and custard for pudding - Anna's favourite. I put Anna in the bath and sit on the toilet whilst she talks nonsense about her day. After brushing her teeth, we settle in her bed, and I read her a story. This is my favourite time of the day. Anna smells so fresh and clean and loves to hear me read to her. I even put on these terrible American accents, but she laughs anyway. I give her a big kiss and hug and leave her room with her little pink lamp on 'in case of spiders'.

Confidential

I do my daily Joe Wickes you-tube video. I say daily, who am I trying to kid? It's not daily at all, it's not even bi-daily. Ok, so it's more like 2 days a week, but hey, whose counting? I can't believe how much I can puff and pant over a 15-minute exercise. When Joe says '1 minute of burpees', it sounds easy peasy. I mean, it's only 60 seconds, you can't really achieve anything else in 60 seconds. Whilst I'm jumping up and down, with press ups in between I take my mind off it by thinking what you can actually achieve in 60 seconds.

Making a cuppa? – nope

Making toast? – nope

Doing your hair? – nope, unless you want it to look crap

Painting your nails? – nope

Tying up your trainer laces – hold on. I think this can be done.

I drop tools, undo the laces on my trainers. Pause Joe Wicks, and set the timer, 5/4/3/2/1…go…….yep, I did BOTH trainers under 60 seconds……………..boom.

OK, so that's a poor excuse to stop my measly 15 minutes of exercise. But equally, the relevance of proving that things can be done under 60 seconds seemed equally important.

As my mind has wondered somewhat I decide to turn off the video – it only had 4 minutes left anyway. Do I feel cheated? Possibly. Will I get over it? Too right, after 5 minutes I've forgotten all about it. I decide to have a lovely hot shower, moisturise and pop on some fresh PJs and get into bed.

I don't know what it is about getting into a fresh bed, but there's nothing better. I also feel cheated if I haven't had a lovely shower, clean pjs and hair washed for this special occasion (this makes it sound like I only change my sheets on special occasions like birthdays or Christmas, Bar mitzvahs).

The next day its school run day. The day every parent that has to drive their child to school dreads, with all the traffic and the drivers that are late for work and drive like a maniac. No matter how early I leave to go to school there never seems to be any car parking spaces. I don't know who decides to build schools on an estate that is full of houses with limited parking, or that the fact that more houses have been built around the schools, either way, there is never enough parking for us parents. It seems like a daily challenge, fighting every other parent in the same predicament to get 'that' space. I know we should encourage walking with our kids to school, but as most working parents, it's not always possible to do.

So, I have the ever-fighting battle with the car park parents. There always the same parents that seem to get the best car park spaces. I honestly don't know how they do it. Remember 'those parents'?. The ones who are always at the front of the queue for every child event. I once turned up 1 hour early for Anna's first Christmas production, as she was playing the 'star' in the nativity. Even then I somehow seemed to be stuck behind 'them'. I was fuming. I was trying to film Anna for her first starring role and all I had was those flipping heads in the way. They didn't even have extra-large heads or anything, but either way when I was showing family/friends the recording, all I could concentrate was there

Confidential

massive heads in the way. Like a portray of Alien heads, slightly bigger than usual.

Next time I will get there 2 hours earlier. I will arrive earlier than them one day – you mark my words !!!

After the school run, which surprisingly didn't involve in parent road rage, I head back home. As there are no events on I can have a 'work from home' day. This day typically involves responding to enquiries and planning the next month's events. Seems easy but believe me it is not.

February is typically a busy month with Valentines Day. We are currently holding a Valentines 3-course dinner with a Michael Bublé tribute. That usually books up really quickly, so I am busy ensuring this is promoted, checking bookings are going well and start ordering the extra touches.

We usually go all out on the Valentines night. It's not a cheap event, so we don't just do the 3-course meal. I like to add the additional touches to make the night special. The tables are decorated with red tablecloths with little gold heart shaped decorations on each table.

I know these are cliché, but hey, the tables look bare without them. I remember many a time going out on a night out with these stupid decorations, if you lick them they are pretty good at sticking on your face. I've spent many a night after an event going out after with 'hearts/stars' stuck on my forehead. And even more time finding them in my bed in the morning.

Each table has a lovely small vase with some fairy lights inserted inside. Gone are the days are having candles (the risk assessment is far too much)......and who wouldn't want Mr Bublé serenading you with some romantic tunes whilst you're eating your tomato soup/prawn cocktail for starter?

I'd been working with the head chef, Alberto for a while deciding what to incorporate in the 3-course meal. I'm not going to lie, it's getting even more difficult with dietary and allergy requirements, so we must cater for all. But luckily I have a great catering team and head chef, who I know I will come up trumps (and yet again – where has this saying come from? The only trumps I know is another word for 'farts' that I say when Anna is around).

We've also got a Valentines wedding, so extra pressure this month. I call Greg to check in on things. As I have said previously as Greg works as a waiter/bartender/reception when he is not helping me with events, he's on hand to take my calls.

'Hey Grey, how's it going?. How did the date go the other night?'

'OMG, OMG, OMG. My date was A..M...A...ZING. OH Em, you would love him. Are you sitting down for this?'

The thing I love about Greg is that he does love to tell a good story. So whilst he's talking I turn on the kettle, make myself a brew and return back to my seating plan for the Valentines meal. It's a good job I can multitask.

Confidential

'So, we arrange to meet at the new bar in town. Its really nice with wooden bench tables and chairs and funky lights that are made from different house taps. Well anyway, I got there first, and I was really nervous, so I decided to go for a cocktail. The cocktail menu was surreal, so much choice. I have to sample all of these cocktails each time we go out.

I go for Sex on the Beach, which is ironic, because living in the Midlands, we are as far away from the beach you could get, so I know he wouldn't think it was a hidden agenda me ordering that cocktail. So, I'm dressed in my new white skinny jeans and black shirt - thought I'd tone it down abit - and my black cowboy hat. Come on, I couldn't tone it down THAT much and in he walks. Wearing a white shirt and black jeans. We took one look at each other and couldn't stop laughing. We looked like Minstrels. I was just disappointed he didn't have a hat either.

We didn't stop talking all night. He's soooo funny, I think I even did a little wee at one point he was making me laugh that much'

As he finally takes a breath I interject

'I'm so happy it went well for you Greg. So, what happened after the pub? Did you have a sneaky kiss? Are you seeing him again'?

'Well, I really shouldn't spill the beans !! But of course, we had a sneaky kiss before he got in the taxi. He had to go home early as he has to get up really early the next morning for a flight. But I am seeing him on Thursday evening after I've finished my shift. I'm sooo excited, I've got my outfit ready already. I'm thinking of going all-out and going for bell bottom jeans, pink shirt and denim jacket. I'm going 70s baby'

I love how Greg has his outfit ready and reply

'Well, I'm glad you seem to have hit it off. Sorry to change the subject but is there anything I need to know regarding work? Its quiet events wise over the next few weeks, so I don't think I'll need your help until nearing to Valentines. But I'll give you a shout if anything changes. I've got a 70th party Friday early evening, then nothing on Saturday so I might book the evening off. Do you fancy going out for a few drinks Saturday if you're not on a date? I am dog sitting for Becka, but it's no problem going out, just need to go back to hers after'

'Yes of course for Saturday. Let's go to the new bar and we can drink ourselves silly with Tequilla and Cocktails. I've gotta go hunny, customers to deal with. But text me on Saturday'.

'Will do, enjoy your date on Thursday. Bye'

I'm so happy Greg's date went well. Although I know he tends to exaggerate abit, I just hope this one really is as nice as he says he is. Although Greg is still young, he hasn't got the best history when it comes to relationships. He was dating a girl during school and all through college, but finally came out when his then girlfriend finally realised he wasn't actually into women. He's gone from relationship to relationship ever since. Nothing ever lasting more than a month. I'm not sure if it's because Greg is so sweet natured that he falls too hard too quick, and that puts people off. His parents are childhood sweethearts and are still so in love, they are constantly giving each other little kisses and holding hands. So Greg thinks that how all relationships should be, and that's what he so desperately craves for. But at a young age, unfortunately that's not what everyone wants. I know his time will come, he just needs to 'have a little patience' (did anyone sing that in their head or is it just me?).

Whilst I'm working on the Valentines table plan I receive an email from the mother of the bride for Valentines Day wedding.

'Dear Emily,

I am sorry to contact you direct, but I am really concerned about the current wedding seating plan. I have tried talking to Louise, but she doesn't seem to be listening. Can I be clear, that under no circumstances do I want to sit on the same head table as my ex-husband's partner, Elizabeth. As far as I'm concerned, she can be sat outside.

So, can you please ensure Elizabeth Green is NOT on the main table. I would also suggest that Joan Phillips does not sit anywhere Graham Bans as they simply do not get on (that is my Auntie and her brother).

I hope you understand the situation and thank you again.

Kind Regards

Cecila Manners

Mother of the bride'

Confidential

CHAPTER FIVE

Early 30's lady looking for a relationship. Looking for the following;

1) *Loves socialising*
2) *Funny*
3) *Kind*
4) *Enjoys holidays*
5) *No d---pics*
6) *No pictures of your kids*
7) *Drives a car bigger than a mini*
8) *No complicated families*

The next few days seem to mould into one. I do the usual school runs, never finding a car park space. Cooking nice, healthy meals for Anna and myself. I even manage to do a full Joe Wickes video without thinking about what else I can achieve in 60 seconds.

I manage to discuss the table plans with Louise, the bride, and she agrees to discuss the seating plan further with her mum. Joan Philips and Graham Ban are on different tables, at the opposite end of the room.

I've been sending the odd messages, here and there to Tim and Evan (yes they did message back). They both seem nice, but again its early days.

I joined the POF dating web site a few months ago. It wasn't something I was very keen to do, but after spending a few months going out in bars and not really getting anywhere, I realised it was probably the best way of meeting someone. Problem I found is that when I went out with my friends, it was to go out with my friends, not to pick up men. The few times I did get chatted up I felt it wasn't fare on my friends who have relationships and don't want to spend the rest of the evening as a third wheel or having to talk to their friends. So, I thought joining a dating site was the best way forward.

It really does have some positives. For instance, you can check out their photos beforehand. You can chat to them without having to commit to any dates. There's nothing worse than spending all day getting ready for a date and it not being a good fit. When you make an effort into buying a new outfit (please note – I don't do this for every date), making sure your legs are shaved. Not that I'm expecting any 'coming back to mine for coffee', but it must be a psychological thing, having nice shaven legs and matching underwear just makes you feel more confident on a date.

Its abit like try before you buy. However, it does have it negatives. A lot of the photos can be filtered. And it does seem like a lot of males go for the females with the 'good-looking photos' rather than your average Jane (what did Jane ever do wrong)? It seems like a lot of men go to the gym frequently, is looking for someone to settle down with and has kids who are 'their world'. Abit too superficial for my liking.

I've tried really hard to put pictures of me that are not filtered, more natural looking. Don't get me wrong, there not the ones where I've got my double chin out, or I'm sitting down with the over hanged rolls showing, but they are an actual measure of what I actually look like. And my profile, albeit very brief, is exactly what I'm looking for. Its straight to the point, which I think suits my personality. Although I can be very judgemental and can suffer from 'unconscious bias'. I would prefer not to have someone who lives in their parents back bedroom, but equally I do understand that some men have it hard financially when they break up with their partner – especially when there's kids involved. I, however, chose not to date anyone like that. It's just my opinion. I'm not judging.

By Friday I drop Anna off at school and go into work to start setting up the room for the 70th. It's an early event, starting at 5, so hopefully that will mean an early finish for me. The lucky lady who is 70 is a wonderful woman. She's recently widowed, but that isn't stopping her. Edith is so full of life, has a great circle of friends and is loving her retirement. Apparently she has Aerobics on Monday, lunch with her girly friends Tuesday, grandkids Wednesday and Thursday and Aqua Aerobics Friday before spending the afternoon shopping combined with the pub. Now that's the retirement I want.

Edith turns up at 4.00pm, looking very glamours in a bright yellow long-sleeved maxi dress. She had obviously been the hairdressers as her normal long brown hair is tied up beautifully in a high bun with curls hanging down. She looks so elegant I'm very envious and wish I had that figure now, let alone when I'm 70.

Edith's friends and family start arriving, and so I greet them and show them to their tables. When everyone has arrived, the food starts arriving. It's a 3-course meal, a choice of prawn cocktail, tomato soup or pate. Mains are chicken and mushroom pie, roast beef or wellington with all the trimmings. Puddings are either apple pie and crumble, black forest gateaux or cheese and biscuits.

Whilst the teas and coffees are being served Edith makes a very heartwarming speech about her late husband, her family and friends. It makes me feel very warm inside and I find myself heading back to the kitchen to give my mum a quick ring.

'Hey mum, just calling you quickly to see how you and dad are'.

'Hey love, great to hear from you. Yeah we're good, just watching last weeks recording of Strictly as I haven't had chance to watch it yet as I've had to wait for your dad to bugger off out. My favourite dancer is due to do the La Mamba in a minute. He looks so good in his sparkly blue outfit, and you should see his hips. He does things with his hips I could only dream about. Your dad is at the pub with his darts mates, so whilst I've finally got an hours peace I thought I'd watch it before Saturday's live show'.

'I'm glad you're ok mum, I'll have to come and see you and dad soon and bring Anna. Have you managed to sort out how to video call yet?'

My mum and dad live in Bristol. They moved there a few years back to look after my Grandma. Unfortunately my Grandma has passed away now, but my parents made a great social life and decided to stay. So I don't get to see them as much as I want too. Especially with me working shifts and Anna at school.

I've been trying to explain to my mum how to use the video call on WhatsApp, but the couple of times we've tried it I've spent the whole call looking at my mums' chins. So I gave up.

'Not yet love, but Michael from next door says he'll have a look next time we arrange face call or whatever you call it. It would be great if you and Anna could come and see us soon. I miss my little sweet cheeks, that's Anna, not you!.'

'Hey, I've got some time off February half-term, can we come and stay with you for a few days then?'

'That sounds great. Let me know the dates and I'll cancel my plans for that week. We could take Anna to Bristol Zoo; I've heard that's great for kids'

'OK mum sounds like a plan. Send my love to dad and enjoy strictly. I need to get back to work. Love you'

I always feel better after talking to mum. I do miss not seeing her nearly every day, but then when we do get together we always ensure we spend quality time together. Anna and I will look forward to spending a few days with them over February.

I get back to the party, the music seems to have been turned up and Edith and her friends are having a dance to some Beatles tune. I help the waitresses clearing up the tables and ensuring the wine is topped up. At one point, Edith grabs my arm for a dance. I join in, but it's so hard having to dance when your sober and everyone else is a little tipsy. Sober dancing makes you paranoid. You do your usual 'mum' dance, moving from side to side with your feet, one step, two step. Definitely not one for Strictly. My mum would be devasted !!

At about 9.00pm, the party comes to an end. Edith and her friends have decided to carry on partying back at Edith's house, they ask me join, but I decline. I know it would have been lovely, but I'm on a different wavelength to them, and by the time I'm ready to start partying their night would be coming to a close.

After they have gone, I clear up as best I can and leave. Nat has messaged me asking me to go round as Adam is out for the night, so I decide to 'pop' round. When I say 'pop' round, if the wine is open then I'll probably end up staying.

I turn up at Nat's at about 10. Her other friend, Becka is already there. They've clearly been on the wine for a good few hours and are proper slurring and talking rubbish. I decide to stay for 1 and then head off home – just feeling really tired and if I am honest I'm looking forward to my bed.

Tim and I are still messaging. It appears Tim is a Team Manager for an Engineering company. Works long hours during the week, and every other weekend has his son, whose 10. He also has his son twice in the week, which I feel really appealing.

The gym thing he put on profile, may be a little over-exaggerated, as he seems to go the gym as many times as I complete my Joe Wickes workout. He did admit he put that

Confidential

to keep up with his competitors. He seems really amusing and funny. And no d--- pics, which is always an added bonus.

Tim asks if I want to meet up with him. I agree and we decide to meet on Sunday around 6:00pm. I don't want it to be a late one as sods law I'll be working Monday as I have some visits at the Elliott for some potential future bookings.

I can't wait

CHAPTER SIX

Early 30's lady looking for a relationship. Looking for the following;

1) Loves socialising
2) Funny
3) Kind
4) Enjoys holidays
5) No d---pics
6) No pictures of your kids
7) Drives a car bigger than a mini
8) No complicated families
9) Enjoys life
10) No photo filters

Its Saturday morning, I'm lying in bed checking emails and thinking about getting up.

What I would give for someone to bring me a cuppa in bed. I remember when I was little I used to stay round my nans at the weekend and she'd have a tea-maker in her room. She'd set the clock in the morning so I could have a cuppa in bed. It was amazing. I wonder if they still sell them?

I've been messaging Evan a few times. It's very strange, but he seems to message non-stop for a day, and then it all goes quiet for a week. If I was a suspicious lady I would seriously think he was married !!! Perhaps he is, I will tred this one with caution. See how it goes.

Evan does seem funny though – even for an accountant. I bet he'd love to see my work spreadsheets (wow, I should use that as a flirty chat up line), that should get his juices flowing…..ha ha

There are another 3 guys on the scene as well. So there is Will, who has suddenly appeared back on the dating site. We were chatting for ages when I first joined, but nothing further. He then disappeared, so I'm assumed he'd found someone. But he's back again, which I'm happy about as he did seem pretty smart and switched on with his life. He must have saw I am still on the site and started messaging me again.

And then there's Mark, and Mike.

So, let's have a look at who I'm messaging at the minute. It might sound really bad, but I have to make a note of this, so I don't get confused. Last thing I want is to do is say the wrong thing to one of them, like getting their kids sex wrong, or their job.

When I was doing some serial dating a few months back, I even used to make a list of what I wore for each date. I would not want to wear the same outfit twice with the same bloke. And I need to know who I've wore 'that special dress' too – not that I have yet mind, but there is hope.

This serial dating sounds like fun (it certainly made my friends envious), but it certainly isn't. Its hard work. Especially shaving and there's only so many matching underwear a lady owns. Like I said before, not because of that, just wearing nice underwear makes you feel sexy and confident on a date.

So, here's my current list, in no particular order of preference.

Tim;

- Date on Sunday (so keen)
- Recently divorced (so maybe not ready for a relationship yet)
- Isn't a gym freak
- 1 child, 10, has him often
- Has travelled
- Team manager (career minded) – but works long hours
- Is really funny, has me in stiches over random things, so has my personality
- Seems like he's close to his parents
- Spends his nights off going to club quizzes or playing pool with his mates

Hot-Guy;

- Is now blocked

Evan;

- Goes rock climbing (so must be pretty strong)
- Fan of rock music (I love watching live bands – not so keen on rock though)
- Has cats
- Is an accountant (gotta be clever)
- No mention of kids
- Seems off and on with messages

Harry;

- Zombie lover (made my excuses and no longer message)

Will;

- Back on the dating scene (so could mean he really is serious into finding someone and did find someone)
- Gas Engineer (oh, he could service my boiler – no pun intended)
- Has 3 boys, doesn't see them as much as he wants too (I haven't divulged enough into that one)
- Loves films and crime documentaries (a serial killer in the making)

Mark;

- A fireman (oh the innuendos I could have here)
- No kids, but married young for about 10 years
- Doesn't drink as like to keep fit a lot (could be a problem as I am partial to the odd drink – or 3)
- Would be my taxi driver

Mike (not magic)

- 2 teenage girls
- Doesn't seem to have many hobbies
- Estate agent

Wow, looking at the list it doesn't seem so bad. And I promise you I'm not a serial dater anymore. Too complicated. But I'm doing no harm in messaging different people, it's what we all do being on these sites. And I would have no problem telling these guys that should they question it of course.

CHAPTER SEVEN

Early 30's lady looking for a relationship. Looking for the following;

1) *Loves socialising*
2) *Funny*
3) *Kind*
4) *Enjoys holidays*
5) *No d---pics*
6) *No pictures of your kids*
7) *Drives a car bigger than a mini*
8) *No complicated families*
9) *Enjoys life*
10) *No photo filters*
11) *Has a tea-maker*

So, I finally get out of bed. Still in my pjs I do all the house chores. Then I throw on my comfy leggings and jumper, wrap myself up in my big coat, scarf and hat and go food shopping.

I absolutely detest going food shopping. The whole activity to me seems like a difficult task. I do a weekly food shop as I when I'm a home I can spend my lunch breaks prepping the dinners or popping it into a slow cooker.

I have friends that go shopping every other day. Going once a week is bad enough. I try my hardest to ensure Anna gets some variety, luckily she isn't a picky eater. I try and eat healthy as well, but I do tend to sneak the odd 'beige food' in the trolley as well. I'm not superwoman after all.

Confidential

Once I'm back from the dreaded shop, I decide to take an afternoon nap. I absolutely love my naps. I seriously think I should be Spanish, as I'm all up for those siestas they have. How great would that be? A lovely nap every day. They just make me feel so refreshed and I'm gutted when I don't have chance to have one.

Upon waking from my nap, I make a chicken salad, but decide to have a few sneaky pieces of bread with it, you know to line the stomach up for later – well that's my justification for some carbs anyway.

I have a shower and start getting ready for my night out with Greg. I always love my nights out with him, his dating disaster stories crease me.

I head over to Becka's house with my overnight bag and remainder make-up and outfit for tonight. Becka and her husband have gone to a wedding for the night and are staying over in some swanky hotel, so I've agreed to stay over their house to look after the dogs. They've got 2 labradors, who are absolutely gorgeous.

Upon entering the house, I hear Luna and Lala in the kitchen, I immediately drop my bags and open the kitchen door and are greeted with 2 massive balls of fur. They go mad, jumping up and down, twirling round for attention. I give them loads of fusses before opening the patio doors to let them out.

I know Becka through my friend Nat, they used to work together at the supermarket Nat works at with Becka in the clothing line section. Becka has since moved on and has a really successful job in retail. She is doing so well for herself in her career. She is definitely the career-minded one in the group. When we were younger and Nat and I would go out and Becka would sometimes join us. Becka then found her now husband, and stopped going out as much but then I bumped into her at a wedding I was hosting, and we decided to meet back up. Along with our other group of friends we try and meet up at least once a month.

Becka absolutely loves dogs. At one point, she was even thinking of owning a doggy day care in her home, but I think her husband soon talked her out of that one.

Becka lives in a massive house in a village about 20 minutes' drive from mine. She has large bi-folding doors which opens up to a beautiful view of fields. Her dogs have so much room to run around in and it appears she spends a lot of her spare time doing her garden as its amazing. Full of flowers (I would tell you the names – but I have no clue). She has a pond with a massive waterfall that I could sit and listen to all night on a summers evening. Her husband is currently in the process of building one of those rooms in the end of the garden. I think Becka wants it for a gym, but I know her husband is thinking more of a man-cave (I'll let them fight the battle).

Becka is very petite and has amazing long red hair. She always seems to have a new style every time I see her and is always up to date with her fashion.

Whilst the dogs are running around in the garden, I get their dinner ready and finish getting ready myself. I've booked a taxi for 8 so I have plenty of time.

I've decided to wear my faithful black skinny jeans and a nice black and red long-sleeved jumper, which shows great cleavage. Finished with my black heeled boots and my leather jacket. I even take my red fancy scarf which completes the outfit.

I let the dogs back in, and whilst there scoffing their dinner I make sure all the doors are locked and wait for my taxi. I have a vodka and coke whilst waiting, hey would be rude not too.

CHAPTER EIGHT

Early 30's lady looking for a relationship. Looking for the following;

1) Loves socialising
2) Funny
3) Kind
4) Enjoys holidays
5) No d---pics
6) No pictures of your kids
7) Drives a car bigger than a mini
8) No complicated families
9) Enjoys life
10) No photo filters
11) Wouldn't mind if you had pets

I enter the new cocktail bar in town. Greg is right – this place is pretty decent.

The bar seems to have every spirit you can think of. It has pipes that have been decorative placed around the pub. Its painted a dark green but has lots of windows so it seems to have a really light and airy vibe. The tables and chairs are all made of rustic oak, with oak stools at placed at the bar. There's an old juke box in the corner but it seems they are currently playing some light music in the background. It also looks like there's a band being set up in the corner of the pub.

I place myself on a stool, which isn't the most glamourous when your relatively short and take a look at the extensive cocktail list. I decide to order a pint of lager, although the cocktails look great, I need to steady myself as I do have work tomorrow.

''''Ooohhhhhh, excuse me, excuse me, hey babe, how you doing? Hey hunny, how's that sexy husband of your?s'

I recognise the voice. Its Greg, making his grand entrance as usual. He rocks up, dressing quite tame for a change, in a green tweed blazer and light green button up shirt, cream trousers finished with some green doc martins.

We give each other a massive hug and Greg decides to order a Passion fruit martini.

'So, Greg, tell me all about your date with mystery man on Thursday. How did it go?'

'Oh Em, it was even better than the first. We decided to go bowling. Well what do you wear for bowling? I wore the skinniest of jeans, and I was struggling to breath in them, let alone do any strenuous activities.

'After bowling, Ethan decided to book us into crazy golf. OMG, I played so terrible. I was dying to fart all evening cus I made the mistake of having my mums beef stew before we went out, and you know what broccoli does for my bowels. I ended up making my excuses to go to the toilet and spent a good 10 minutes in the bog just letting off wind. It felt amazing. I had to tell Ethan that I wasn't feeling too good (blamed it on my mum's food poisoning). Ethan was so concerned about me. Got me some water and even offered to go the shop for some paracetamol. Bless him, I didn't have the heart to tell him I just had wind'.

'So obviously we couldn't take the date further. Not exactly a great night of passionate sex when I'm farting all through the night'.

Greg talks endlessly about his date, all the details. I don't interrupt apart from ordering 2 long island ice teas and let him continue.

The band starts playing now, it's a 3-piece band, a singer, who is also on main guitar, a drummer and bass player.   They start by playing Stevie Wonder 'Superstitious', so I'm delighted, it's a great choice of a song.

My music taste is very varied. Depends on my mood. When I used to go out every weekend I loved R n B. I also grew up with a cousin who loved House music (not so much a fan), and 90s music such as Blur, Oasis and the Verve.

My mum used to listen to the old classics, Aretha Franklin, Diana Ross and the Supremes and Tina Turner. And my dad, well he loved Frank Sinatra, so I grew up being accustomed to lots of different genres.

A friend of Greg's comes over to have a chat, and we suddenly find ourselves joining Greg's friends at a table. I already know Max and Mai from previously nights out, but there's also Joe (whose very hot looking. He's got a jaw line I can only dream about), Teddy (who appears to be very drunk) and Carla whose celebrating her 28th birthday. They all move up on the benches to make room for us, and before I know it the shots have started. First its Jagger bombs, which are my absolute favourite, then some green thing which is very sour.

I take them graciously and down them even more graciously. The band has stepped up a notch and are playing Bon Jovi, living on a prayer, which the crowd seems to love and are singing loudly at the chorus.

After nipping to the toilet - why is it with going to the toilet when you've had a drink? Once we've broke the seal, us women can spend half our night in the toilet. There always seems to be a queue, and then after you've done your business you spend 5 minutes touching up your hair and makeup, and you can guarantee you can always find someone who wants to either borrow your makeup or has a funny story to tell/drama to discuss. It's never a quick 5-minute toilet break anymore !!

I go to the bar, feeling really tipsy by now. I think I even did a little jig to 'proud Mary' whilst I'm walking to the bar, head bopping away. I try to focus on the cocktail menu and decide on ordering a vodka and coke as its probably less potent than the cocktails currently on offer. I don't know if I'm drunk, but I feel from the other side of the bar there are eyes on me. I look over and realise its Sam from Celebrations waving at me for my attention. When he realises I've finally clicked who it is he comes over

'Hey Sam, fancy seeing you here'.

'I thought the same Emily. My mate is the guitar player in the band, so I thought I'd come along and support them. This new bar is great. Loving the vibe, although I tend to spend my drinking days in the local social club whereas there perception of a good night out is the cheese and biscuits they offer after the darts team have played'

Greg suddenly joins us, gives Sam a massive hug (oh God are we really that drunk?).....and insists Sam joins us, which he does reluctantly.

By now the band has done his last Finale of 'Hey Jude'. We're all up on the made-up dance floor of the pub by now and I'm having a great night dancing away like no one is watching !!

By 12.00am I'm done. I'm tired, drunk and hungry and for the last hour all I've thought about is a dirty kebab wrap with mayo. Greg and his mates are continuing onto Pop World, but I decide to be good and go home. Plus I've got to let the dogs out....(tell me, did you think of the song?).

Luckily the pub is only a 5-minute walk to where Becka lives, so I decide to stagger home. I say my goodbyes and wave Greg and friends off and start walking.

'Hey, are you leaving?. You didn't say goodbye'.

Its Sam, jogging over to me to catch me up

'Sorry Sam, I thought you was with the band, being a groupie and all. I really want a kebab and I'm tired, I have work tomorrow'

'Well I'm also up for a takeaway so I'll walk with you if that's ok?'.

We start walking together, and I start thinking about this greasy kebab. It's all I can think about.

'So' says Sam, 'how's things with you'?

I'm drunk, I'm thinking about nothing else apart from this food I so crave.

'Well, I have a date tomorrow with some guy I met on the dating site. He's really nice'

And before I know it I'm telling Sam all about the dating site and my current dating disasters. I must have whittled on, because before I know it, my order was ready and I said my byes to Sam, pointing to the house I was heading too (within pointing distance).

'Good luck on your date tomorrow' he calls. I think that's what he said. I'm too busy sprinting home with the last power I have to ensure the food doesn't go cold.

I open the door to Beckas and that's when the smell hits me.

Dog poo.

Jesus

It's the last thing I want.

It appears the dogs should have gone outside after eating their dinner. I can't let the poo stay in the kitchen, they'll be walking in it all night and it will be like something from Drop dead Fred 'dog poo, dog poo, smelly smelly dog poo'.

I let the dogs out, pick up the poo and get ready for bed. I turn on the TV to some mindless channel that I have no intention of watching, it's just some background noise whilst I'm eating.

I warm up my kebab and finally take a bite. MMMM this tastes so good, but hey, what the hell is that? In my nails I see brown bits. Turns out I was drunker than I thought. I had dog shit in my nails and was eating my kebab !!! I was retching at the thought.

I make sure the dogs are back in the kitchen, house locked up, thoroughly clean my nails and go to sleep. Putting my kebab in the bin

Gutted

CHAPTER NINE

Early 30's lady looking for a relationship. Looking for the following;

1) *Loves socialising*
2) *Funny*
3) *Kind*
4) *Enjoys holidays*
5) *No d---pics*
6) *No pictures of your kids*
7) *Drives a car bigger than a mini*
8) *No complicated families*
9) *Enjoys life*
10) *No photo filters*
11) *Wouldn't mind if you had pets – but need to be house-trained*

OMG, my head is banging. I can hear the dogs barking letting me know they want to be let out to go the toilet – don't want to make the same mistake as last night

I get out of bed and head my way downstairs. Open the doors and put the kettle on. As I open the bin, I see my kebab sitting there and remember about the shit in my fingernails. I check my nails, luckily they are clean. But equally it may have put me off for kebabs all my life (I say 'may'...who am I trying to kid? – it won't last long).

I take some paracetamol and check my phone.

Greg messaged at 3 in the morning to tell me he loved me and hoped my kebab was nice (if only he knew).

Confidential

I got a message from Tim to say he's looking forward to our date tonight (oh crap, I'm going to have to go sober). Then the usual chit chat from Evan, Mark and Mike.

Evan telling me about his eventful weekend going to a rock concert and ending up spending a night in a single bed with 2 of his other mates as they got too drunk to drive home and there were no other rooms at any of the hotels nearby.

Mark telling me he'd been working Saturday night, and luckily no fires, just a house call from an elderly lady whose smoke alarm kept going off. Bless her, the poor thing didn't realise it was beeping as the batteries had run out.

Mike saying he went to the cinema but the film was very boring he fell to sleep during the second half and only woke up when all the lights turned back on after the film.

I decide to reply later. I need to sort myself out first. I have work in 2 hours and need to do something to wake myself up.

An hour and half later, I'm showered and off to work. I haven't got any events today, but I have a Christening next Sunday that I need to check all the orders have been placed and will arrive on time. The Valentine's meal is pretty much arranged. The wedding next month has a few more requests, including a firework display in the evening. That's no problem at all, but it'll mean I'll have to stay and play H&S representative and fire marshal. I dig out the previous Risk Assessment and update to reflect on the event.

I also start checking the calendar so I can plan some tribute evenings. I've also decided to host a Bottomless Brunch Day,

Confidential

as they seem to be popular at the minute. And I've been researching Bongo Bingo, as that seems like a fun event as well. I also update our web-site to say that we can host 'Baby Gender Reveals' parties.

I get so carried away with all the planning I suddenly realise the time. Its 5.00pm, so I have 45 minutes to get ready. Thankfully I've already had a shower and brought my outfit and makeup to work. But even still, I hate rushing to get ready.

I decide to keep it pretty casual, some dark denim jeans, a long-sleeved see-through blouse thing (with a vest top underneath)….no one wants to be seeing my midriff rolls in my see-through top. I wear a nice black jacket and my patent stiletto heels (ok, so the heels make it smart/casual).

I head off at 5.50pm and realise I haven't eaten. I decide not to have a drink tonight and drive instead. It will be easier that way, and plus if I haven't eaten I'll get drunk too easy, and I need to make a good impression on my date.

We have decided to meet at a bar just outside of my town. Tim lives about 40 minutes from me, so we found a place that was halfway for both of us. It also means it's unlikely we'll bump into anyone we know so we don't have to do the awkward introductions.

I walk in the pub a little nervous, especially being sober. It's a very old-fashioned pub. With green and brown leather chairs and a lovely fireplace which is roaring away. It's so cosy. There's only a handful of people in here, a couple of lads playing pool in one area, and 2 blokes having a game of darts.

There's a few 'old boys' dotted around, probably gloating they haven't got work in the morning. I can't wait to retire and join in on the Sunday drinking, very much gloating and not having the Sunday night blues, although Monday it is technically my day-off – but that doesn't always happen.

I see Tim at the bar, he's dressed in a checked blue and green shirt, denim jeans and some black boots. He's got black hair that is nicely styled . He's shorter than I thought he would be, probably about 5'5, but that doesn't bother me as I'm only 5'2 anyway. So, with my heels we are about the same height.

Tim orders me half a shandy and a pint of Guinness for him. Then we sit down near the fire and start chatting. I notice Tim seems a little tipsy, it turns out he's had a few drinks this afternoon watching the football with his mates. The more he talks the more visible it gets. It's probably more noticeable because I am sober, is this how I sound when I've had a couple?

I order Tim another Guinness and I have an orange J20. He does seem nice, but he's getting drunker by the minute. Tim then wants to go outside for a cigarette, I told him I'd join him after I've been the toilet. The fire was starting to get a bit too much so the fresh air would be nice.

I text my friend's group to tell them I'm safe and no need for the 'emergency' call just yet.

I go outside to join Tim and find him sitting on the bench table. Not the bench seat, but the table, with his feet placed on the seat, one elbow placed precariously on his knee, other hand on hip, cigarette in his mouth. He looked like he was practising to be a model. He looked like a dickhead, and I was so glad no one else was around to see it.

When I walked over he continued with his Calvin Klein pose, what a prat. He'd snuck to the bar and looks like he'd had a few shots whilst I was in was in the toilet !!!!

About half an hour later, I made my excuses and left. Tim said he'd had a great evening and was looking forward to seeing me again. I however was in two-mind. I mean he was drunk and might be even nicer if sober. However, turning up at a date half-cut isn't exactly the best impression.

By the time I'd got home I had 15 messages and 2 missed calls from Tim. Wanting….no, correction, begging to see me again. Oh dear lord. I do the right thing and tell him I don't think it would work but was lovely to meet him.

Confidential

CHAPTER TEN

Early 30's lady looking for a relationship. Looking for the following;

1) *Loves socialising*
2) *Funny*
3) *Kind*
4) *Enjoys holidays*
5) *No d---pics*
6) *No pictures of your kids*
7) *Drives a car bigger than a mini*
8) *No complicated families*
9) *Enjoys life*
10) *No photo filters*
11) *Wouldn't mind if you had pets – but need to be house-trained*
12) *Doesn't turn up on a first date drunk*

Auurrgghh, Monday mornings. Everyone's worst nightmare (apart from those retired people, or those weird people that live for their jobs)....

I go into work where I have scheduled 3 appointments. 2 potential weddings and another 30th party (did I say I don't normally work on Mondays?) – it appears I may have lied !!

The tours go pretty well, and fingers crossed I've secured at least 2 of the bookings, although they did say they had other venues to view. I do try and price the events fairly, but the cost of organising a wedding and all the additional 'fancy' bits

Confidential

soon add up. I try to gauge the customers budget, by the way they look (I know that sounds so judgemental), the way they sound when I mention 'oh we can add chair covers/an orchestra/canapes upon arrival'. I appreciate how much weddings can cost, but unfortunately the additional touches do cost – and I do need to make a profit to justify my job.

I update our website with some event photos we recently took of our newly refurbished function/conference room and add an new bottomless brunch event in the calendar.

I pick Anna up from school and I decide to take her to the Harvester for dinner. Because quite frankly I can't be bothered to cook.

Anna is her ever talkative self and approached the subject of swimming lessons. For some reason, Anna has always been nervous going swimming. Her dad and I have always tried to encourage her to go, even took Tilley and Flo to entice her, but she seemed so unsure.

Luckily, she seems to have got over that now so I call the swimming baths for availability, and they advise they would get back to me.

The next few weeks passed by uneventful. The bottomless brunch is completely full already, so I decide to book another more. I've also scheduled a bingo bongo in March. The valentines evening and wedding at the end of the month is all on schedule.

So, back to my dating update. I'm still messaging Evan on and off. We have now exchanged numbers and we've had a few

Confidential

phone calls, but it's still hit and miss with his exchange of conversations. No mention of a date and I'm still very wary, but when we talk we seem to get on really well.

I did end up meeting with Mark (the fireman) one evening when I had a night off from Anna. I decided to drive closer to his as he had an early shift the next day. No word of a lie, it took me over an hour to get to the pub we were meeting, full of horrible country lanes that only 1 car could fit. I was praying there wouldn't be another car coming the other way, especially driving in the dark.

By the time I arrived, I was in a pretty bad mood with the horrible drive. And then I spent most of the evening listening to Mark talk about his bad dating experiences. One where his 'date' turned up, let him buy her a drink, she downed it and then made her excuses and left. So naturally I joined in and spoke about my dating disasters (so at least I thought we had 'something' in common).

After an hour, I was envious of that woman. He was soooo boring. Had nothing else to talk about apart from his work. He hadn't really done anything in his life, hadn't been on holiday in like forever, and spent his evenings (when not at work) sitting in his room all evening. He didn't seem to have any friends (although that is quite sad) and had no hobbies.

Let's just say, I was bored shitless.

So, after 2 hours I made my excuses and took the long drive home. I was fuming I'd wasted my evening on this boring bugger, and now my petrol light came on which added to my annoyance.

When I got home I'd got a message from Mark to say 'he'd had a great night, and we should do it again some time'

My response 'thank you for a lovely night. However, I don't think we're quite suited. I wish you all the best and good luck on the dating site'

Then he turned nasty

'Well, you won't have any luck with your dating disasters. There is clearly something wrong you with to have that many dates, and it just so happens they all have something wrong with them. Perhaps you should reflect and think its not actually them, and perhaps it's actually you !!!'

I sighed, obviously doesn't take rejection very well. Although maybe he is right. I don't have much luck, and perhaps it is me? I give my head a wobble. No its not me, I know what I want in regards to a partner. And I know I am normal (ish). Sod Mark making me even think that. I know my worth !!!

So now I am left with Evan (texts on and off/married and no sign of a date), Will (think he is a serial dater) and Magic Mike (do not know enough about him yet).

What choices I have !!!!!!

Confidential

CHAPTER ELEVEN

~~Early~~ Mid-30's lady looking for a relationship. Looking for the following;

1) Loves socialising (and actually does socialise)
2) Funny
3) Kind
4) Enjoys holidays (and actually goes on holiday)
5) No d---pics
6) No pictures of your kids
7) Drives a car bigger than a mini
8) No complicated families
9) Enjoys life
10) No photo filters
11) Wouldn't mind if you had pets – but need to be house-trained
12) Doesn't turn up drunk on a first date

I take Anna for her first swimming lesson. The local leisure centre has managed to book her a place at 4. I can just about manage collecting her from school, drive to the centre, have a quick after-school snack. That should give her enough time for the snack to digest before getting ready into her swimming costume (don't want her getting cramps in the pool after her snack – if that's even a real thing – its what my mum used to tell me anyway!!).

I could tell she was nervous, but luckily I manged to get a seat right by the window so she could just about see me if I waved frantically. The instructor was very patient with her, and she

Confidential

even managed to pretend to swim a little bit – her arms and legs flapping everywhere.

After her lesson, I meet her at the side of the pool, wrap her in a big fluffy towel and take her to the showers. I've decided it's easier that she washes and showers now and then it's done for the evening, rather than drying her and then showering her later on this evening. It's a win-win.

After queuing for the showers for what seemed like forever, I mean how long does it take 5/6-year-olds to shower?, we finally get a cubicle. It's not like this kids have got to shave their bits or anything !!!

I help dress Anna into her 'bear' onesie and pop her into her wellies. Don't judge me, the swimming pool floors are always wet, and the onesie will only get wet at the bottom with her normal shoes. So, I copied one of the other mums I overheard saying at the school gates one and brought some wellies for her – it's a game-changer for sure.

We head off home, singing along to 'frozen' (yep, I know all the words). I make a lasagne (does anybody fancy a lasagne – sorry 'Oasis'), and we sit at the kitchen table eating lasagne, salad and garlic bread, listening to Anna talking gibberish – but God I love that kid !!

After reading Anna a book about farm animals, I kiss her goodnight and have a quick shower myself, pop on my pjs and start flicking through Netflix for some 'girly trash' to watch.

Confidential

I respond to Will's and Evan's messages and have a quick look on the dating site for any newbies. Nothing new, but it has only been 2 days since I last looked.

At around 9.00pm I hear a faint tap on my front door, and I immediately panic. Who could it be at this time of the night? Well a burglar wouldn't knock, the police would though so my immediate reaction is 'oh god, whose dead?'

My mobile suddenly starts vibrating, its Greg

'Open the door, its bloody freezing out here' Greg says when I answer my mobile.

I open the door and Greg barges in, half a bottle of wine in his hand. He's dressed up to the nines, even for a mid-week and I immediately know something is not right.

'Oh Em, it's been a disaster. I thought me and Ethan were getting on so well'.

He plonks himself down on the settee whilst I get him a wine glass. It's obvious he's here for a while. I make myself a cup of tea and settle myself down on the sofa chair.

'Well, Ethan invited me round tonight. He was cooking me dinner, a lovely pea risotto with salad and a tiger loaf - he didn't bake it himself.

We had a lovely dinner, laughing, talking about random stuff. We'd already drank 2 bottles of wine by then, and I was looking forward to snuggling up on the sofa and watching a film. I'd seen a great film on Netflix, a true story about some chap saving loads of Jewish kids in the War. Anyway the

Confidential

doorbell rang. Ethan didn't seem surprised at this and off he went to answer the door.

A few minutes later, another two blokes walked in, who Ethan introduced as his friends that he'd met at a Gay bar over Birmingham. The two blokes seemed nice, quite chatty and a little tipsy. They'd brought some vodka with them, so it was clear they hadn't just 'popped' in for 5 minutes'

Id finished my cuppa by now and was contemplating helping Greg finish off his wine but thought against it. Not on a school night and with Anna in bed.

'Ok Greg, nothing too strange so far. Perhaps Ethan just forgot to tell you they were coming over? Or perhaps he didn't want to freak you out by letting you know he was going to introduce you to his friends?. You know what you're like, and you'd be worrying about giving off the wrong impression all week. Really you should be happy Ethan wanted you to meet his friends' I reply, trying to sound encouraging.

'Em, well that is what I was thinking BUT, let me finish…..Oh, have you got any more wine or anything containing a percentage please? I need it to calm my thoughts'.

I pop into the kitchen and grab a cheap bottle of plonk I save for emergencies when I have completely run out. I pour Greg another glass and pour myself a pint of squash (go me).

Greg continues 'So, Ethan starts playing some songs on his Alexia. Some 60s disco tunes where he encourages us all to get up dancing. Of course, I am the first one up and start doing my John Travolta moves. I can see Ethan's friends are

Confidential

perhaps a little more than friends and start dancing together. Then Marvin Gaye comes on, and suddenly Ethan and one of the friends are grinding up each other, proper dirty dancing. I laugh at this point as I thought they were just being silly'.

Suddenly this has my attention, sod the squash, I am pouring myself a drink, even though it tastes like vinegar.

'Anyway, all of a sudden the two of them start kissing. Like Ethan and his mate. Proper full-on tongues and everything. I didn't know what to do with myself. I mean, it's not like we were an official item, but not in front of my face. Then a few seconds later the other bloke comes over to me and starts trying to kiss me. I look over at Ethan and he smiles and signals to me that it is ok'.

'So I am all confused at this point and start backing off'.

'Ethan then suddenly says 'its ok Greg, we are all friends here. Why don't you come and join in with me and Simon?'.

'I looked shocked and then he says 'Oh come on Greg, you don't seem like the shy type to me. I thought this would be your thing.'

'I suddenly realise Ethan was a swinger. I know he'd mentioned having couples round his house, but I just assumed he liked entertaining....but not this type of entertaining'

By now, I can see Greg is getting quite upset and I go and sit next to him with my arm around his shoulder for comfort.

'Oh Em, I really liked him. How could I be so naïve?'.

I let Greg have a cry. I am lost for words on how I can comfort him. Instead, I go and get a spare duvet and pillow, stick on an old film and let him cry on my lap until he nods off.

CHAPTER TWELVE

~~Early~~ Mid-30's lady looking for a relationship. Looking for the following;

1) *Loves socialising (and actually does socialise)*
2) *Funny*
3) *Kind*
4) *Enjoys holidays (and actually goes on holiday)*
5) *No d---pics*
6) *No pictures of your kids*
7) *Drives a car bigger than a mini*
8) *No complicated families*
9) *Enjoys life*
10) *No photo filters*
11) *Wouldn't mind if you had pets – but need to be house-trained*
12) *Doesn't turn up on a first date drunk*
13) *NOT into swinging*

The next day its Valentines day, the day every singleton dreads. I feel so sorry for Greg, I know he had booked a lovely meal at a fine dining restaurant for him and Ethan once he had finished work. I also know he would have had to pay an up-front deposit. My only hope is that he finds someone he could take instead. Of course I would offer, but this is a really busy day at work for me.

Anna wakes Greg up by jumping all over him. Anna loves Greg, and the feeling is mutual. I make Greg a cup of coffee, get ready for work and Anna for school.

Confidential

I have to force Anna in the car as she now refuses to go to school now she knows her 'bestie Greg' is around. She was equally upset to find out he'd had a sleepover without me waking her up and telling her.

I drop Greg off home on my way to do the school run. He looks terrible, but unfortunately I need his help tonight else I would let him have a night off.

Once I have dropped them both off (Anna still not happy with me), I quickly call Rob to check he is still ok to collect Anna from school. Although its not typically my night to have Anna, I still wanted to make sure he was ok to have her as its Valentines night after all.

'Emily, with a toddler, it's not like I have any other plans on the most romantic night of the evening. And besides, Anna and I are going to have our own romantic meal of our own – spaghetti hoops, nuggets and chips'.

As I am laughing I quickly say 'enjoy your romantic evening, I owe you one. Her PE kit is in her bag, make sure you take it out after school else it will sit in her bag all over the weekend and be all creased'. And hang up

Right, now back to work to get creative.

When I arrive at the Elliott there is lots of activity going on. Chefs busy creating their master pieces for tonight's dinner. The tablecloths and chair covers are already being done. Glasses are being polished and the drinks being stocked up well in the fridges.

I grab my table plan and start re-organising the table and chairs accordingly. The balloons and table decorations have arrived curtesy of Celebrations and they look wonderful (mental note – must thank Sam for his wonderful job).

I check the food is in full preparation and grab myself a quick sandwich. That's the bonus of working in a hotel that serves food, there is always something I can make to eat. The best days are when the Chiefs are trying out new menus and we all get a taster-session. The food is so delicious.

Mr Buble and team arrive and start setting up their equipment.

A table is laid out in the entrance to the suite which has a selection of wines and orange juice to choose from upon arrival. Another mental note - I must remember to take them out of the fridge an hour before the first set arrive.

We have couples arriving at various times, first one to arrive at 6.00pm and then in 30 minutes intervals until 8.00pm. Everyone has pre-ordered, but you can guarantee someone always changes their mind and asks to swap. I have made a note of what everyone has ordered as well, as I can bet people have forgotten.

Luckily Greg has been busy, so his mind has not gone onto overdrive. Greg was meant to finish work at 7.30pm so he could go for his meal, but to keep his mind off things he has decided to stay and help work behind the bar in our lounge area, and it appears some couples have popped in just for a drink. So the bar staff are thankful for the extra help.

Greg working over has done me a favour really as it saves me worry about him all evening.

The evening goes so well, apart from the odd dietary requirement that someone forgot to mention, or the odd glass having a 'smear' I think we did pretty well.

It was so lovely to see the mixed array of people of all ages. Some young couples (far too young to settle down), some elderly couples (I played a guessing game as to whether they had been married for years, or whether they were widows and trying to find a spark again), or your couples who were clearly using tonight to have a night off from the kids and not having to cook.

I was sad to see there was no proposals this year, as I remember fondly there was 2 the year before (both said yes). But equally, both couples were annoyed their night was outshone by the other couple being proposed to on the same night – but what did they expect, it's meant to be the most romantic day of the year.

By 10.00pm we are finally done, and I suggest going for a quick drink to the pub with Greg to try and cheer him up.

'OK Em, we'll go. But I am not going to the swanky cocktail place, it will be full of lovey dovey couples. Can we go somewhere where we are highly unlikely to meet romantic couples?'

CHAPTER THIRTEEN

~~Early~~ Mid-30's lady looking for a relationship. Looking for the following;

1) Loves socialising (and actually does socialise)
2) Funny
3) Kind
4) Enjoys holidays (and actually goes on holiday)
5) No d---pics
6) No pictures of your kids
7) Drives a car bigger than a mini
8) No complicated families
9) Enjoys life
10) No photo filters
11) Wouldn't mind if you had pets – but need to be house-trained
12) Doesn't turn up on a first date drunk
13) NOT into swinging
14) Celebrates Valentines night

Greg and I decide to head off to an old working men's club. It's bound to not have 'those couples' in there. A few other singletons from work decide to meet us there after they have finished their shift.

We walk into the club, it's not very busy at all which is a relief. A couple of locals sat at the bar, 1 reading doing a crossword puzzle, the other talking to the owner working behind the bar.

There looks like to be a pool match on between the club and another local club. There are some stale sandwiches sitting in

Confidential

the corner for the pool players, and some pork pies and crisps. The catering is very different to what was just served at the Elliott. But hey, I am not knocking it, this food was probably free – whereas let's not discuss how much the 3-course Valentines meal was!!

Greg and I take a seat on the very many seats that were available. There is some music playing quietly in the background. I look at Greg, and I can see how low how he is feeling. He must be sad, as he has not even bothered changing out of his work uniform. Luckily for me, I always have a spare pair of clothes at work for these occasions. Just black jeans, and t-shirt and cardigan to keep me warm and my black suede, flat boots.

Suddenly there is an up-roar from the pool table. It appears the home team has won, and the pool captain shouts, 'shots on me' (well, I do not want to sound unreasonably, but there is only about 20 people max in the club).

Next thing we know, the pool captain comes over with a Sourz Apple. Greg takes two (after asking permission) and I (obviously) very gracelessly take one.

Suddenly the atmosphere seems to change. The away team are leaving now, but the music is suddenly turned up and the party tunes begin, starting with 'Hey baby, oh ah, I wanna know, if you'll be my girl'. It appears, tonight was the finals and the home team won – so no wonder it was 'shots all round'

I decide to try and cheer Greg up abit and stick a pound in the jukebox. I was trying to remember whether there were any songs relating to 'swinging' that I could avoid when suddenly Sam walks over.

'Happy Valentines Emily' and gives me an unexpected hug. He is obviously drunk.

'Hey Sam, are you in the pool team? I didn't know you played'. Responding to the awkward hug

At this point, Greg, delighted to see a friendly face, comes bounding over and gives Sam a massive hug (thank god for Greg). Without going too far off track – what exactly does the term 'bounding' mean? Where has that say originated from?

Sam takes us over to meet his pool team members. I can't remember their names at all, something like Craig, Skippy (I think), Alan, Jules and Greeny (who knows).

By now a couple from work have arrived, Lacey and Samantha – our waitresses, and Alberto, the Chef.

Someone turns up with more shots. Out of curtesy I take one (taking one for the team and all that).

Then someone decides for us all to go night clubbing. Well why not? If my work mates are going I have nothing better to do apart from going home and seeing all the loved up couples on facebook.

In our town there are two places that open till after 12. There's the nightclub which I avoid as I'm far too old. Its dark and dingy, your feet stick to the floor and full of young people. And plus I have no idea of the music they play – which makes me feel even older.

The other place is Pop-world, which is equally bad with sticky floors but at least they play better music and its usually a mixed clientele. As its Valentines night I was surprised at how busy it was, obviously single people like me not wanting to waste a night out or drink themselves silly at home alone.

I order drinks for my work mates, Lacey and Samantha opt for a bottle of wine (apparently they are on the pull). Alberto has a pint of lager (his wife is away on business), and Greg decides to go for a Rum and Coke. I go for a Vodka and coke, no wine tonight – it gets me far too drunk.

Greg helps me with the drinks and join all the others on the dance floor who are currently dancing to Shaggy 'It wasn't me'. We put all the handbags in the middle of our crowd and dance around our bags, taking it in turns to do silly dancing, I've never laughed so much in ages.

After about an hour of non-stop dancing I go and sit down with Greg. Samantha and Lacey are being chatted up by the pool team lot and loving the attention. After about 10 minutes Sam comes over to join us. By now, Greg is in full swing (excuse the pun) telling Sam about his swinging disaster. Luckily Greg was finding it funny at this point and was exaggerating the story even more, and the more he drank, the more bits he added which was hilarious.

I nip to the toilet, whilst walking I'm checking my phone and clearly not looking where I am going and bump into someone.

'I'm so sorry, I wasn't looking where I was going'. I look up to see a really tall man which mousy brown hair that is gelled upwards. I recognise him but can't think for the life of me where from.

'No problem' mystery man says and off he goes.

I do my business in the toilet, checking my hair and re-doing my lipstick racking my brains where I know mystery man from then realise I think its Mike from POF.

I head out of the toilets, hoping to see him again but can't see him anywhere. I go back to Greg and Sam and on my way I see Mike again. He looks up and smiles

'It's Emily isn't it? I'm Mike'.

'Hey Mike, I thought it was you. How are you? What are you doing here on a Valentines night?'.

And that was how the remainder of my night went, talking to Mike all night. Turns out he had gone on a date but didn't seem to go very well as they went out for a meal, and she kept talking with her mouth full of food. He had me in stitches when he told me that his date was eating chocolate cake for pudding and some chocolate even landed on his face. He was not impressed. Then to finish him off she still continued to talk with chocolate teeth.

I was in hysterics. He was so charming and funny. He got me another drink, and I brought one back (equal rights and all that). At one point I did go over to Greg and Sam to tell them I was talking to Mike. I pointed Mike out to them, and Greg was all 'oooohhhhhhh's and arrrrrrrrrr's', but Sam didn't seem impressed, not sure why, but I shrugged it off.

At the end of the night Mike walked me to a taxi and before I got in we had a sneaky kiss. It was a lovely kiss, and I jumped (not literally) into the taxi after promising me he'd message me tomorrow and arrange a proper date. Mike even paid for my taxi which I thought was really sweet.

I was on cloud 9. It turned out my Valentines night wasn't so bad after all !!

CHAPTER FOURTEEN

~~Early~~ Mid-30's lady looking for a relationship. Looking for the following;

1) Loves socialising (and actually does socialise)
2) Funny
3) Kind
4) Enjoys holidays (and actually goes on holiday)
5) No d---pics
6) No pictures of your kids
7) Drives a car bigger than a mini
8) No complicated families
9) Enjoys life
10) No photo filters
11) Wouldn't mind if you had pets – but need to be house-trained
12) Doesn't turn up on a first date drunk
13) NOT into swinging
14) Celebrates Valentines night
15) Does not talk with their mouth full

Next day I wake up to a text from Mike to say he had a lovely evening and would love to arrange to see me again. He asked me for his change from the taxi (a joke). I tell him I'll let him know when I am next free and of course he can have his change.

I head off into work with a massive smile on my face, and Greg notices it as soon as I walk in the Elliott.

'And what did you get up to last night – you left without saying goodbye, was Emily up to no good?' Greg asks with a mischievous grin.

'Actually no, although I do not kiss and tell, I got a taxi on my own thank you very much. But we are going to see each other again. He seems really nice and has great hair.

'Fair play to you Emily, and yes I agree, I did notice his hair. If only he batted for the other team' He laughs

We start tidying up the remainder bits of the Valentines dinner and salvage anything we can use until next year. Greg is also helping behind the bar and waiting on for the lunches.

I arrange a few more appointments for some potential further bookings, a christening, 18th birthday party and another wedding.

The Bongo Bingo event really seems to be taking off, with tickets already being sold. I've also decided to hold an children's Easter party. It doesn't seem too difficult to organise, I could arrange an easter egg hunt in the garden, have someone dress up as the Easter bunny (well volunteered Greg), and throw in a few party games. I can organise a buffet for both the adults and the kids. And maybe even look at a face painter. I am sure Anna would love it. And hopefully the adults will buy drinks at the bar.

Tomorrow I have a christening party which is all going to plan, and I make a start re-arranging the tables back into groups as opposed to the couple tables we had last night. I have changed the tablecloths from red to a lovely white colour. It's a buffet and no wine on the table or on arrival. It's also free seating, so I just ensure there is a table placed near the front door so that any cards and presents can be placed there.

We do have guest in a wheelchair, so I have to make sure the tables are not placed too closely together to allow easy access to the toilets etc.

I finish off and head off home. I'm absolutely shattered from Valentines night and decide to have a lovely nap. Mike has been texting me which has been making me smile all day.

I've also had a few messages from Evan and Will. Obviously I respond as its far too soon to put all my eggs in 1 basket.

After my nap I take a quick shower and get a lovely photo of Anna and her dad having a romantic dinner spaghetti hoops and nuggets with a candle at their dining table. They even do the Lady and the Tramp moment when eating the spaghetti. Its so cute.

I'm off to Nat's house for a girly night tonight. So that means even more wine and some dinner, she has sent Adam off at the pub. Becka comes and picks me up and she will leave her car at Nat's. I would usually stay over, but I really fancy my own bed tonight, and plus I do want an early-ish night as I have the christening tomorrow.

In Beckas car is also our friend Rachel who is joining us for the evening. Rachel is a massage therapist. She also has 4 kids (triples aged 3 and a 14-year-old) and lives with her husband who also works full time as a Car Mechanic. They also have about 6 guinea pigs, 2 cats and 3 rabbits. I honestly do not know how Rachel copes, she's an absolute warrior.

We arrive at Nat's and the girls are already dressed in their cute pj's watching The Little Mermaid in the living room whilst Nat is in the kitchen busy cooking dinner. It smells like she's doing us a curry…..yummy as I am starving. There is also our other friend, Kerry, already in the kitchen helping out Nat. Kerry only lives 2 minutes' walk from Nat's, and she met Nat as her girl is the same year at school as Tilley. Kerry is abit of a gym freak and I'm very envious of her nice, toned stomach and her non-bingo wings. She's definitely the more sensible one out of us 3, and always ensures we get home ok after a night out.

Becka and Rachel go into the kitchen to get the wine and chat to Nat, and I sit down with the girls for abit. After 10 minutes of briefly chatting about school, drama lessons and favourite Disney movies, I can see they are far more engrossed in watching the Seagull 'the witch is watching the which' as opposed to talking to me (so much for being their favourite Auntie Em), so I join Nat, Rachel, Kerry and Becka in the kitchen.

Nat's house has a massive kitchen/dinner which is perfect for parties and hosting. She has a lovely oak table which is laid out already for our dinner. The kids have already eaten so it's just us 5 (and saving some for Adam because he is bound to be hungry when he gets back from the pub).

We sit down to eat the curry whilst catching up over the last few weeks. Becka has applied for a new job as Buyer in a very large Corporate Firm, and her and her husband are

Confidential

currently fighting over the colour scheme to go into the new gym/man's cave. Nat has decided to take up jogging so was telling us about her progress on this Couch to 5k plan she is doing, and Rachel is just surviving each day as it goes. She was telling us about her attempt at her and husband having a romantic valentines meal, but as soon as they sat down to eat all 3 of the triplets started crying and by the time they managed to settle them the dinner had gone cold and was ruined. So they ended up ordering a Just Eat and was more than happy having a chicken chow mein and pork balls. She is very grateful to have a night off as she is drinking her wine very quickly.

Kerry starts telling us about how her husband surprised her with some beautiful earings, although they had promised not to buy each other presents. And now he is giving her the guilty treatment and keeps dropping hints that he received nothing. She is having non of it though and says its his own fault for not sticking by the rules.

Tilley and Flo have gone to bed by now, and I start telling them the story about Greg and Ethan.

This immediately raises their interest, and Nat starts researching swingers websites. We find one and Nat decides to invent a profile. We all gather round her laptop and start looking at other couples. We were surprised as they all looked completely normal - what did we expect that they had 3 heads of something? Then we come across a couple we knew. OMG............we have a right nosey at them. I would never have thought it. We will never look at them the same again !!

Confidential

We are quite tipsy by now, and Nat decides to set up the Wii and puts on a Michael Jackson just-dance. Rachel is more than happy as she's been complaining at how much weight she's put on since having the triplets. I don't think she has put hardly anything on, and she did have triplets after all. She looks great to me.

We have such a laugh having a dance, I am absolutely hopeless. Becka seems to pick up the dance moves really quickly; it must have been due to her being a dancer when she was younger. And Kerry is like a trojan and doesn't even break a sweat. However, she does try to sing louder than me, but I am having none of it – I am MJ's greatest fan after all.

At around 11.00pm I kiss my girlies goodnight, make the usual promises of not leaving it too long next time to arrange another catch up and get a taxi home. I am shattered, and I really need a shower again – who knew how much I could sweat after dancing at home. Next time I'll take a sports bra.

CHAPTER FIFTEEN

~~Early~~ Mid-30's lady looking for a relationship. Looking for the following;

1) Loves socialising (and actually does socialise)
2) Funny
3) Kind
4) Enjoys holidays (and actually goes on holiday)
5) No d---pics
6) No pictures of your kids
7) Drives a car bigger than a mini
8) No complicated families
9) Enjoys life
10) No photo filters
11) Wouldn't mind if you had pets – but need to be house-trained
12) Doesn't turn up on a first date drunk
13) NOT into swinging
14) Celebrates Valentines night
15) Does not talk with their mouth full
16) Can challenge me to just-dance but isn't that good

Next day I wake up to loads of messages from the girly group chat. There're some great pictures of all together, and some videos of us dancing. There's one of Rachel fast asleep, bless her.

I didn't hear from Mike all evening, although Will had messaged saying it's about time we met up for a date and did I fancy going the cinema. I agree to meet up that evening as it's the only chance I'll have over the next few weeks.

I head off to work to finish off the final touches for the Christening. They are due to arrive at 12, but luckily everything is in place after yesterday.

Whilst I'm waiting for them to arrive, I start transferring the buffet food onto the table. I'm still smiling at the swingers website we went on. I must remember to tell Greg when I see him next week.

The guests start arriving including the very proud grandparents and even prouder parents. The baby, Charlotte whose 3 months, looks so cute in her christening gown. It reminds me of Anna's christening.

Although I am not religious I wanted to get Anna christened as that's something my Nannan would have wanted. Nat and Kerry were godparents as well as Robs brother and best friend. We had the ceremony at a local church where my parents got married and then had a small party at our house. Just a few friends and family came, but it was a lovely day. Anna was 6 months and was just started to bum-shuffle, yes she bum shuffled rather than crawled. I hired a bouncy castle in the garden for all the other kids and Rob did a BBQ. Anna's dress was filthy at the end of the party, but it was worth it.

Whilst the guest are eating I update my event spreadsheet of upcoming events, its looking quite healthy already which I am happy about and check on anything outstanding for next week's wedding. It's the biggest wedding I have ever organised, with 200 guests expected in the day and a further 150 in the evening. Although our function room doesn't actually hold that many guests, we are using another room adjacent to our biggest function room. The brides mum insisted on having the event at the Elliott due to a family tradition. It has actually worked out quite well as we have put the elderly friends/relatives in the smaller room which will be quieter for them due to the band and disco being in the bigger room. The hotels rooms are completely full of the wedding guests, so everyone will be really busy.

They are also getting married here at the Elliott, which we have only just recently introduced. Most couples decide to get married elsewhere and then come here for the party. But as this is such a big event we decided to arrange for a license to arrange the ceremony here, so hopefully that we grow the business – not that we are struggling at all. But I am so career minded and my ambition is for the Elliott to be constantly busy and the 'place to be'. It's just something else we can offer.

This wedding really is the big trail for me. It is the biggest event I have organised so far in my career. But I have been planning this for over a year now, and plus I have managed to purchase most of my items from Celebrations, which must be making Sam happy (big bonus for their team – you're welcome). The only thing Sam could not help me with is the Doves the bride has requested, which is to be let off after they make their vows. It's the main thing I am dreading, as this is certainly nothing I have ever done before – but I do like a challenge.

After work, I have a quick shower and change ready for my date at the cinema. I decide to wear a nice brown suede skirt and tights, with my little brown boots, black jumper and I have just purchased a lovely brown fur coat which perfectly complements the outfit, especially as it seems so cold outside.

We have arranged to meet at a bar at 7.00pm next to the cinema so we can have a chat before we actually watch a film which starts at 8. That's the problem with a cinema date, you don't actually get chance to talk. But I am more than happy to go to the cinema rather than the pub – dare I say it, but I really need to lay off the drink abit.

I arrive on time, and there is currently no sign of Will. I order a lemonade and decide to sit at the bar so I can see him arrive. I am a little bit nervous, not sure why. Probably because

   a) I am sober
   b) I have been messaging Will off and on for ages, so I have high expectations
   c) This skirt seems to be a little tighter around the midriff since when I first brought it

By 7.30 no sign of Will. I have messaged him but no response. I wonder if he is caught up in traffic and cannot text whilst driving.

By 7.45 I try calling him, but it goes straight to voicemail. I tell him I am going to head into the cinema and order the tickets and wait for him in there. Although the film is meant to start at 8, it is usually 8.15 by the time they have finished with the ads and trailers.

At 8.30 still no sign of Will. I do not know what to do, shall I just go in and watch the film just in case he does show? I try texting and ringing him again, but still goes straight to voicemail.

At 8.45 I decide to give up and go home. What a waste of an evening. At least I can take this skirt off which is proper digging into my belly. I even have the marks to prove it.

I get my pj's on, do my moisturising regime which I seem to have neglected the past few weeks and give Becka a call. Her chap usually goes to his mates on a Saturday for a few hours, so I know she is typically at home. She cannot believe I have been stood up and tells me to send him a voicemail giving him a load of abuse ! I won't do that as I am sober – if I was drunk then it may be a different story.

We have a laugh reminiscing about last night and then hang up. Promising to catch up soon and for me to message her if Will decides to contact me and what his excuses are. I check my phone, and still nothing from Will. In fact nothing from Will, Evan or Mike.

Where am I going wrong?

CHAPTER SIXTEEN

~~Early~~ Mid-30's lady looking for a relationship. Looking for the following;

1) Loves socialising (and actually does socialise)
2) Funny
3) Kind
4) Enjoys holidays (and actually goes on holiday)
5) No d---pics
6) No pictures of your kids
7) Drives a car bigger than a mini
8) No complicated families
9) Enjoys life
10) No photo filters
11) Wouldn't mind if you had pets – but need to be house-trained
12) Doesn't turn up on a first date drunk
13) NOT into swinging
14) Celebrates Valentines night
15) Does not talk with their mouth full
16) Can challenge me to just-dance but is not that good
17) Actually turns up for a date

So the ever optimistic I wake up and check my phone thinking I will have a very apologetic message from Will with a believable excuse. But nothing.

I work from home today and manage to get the odd sneaky house chore in in-between emails.

I have decided to come off the dating site for now. I am not in the mood to meet any more prats and be set up for more disappointments. But I still keep my ever-growing list going. It reminds me of what I want (what I really really want) – girl power.

At 3.15pm I collect Anna from school. I love picking her up on a Monday when I have not seen her all weekend. I do get the guilty feeling that I am missing out on spending quality time with her, so that's why I will value our week off together for February half term. I will try and cram in as much as possible. It will also be important for her to spend some quality time with her grandparents as she does not see them as much as I would like.

Before we head off home I nip into Celebrations to check out their current array of Easter Bunny costumes. I thought it would be ideal for Anna to come along, as she no longer believes in the Easter Bunny and would be a great judge of character to see what costume look realistic. I certainly do not want to order a costume that looks like something from an Easter Bunny horror movie – you can just imagine all the kids running round the garden at the party, screaming in terror.

When I arrive at celebrations Edith, Sam's mum, is sitting in reception doing some work on her computer. Edith is lovely, should be retired by now but clearly is reluctant to give the business up completely.

When I explain what I am after we go into the warehouse and have a look at the costumes. It is really difficult to decipher the good from the bad ones, so Anna and Edith convince me to do a try-on. This is not how I envisaged my pretty woman debut would look.

Confidential

After the second costume try on I cannot believe how hot these costumes are (as in 'warm', not like Jessica-Rabbit'). I decide to make an extra effort and do a little silly dance when I come out of the toiles from getting changed.

Anna and Edith are laughing their heads off when Sam appears and starts laughing at my dance. When I take off my head part I take a bow, and suddenly Sam's face changes. He is no longer laughing and seems a little annoyed and walks off. After my third try-on thankfully we decide on a costume which will not scare the kids away (just like my mums tosh – Peter Kay – only kidding, my mum doesn't have a tosh).

Edith shouts over to Sam to sort out the booking with me whilst she kindly takes Anna to look at the frozen costumes they have available.

I go over to reception and begin the booking process. I explain to Sam that I am hiring the easter bunny costume as I am organising an Easter party at the Elliott. I also decide to take this as an opportunity to see if it my imagine or does he seem very weird around me.

Yes, I am definitely right, Sam is acting very professional and abit cold. I understand we are not exactly friends, but I was only dancing with him only the other night. Perhaps he just wants to keep it professional. Sod that, I need to ask.

'Sam, is everything ok with you?'

'Yes sorry Emily, everything is fine. Perhaps I am just abit stressed with work – taking over my grandparents business is a lot of pressure to keep up with their standards. But I want

Confidential

to change things, I want to expand, but my parents seem to be holding me back'.

"Anyway, how is the dating going?" Sam suddenly asks

I hesitantly reply 'I must imagine that it's hard, trying to expand your wings but having some blockers. I am sure if you spoke to them and explained your ideas they may be open to it"

"On the dating side, well I went for a date last night and the bugger didn't even show. How rude is that? But I am planning on a date with Mike, you know, the guy I introduced you to on Friday night?'

'Mmm yes about that.....' – Sam responds.

Before I get chance to ask Anna comes bouncing in.

'Mummy, I have been dressing up as Anna from Frozen, I looked so pretty. You missed it, but that lady has taken some photos of me'

Anna suddenly goes shy when she sees Sam. Luckily Sam picks up on this and goes over to her, bending down so he is at her height.

'Hey, are you Anna? Are you really Anna from frozen? I am Sam. I work here and I know your mummy. Would you like a lollipop?'

Anna giggles and nervously says 'Yes please'.

Sam retreats a magic jar of lollipops and offers this to Anna to take one. She picks one and gives it to me to take the cellophane off. I do this why finishing off the work details with Sam. Thank him for the lolly and head out

'Bye Anna from Frozen' yells Sams

'Bye Sam. Fank you for the lolly' Anna yells back.

Anna gets in the car, and I help her with the seat belt which she hasn't quite got to grips with yet. As I go to get in the driver's seat I see Sam come over.

'I'm sorry Emily, but please do not date Mike again. I promised myself I would not get involved, but it is too wrong. He has a long-term girlfriend. I am sorry'

And he walks away with me standing there with my mouth wide-open, for once speechless.

I quickly regain composure and drive home where I spend the night helping Anna with her spelling homework, doing dinner of sausage/mash/veg and gravy, bath and reading some books.

After Anna has settled down to bed I do another you-tube 10-minute boxing work-out. I figured I would let out my stress by boxing into mid-air thinking of a particular person.

I call Greg to tell him what has happened and have a good catch up whilst I am ironing. Best thing is Greg doesn't even seem surprised, although he promised me he did not know.

I am debating on what to do next. Thing is, I do not even know Sam that well. Is he sure? Is that the right person, he was drunk after all? Could he have made a mistake? What if they have split up since we started messaging?

Confidential

There is only way to find out.

I message Mike

'Hey Mike. How are you?'

After about an hour I get a response

'Hey yourself. I have been thinking about you a lot. How are you?'

'Sorry Mike, but I have got ask, and please do not take offence – but do you have girlfriend?'.

Message is deleted………………………………….You are blocked

Well that answers that one then.

CHAPTER SEVENTEEN

~~Early~~ Mid-30's lady looking for a relationship. Looking for the following;

1) Loves socialising (and actually does socialise)
2) Funny
3) Kind
4) Enjoys holidays (and actually goes on holiday)
5) No d---pics
6) No pictures of your kids
7) Drives a car bigger than a mini
8) No complicated families
9) Enjoys life
10) No photo filters
11) Wouldn't mind if you had pets – but need to be house-trained
12) Doesn't turn up on a first date drunk
13) NOT into swinging
14) Celebrates Valentines night
15) Does not talk with their mouth full
16) Can challenge me to just-dance but is not that good
17) Actually turns up for a date
18) IS NOT IN A RELATIONSHIP

The next few days I am really busy ensuring everything is in place for the wedding and the following week whilst I take annual leave.

We do not have any bookings next week apart from an Afternoon Tea party but that is booked for the Sunday, and I come back on Friday. I have managed to re-schedule any viewings for the week after I return. I will still have to check my emails whilst I am away, but that won't be a problem.

Will messages me 2 days later after he stood me up, apologises profusely and comes up with an excuse that his phone was broken, and he contemplated turning up at the cinema to wait for me, but he couldn't remember what time we were meant to be meeting. I thought it was a bit of a poor excuse, and he could have made more of an effort than that. I don't agree to meet up yet, he can grovel a little bit more.

Evan too has stepped up his game and has been messaging me abit more. We continue to exchang the odd phone call during his lunch break, but it was always abit rushed as I was at work as well.

The day of the big wedding finally comes around. Luckily we did not have an event on the night before, so I spent Friday arranging all the seating plans. The colour scheme is gold, so the chairs are covered in white with a lovely gold stash decorated into a bow.

The tablecloths are white, with a beautiful gold runner across the table. Each table place has a main plate and side plate trimmed in gold. The napkins are black with gold napkin holders placed delicately onto each main plate. I even managed to source gold cutlery and wine glasses with a gold trim to compliment the table even further. The name place settings are black with beautiful gold calligraphy named on them. The favours are matching black bags tied with a gold ribbon. Even the children have their own special favours with bigger black and gold bags and inside there are lots of activities to keep them occupied, colouring, crayons, bubbles, sweets, orange/apple juice and a disposable camera.

In the centre of each table are mid-height, elegant sparkly black vases with gold painted flowers inside each vase. As the tables are round I am conscious that table centre pieces can block the guests views from each other, so these vases are perfect.

In the quieter room I have an array of tables in the back of the room. I have placed the Guest book with some gold pens for the guests to use. I also have a post-box for any cards they receive.

The table plan is a large black board with gold printed cards and matching calligraphy writing of the guest names. The board is decorated in gold painted flowers which is the same as the centre piece decorations.

Celebrations arrive with 150 black and gold balloons which are being hung in a net over the dance floor ready to be let off after the newlyweds first dance. I was hoping that Sam would drop off the balloons so I could thank him for the heads up on Mike, but disappointedly he sends two other members of staff. Maybe he is avoiding me.

Greg informs me that the cake has arrived which is placed in the kitchen's fridge. The kitchen staff seem very busy, preparing as much of the 3-course menu they can in advance.

The guests are due to arrive in the next hour and I must admit the party rooms looks amazing. The band has turned up and are busy setting up ready to play later on in the evening.

I have already gone to visit the bride a number of times today, checking she has everything she needs. She and her bridesmaids are excitedly getting ready wearing matching silk dressing gowns. 2 little girls around Anna's age are having some snacks, I can only assume they are the flower girls.

Greg and some of the other staff have been busy getting the ceremony room ready. With 200 guests arriving it is abit of a squeeze, with a quite a narrow aisle to allow for extra chairs. But the room looks brilliant. We have used the covered chairs from the bigger venue and the aim is after the ceremony the guests can be taken into the smaller room for an arrival drink and we can quickly move all the chairs and flowers into the larger venue. It's going to be a rush job, and I have as many staff on hand to help me.

The photographer is here, and I have already agreed I can use some of the photos for the website, he is clicking away and I am trying my hardest not to be in the photos. The registrar arrived earlier, and he is currently with the bride. The pair of doves are also here, currently situated in a beautiful wicker cage hung on an ornate stand which Greg is currently decorating with flowers. It has been arranged that after the ceremony the handler will take the cage outside for the release as it is a little too cold now.

After all this running around I feel it's best to go and change to a fresh blouse, as it's going to be a long day. I touch up my make-up, tidy up my hair and whilst I check on the kitchen preparations I grab a water. I seem to be so busy that sometimes I forget to drink, so I am making a conscious effort to try and remember.

The guests start arriving by now and Greg and I hand out the order of service. The groom and best man are here, the groom looking very nervous.

I go and check on the bride, she is currently having a glass of champagne with her dad and bridesmaids. Her dad looks so extremely proud. The flower girls look so cute with their cream dresses and little gold flowers in their hair.

The bride's dress is absolutely stunning. It's an A-line satin white dress, with ¾ length lace sleeves. The lace continues all around the top half of the dress complimented with a brush train.

I get the text from Greg to say everyone has arrived and they are ready. I help the bride from the bridal suite to the ceremony entrance, and the flower girls and bridesmaids walk down the aisle. I have allowed the flower girls to scatter some gold and black paper petals (I have promised the cleaner I will help with the tidying up after).

Then the bride starts to walk down the aisle with her dad proudly guiding her by the arm. A beautiful classical song is playing gently in the background – I do not know the song, but the music and the ambience is just so romantic I am trying really hard to hide the tears from flowing. Greg has beaten me to it and has tears streaming down his face.

CHAPTER EIGHTEEN

~~Early~~ Mid-30's lady looking for a relationship. Looking for the following;

1) Loves socialising (and actually does socialise)
2) Funny
3) Kind
4) Enjoys holidays (and actually goes on holiday)
5) No d---pics
6) No pictures of your kids
7) Drives a car bigger than a mini
8) No complicated families
9) Enjoys life
10) No photo filters
11) Wouldn't mind if you had pets – but need to be house-trained
12) Doesn't turn up on a first date drunk
13) NOT into swinging
14) Celebrates Valentines night
15) Does not talk with their mouth full
16) Can challenge me to just-dance but is not that good
17) Actually turns up for a date
18) IS NOT IN A RELATIONSHIP
19) Sympathises when I cry at weddings

After the ceremony, which I think had everyone in tears in the end, a handful of guests head outside to watch the release of the Doves. Some of the elderly guests decide to stay inside, probably choosing to stay in the warm.

Confidential

I usher these guests into the smaller room for a drink whilst our available staff start the laborious task of transferring the chairs and flowers into the main room. By the time the photos including the dove release are done and everyone has managed to get a drink the main room is ready, which is lucky as it was getting abit of a squeeze with everyone in the smaller room.

I make an announcement, to firstly celebrate the newlyweds and everyone can now start making their way to their seats. I help a few of the guests find where they are located, and once everyone is seated the starters are being served. I notice someone trying to invent a place at the head table, but the father of the bride gently takes her away. I can vaguely make out him saying to her 'I am sorry love, but I already told you, you were not to be seated on the main table. It is what Louise requested and she is the bride. So will you please, just for today, sit where you have been placed'.

I realise this must be Elizabeth, the stepmother. Following the email from the mother of the bride in which she insisted she would not be sitting on the head table. Looks like the mother got her wishes. That reminds me, I must go and see if Joan and Graham look happy, I remembered to place them as far away as I possibly could. The seating arrangements was a logistical nightmare to organise.

Suddenly I remember the cake still in the fridge……oh crap. I quickly go into the kitchen which is full of chaos and the waiting staff coming in and out. I locate the cake, and without too many people noticing I manage to put it on the table next to the post-box and gifts.

Confidential

After the meal has been served and all the dishes have been taken away the speeches start. I only manage to hear the best man's speech which was an hilarious story about the groom going to Benidorm for his stag and getting dragged up on stage by Sticky Vicky and, well, let's just say, he will not look at table tennis balls the same again !!!!

Whilst the band is setting up I go outside for a break and some fresh air to cool down. All this running around is giving me abit of a dab on. There's a few of the wedding party outside, some parents letting their kids have a run around, others having a cigarette. A man in his 40s saunters over to me. He's wearing a dark blue suit with some expensive looking brown shoes. He introduces himself as Aaron and compliments me on how great the wedding is going so far.

We stand chatting, Aaron telling me he is one of the grooms friends that he's known since University. He confirmed he was there when they went to Benidorm on the stag-do. He asked how I got into this line of work and whether I enjoy it. I tell him in more detail about my job, but not too much, don't want to over-excite the bloke !!

After about 10 minutes I make my excuses as I really needed to get back to work.

My god, Aaron looked great in a suit. I wonder if he looks as good with it off (Emily – enough of those rude thoughts – I am working). But still, what a suit !!!

I head into the main room and ask the couple to make way to the dance floor for their first dance. They have picked an Ed Sheeran song, and after a minutes a few other couples join

Confidential

them on the dance floor. After the song has finished we release the balloons, hopefully we have managed to capture some great photos.

The band then starts with 'Valerie' which really gets the party started. I start doing some clearing up, moving the gifts and presents out of the way to make room for the buffet. They are having lots of different pizzas and chicken nugget and chips for the children. Just before the evening food has been served we all head outside to set off the firework display. I brought in a professional service to organise this, so one less thing for me to stress about.

The couple have decided not to do the traditional cake cutting but have asked if it can be used as a desert option. I have also got some nice boxes should some decide to take some home instead.

I catch Aaron watching me a few times, trying to catch my eye. It doesn't look like he's brought a partner with him – so no girlfriend in sight – tick.

I start tidying up the last bits and see Aaron going over to the elderly lady in the wheelchair and starts taking her outside. Just as he leaves, he pauses, then turns back around and heads over to me.

'I am sorry if I seem a little direct, but I am taking my Grandma home now as she is tired and wants to draw the curtains. Ha ha, I love Peter Kay. Anyway, I'm mumbling. But may I have your number please? – that's if you are not in a relationship? I really hope you are not'.

I nod at Aaron and Greg suddenly appears out of nowhere with a gold pen and a post-it note (god save Greg). I write my number down; confirm I am most definitely single and hope he contacts me.

And off he goes, wheeling his Grandma out to get settled. It might be against the rules to flirt whilst I'm working, but hey, it was worth it.

Wow, just wow – I think I do a little wee I am so excited.

CHAPTER NINETEEN

~~Early~~ Mid-30's lady looking for a relationship. Looking for the following;

1) *Loves socialising (and actually does socialise)*
2) *Funny*
3) *Kind*
4) *Enjoys holidays (and actually goes on holiday)*
5) *No d---pics*
6) *No pictures of your kids*
7) *Drives a car bigger than a mini*
8) *No complicated families*
9) *Enjoys life*
10) *No photo filters*
11) *Wouldn't mind if you had pets – but need to be house-trained*
12) *Doesn't turn up on a first date drunk*
13) *NOT into swinging*
14) *Celebrates Valentines night*
15) *Does not talk with their mouth full*
16) *Can challenge me to just-dance but is not that good*
17) *Actually turns up for a date*
18) *IS NOT IN A RELATIONSHIP*
19) *Sympathises when I cry at weddings*
20) *Looks great in a suit*

I don't manage a lie-in the next day as I decide to travel to my parents earlier. I finish packing mine and Anna's bits and bobs and go and collect Anna. She is so excited to go and see her Nanna and Grandad.

Confidential

We head off to Bristol, it takes just over 2 hours to get to Bristol centre, and then my parents live another 10 minutes from there. The traffic is quite kind, and we arrive at my parents at 14.00pm. I made a little picnic for the car journey which I was grateful for as it helped to keep me awake and kept Anna entertained.

My parents house is a small 2-bedroom terrace. When you walk through the front door it goes straight into the front room which was converted into a bedroom for my Grandma when she came to live with them. It seems they have now reverted it back to a dining room. The living room holds two 2-seater sofas (one is my mums; one is my dad's) and a small coffee table in the middle of the room.

As its 2-bedrooms, Anna will be going into the second bedroom and I'll be either sharing her bed, or mum has got an airbed that I could put next to Anna's bed.

My mum opens the doors and gives us both a big hug. Dads gone to the pub for his Sunday afternoon session. I can smell something nice cooking in the kitchen and mum confirms she's making us a beef Sunday dinner. MMMM lovely.

Mum gets Anna's toys out and she decides to start making us necklaces and bracelets from her bead set. I sit with mum, and we have a catch up over a coffee.

Dad comes home and later we all sit around the table for a lovely roast dinner followed my apple pie. I am absolutely stuffed at this point and wish I had worn my comfy leggings as these jeans are proper sticking in me.

Confidential

After Anna and I have had a bath, I settle Anna down to bed. I let her watch a film in bed before she drops off. I know she is absolutely shattered as she'd been out with her Rob's family all day on Saturday, so I knew she wouldn't be long before she admits defeat.

Mum puts on an A&E documentary and I am happy just to chill with my parents for abit. After about an hour dad decides to go to bed to watch a film and mum puts on Strictly extra. Whilst this is on I finally check my phone.

Will has messaged asking if I have forgiven him yet and whether I would like to go out for a drink when I get back from my mini break. I tell him I'd think about it, he is not getting away with it that easily.

I have a message from Evan telling me to enjoy my few days off and he hoped the wedding was a great success. It was really nice he remembered. I wonder if we were more in the friends zone, as the messages were never flirty, funny yes, but never flirty. And his messages were very sporadic and definitely no hint of a date.

Mum asked me how my dating is going. I fill her in. She does worry about me, and just wants me to settle down and find the love of my life. I don't think mum realises how difficult it is in these modern days. Mum and dad have been in love for like forever, and although they are not all lovey dovey and soppy, I know they are still in love.

Mum doesn't understand dating web sites either. She is old fashioned in that way and thinks you should meet someone the old way, like going to the weekly 'dance'. If only it was that simple, times are now very different. Getting a divorce in my parents day was frowned upon and so, despite any troubles they would work out their differences and make it work.

Unfortunately it seems to easy now to divorce, again who am I to judge?

I return back to focus on strictly, and wow, these professional dancers are amazing. And they are so fit, no fat on them whatsoever. Perhaps that is what hobby I should take up. Learn some ballroom dancing. I remember taking Anna to Blackpool tower and inside they have a ballroom. We nipped in and watched the dancers, honestly I could have stayed and watched them all day.

A few years ago, Kerry and I decided to go on a 6-week Jive dancing course. It was such a good laugh; the only problem was as Kerry and I were partners one of us had to learn the dance as the male role. As Kerry is a lot fitter than me and would be so much better doing the twirls I took one for the team and learnt the male side.

Now this is where the issue lies, whenever I go to do the jive, I can only do the male part, or when I do try the twirling I end up getting confused and playing the lead role and showing the man what to do !!! Not that I have the opportunity to Jive very often, but still you never know this skill may become useful one day – not sure how, perhaps when I am a professional in Strictly myself. Ha Ha

I decide on an early night, I haven't had chance to blow up the airbed, so I decide to take my chances and share a bed with Anna. It's a Queen's size bed, so hopefully we will have enough room. We are going to the Zoo tomorrow, so mum is making up some sandwiches and snacks to take with us. I kiss her goodnight and head off to bed.

Before I go to sleep I decide that when I retire I am going to take up ballroom/salsa dancing lessons. But I refuse to play the male part again.

CHAPTER TWENTY

~~Early~~ Mid-30's lady looking for a relationship. Looking for the following;

1) *Loves socialising (and actually does socialise)*
2) *Funny*
3) *Kind*
4) *Enjoys holidays (and actually goes on holiday)*
5) *No d---pics*
6) *No pictures of your kids*
7) *Drives a car bigger than a mini*
8) *No complicated families*
9) *Enjoys life*
10) *No photo filters*
11) *Wouldn't mind if you had pets – but need to be house-trained*
12) *Doesn't turn up on a first date drunk*
13) *NOT into swinging*
14) *Celebrates Valentines night*
15) *Does not talk with their mouth full*
16) *Can challenge me to just-dance but is not that good*
17) *Actually turns up for a date*
18) *IS NOT IN A RELATIONSHIP*
19) *Sympathises when I cry at weddings*
20) *Looks great in a suit*
21) *Will go dance lessons with me*

Next day we head off to the Zoo. Mum has done enough picnic food to feed an army and dad is busy complaining that

Confidential

if she packs anymore food there will not be room in the car for us all.

We wrap up really warm as it's a really windy day. Anna puts on her wellies and looks super cute with her woolly hat and bear ears.

We see lots of animals, well obviously we are at the Zoo – it would be abit of a waste of time going if we didn't see any animals !! My favourite is definitely the seals. We manage to watch them being fed and they did a few tricks including a high five, clapping and some really impressive high jumps out of the water. Anna and I found it really funny how they skidded on their bellies into the water to catch the fishes.

After about 4 hours Anna and I are absolutely done-in and completely full after mums amazing picnic. We go and find mum and dad who have gone for a cup of tea and a warm in the Zoo café. We head off home and Anna falls to sleep on the way back, cuddling up to a toy penguin my dad brought her from the shop.

Mum starts on the dinner, tonight she is doing my absolute favourite dinner as a child. Corn-beef, mash potatoes and peas, covered in lots of gravy. The rate I am eating I may have to start up my dance lessons sooner rather than later !!!

Its Monday night Bingo at my mums local, so I decide to tag along whilst dad offers to look after Anna. Apparently she wants him to watch Frozen with her, which I can just imagine my dads face watching that !!

When we arrive, mums three friends have already there. I have met them a few times and seem a great bunch of friends. They have welcomed my mum with open arms (it must be the Midlands accent). They are sitting in their regular Bingo seats, where they sit each week. I dread to think if there was ever any newcomers and they 'dare' sit in 'those seats'.

We manage a few chats in between each bingo session. Currently they are discussing Strictly and how Jolene should have been voted off this week as her Rumba was terrible !!

After the bingo, it seems my mum and friends are a little tipsy. I have drove as its too far for mum to walk back, especially with so much walking we did today at the zoo. And plus, it is freezing outside.

The conversation then turns onto Husband-slagging, all harmless banter of course. Mum is complaining about dad leaving the door open when he goes the toilet, forgets to use the toilet spray and then stinks not only toilet out, but seems to travel through the house. Mum was devasted when the amazon delivery driver could smell it when she greeted him at the door with her parcel. She said he was turning his nose up in disgust.

One of the other ladies is moaning about her husband who seems to start a DIY task, does it wrong, gets distracted and then leaves it. Apparently she has about 5 un-finished tasks and the more she mentions it, the more stubborn he becomes and the longer he takes. She keeps threatening him with paying for a odd-job man to come in the hope that would entice him abit.

Confidential

The last friend is moaning that her husband has decided to take up fixing up an old motorbike for a hobby. But they do not have a garage, so its currently being fixed up in the garden, but suddenly motorbike pieces are turning up all over the house……..apparently the dining room is no longer used for eating, it is covered in newspaper and motorbike parts. And the house smells constantly of oil !!!

I absolutely loved Bingo, who would have thought it was so much fun! Although I did not win anything, one of mums friends won a bottle of chocolate which she opened immediately and shared around the table. I have decided that I must investigate any local bingo venues, as this is definitely something I want to take up as a hobby. I am sure some of my friends will come along with me.

I check my phone and I have a message from an unknown number.

'Hey Emily, its Aaron, you know, from the wedding? I hope this is the correct number'.

Boom – result

'Hey Aaron, lovely to hear from you. You have most definitely got the right number. How are you?'

'I am so glad it is actually you! I was so worried you wrote down a dud number and was even contemplating messaging you in case I ended up messaging someone in Thailand or something'

Confidential

'LOL, no I certainly would not do that. If anything I would give you my mums number, as she certainly does not know how to read a text message, let alone message back'.

We exchange some further messages including me asking Aaron if he would be open for Salsa dancing lessons.

He seems to understand my sense of humour, and we end the conversation with Aaron saying he will message me tomorrow, if that is ok.

How sweet. I really do hope he messages me tomorrow.

CHAPTER TWENTY ONE

~~Early~~ Mid-30's lady looking for a relationship. Looking for the following;

1) Loves socialising (and actually does socialise)
2) Funny
3) Kind
4) Enjoys holidays (and actually goes on holiday)
5) No d---pics
6) No pictures of your kids
7) Drives a car bigger than a mini
8) No complicated families
9) Enjoys life
10) No photo filters
11) Wouldn't mind if you had pets – but need to be house-trained
12) Doesn't turn up on a first date drunk
13) NOT into swinging
14) Celebrates Valentines night
15) Does not talk with their mouth full
16) Can challenge me to just-dance but is not that good
17) Actually turns up for a date
18) IS NOT IN A RELATIONSHIP
19) Sympathises when I cry at weddings
20) Looks great in a suit
21) Will go dance lessons with me
22) Likes bingo

Over the next 3 days we have a lovely time at my parents. We take the bus into Bristol town centre for some shopping and lunch with mum whilst dad takes Anna swimming.

I take Anna to a trampoline park, where I have great fun bouncing around – attempting to be a kid again, although next time I really do need to take a Sports Bra. It's a wonder I don't have black eyes after all that jumping. In the evening I treat them all to a meal out, at the Harvester of course which is Anna's favourite.

Mum spends an afternoon baking with Anna whilst I catch up on some work emails and ensure everything is set for the Afternoon tea party on Sunday. Everything seems to be under control. I make a couple of customer calls for some potential booking enquires and schedule a few meetings.

On Friday, the day before I am due to leave mum is hosting dinner for her friends. Apparently every month her friends take it in turns to host a dinner at each other's house. Anna is busy baking some cookies, I am on starter duty, where they are having prawn cocktail. I am thankful for as I am not the best at cooking, and this is one of the easiest starters to prepare. And plus you can prep it early on and pop it in the fridge.

Mum is cooking a beef stew. I love the fact that my parents are so traditional with their cooking. Apparently my dad doesn't do 'spicy food'. The most 'spicy' they go is Spaghetti Bolognese, which I showed mum how to cook. Dad was dubious at first, but actually quite enjoyed it. I daren't introduce them to the wonderful world of curries. They really do not know what they are missing.

I do wonder when it will be time for my mums friend, the one with the motorbike parts to host. I can just imagine them eating pie and chips around the oil and brake lights !!!

Confidential

It's not a fancy dinner, it is more of excuse for a get-together, and I am delighted mum's night happens to be when I am here, although mmm, on reflection – I wonder if she planned this on purpose?.

Dad decides to take Anna to meet his friends at his local. Apparently, as it is half-term there will be a few other children her age there, so I pack her teddy back-pack full of toys and activities so she will not be bored. Next door to the local is a chippy, so dad has promised he will get Anna sausage and chips. I know Dad will not eat anything; he will be hoping for left-over stew when he gets back home, mopped up with half a loaf of bread.

I raid mums cupboards for some table decorations and manage to find a half decent set which I swear they were gifted when they were married. If I had known mum was hosting dinner I would have brought some of my work hospitality items with me. I just about manage to find 6 matching sets of everything, although all the knives seem to be a different shape, and some have teaspoons instead of tablespoons incase they decide to have some gateaux instead of Anna's cookies.

I place a white tablecloth on the dining table and a grey runner which doesn't quite match, but hey, a girl has managed the best with the tools she has!

I make a mental note to buy mum some matching cutlery sets for her birthday.

Her friends start arriving, armed with plentiful of alcohol, and to be honest, I don't think they care how the table is decorated. Mum puts on her favourite Westlife CD (she does not do Alexa's yet – she is so not ready for that modern technology).

I play the perfect host, taking charge so mum can relax with her friends. They quickly eat the prawn cocktail and mum decides to place the pot of stew on the table so they can help themselves. We have mashed potato and some tiger loaf to soak up the remaining gravy. For pudding, we pop a plate of Anna's cookies on the tables alongside the Gateaux. It appears that the night is more like a piss up than the actual food, to which I am more than game.

I change the CD to 'Best of Tina Turner' and it seems to be a perfect choice. They have not stopped talking and laughing and I smile to myself happy that my mum has found a lovely group of friends since moving away.

I start tidying away the plates and go to the kitchen to wash up. One of my mums friends, Sue comes in to help and we soon have dedicated tasks – I am the washer-upper, and she dries the pots.

We have a general chit-chat but then Sue asks about my dating stories. I tell her a few, including the 'model wannabe', the 'one who has a girlfriend' and the 'one who doesn't even turn up' (it sounds like episode titles from Friends).

She laughs so much and decides to tell me about one of her dates she had many years ago.

'You have got to imagine Emily, this was years ago, in the 70s when it was non-stop partying and drugs'.

'My friends and I went to a music festival. I did not even know who was playing. I just went to meet loads of men. Remember I was young and never experienced anything like this in my life, so was a little naive'.

'Anyway, we watched a band, god knows who they were, but the next thing I know, we were heading back to their trailer van for an after-show party. I do not know how we managed to get through the bouncers, but we did. Although the trailer was massive, it was far too crammed with all the people there, lots of them dancing, some doing more drugs. So I pour myself a drink from some weird cocktail concoction that was on offer and go outside.

Outside I meet the most beautiful man I had ever seen. With grudged black hair, loads of tattoos and it appeared had some great pecs under his vest'.

'So I decide to make a move, bear in mind I am drunk and pretty high by now and we decide to go back to the bedroom in the trailer. We have to kick a few people out who are already getting abit 'jiggy with it' (honestly did you sing Will Smith?).

I proper laugh at this point. I haven't heard the phase 'jiggy with it' in terms of sexual preference for a long time, let alone coming from my mum's friend.

'Anyway, we end up doing the doing the dirty deed. And afterwards, whilst lying there both naked, he finds a guitar in the trailer and starts serenading me with love songs. At the time I thought it was quite sweet, but I was high. But now, when I think back it is one of the funniest things I have ever

Confidential

seen. A naked man, playing love songs on a guitar with his crumpled-up penis hanging down by the lower strings'.

I am in stiches by now, and we join the rest of the group with me still laughing away.

CHAPTER TWENTY TWO

~~Early~~ Mid-30's lady looking for a relationship. Looking for the following;

1) Loves socialising (and actually does socialise)
2) Funny
3) Kind
4) Enjoys holidays (and actually goes on holiday)
5) No d---pics
6) No pictures of your kids
7) Drives a car bigger than a mini
8) No complicated families
9) Enjoys life
10) No photo filters
11) Wouldn't mind if you had pets – but need to be house-trained
12) Doesn't turn up on a first date drunk
13) NOT into swinging
14) Celebrates Valentines night
15) Does not talk with their mouth full
16) Can challenge me to just-dance but is not that good
17) Actually turns up for a date
18) IS NOT IN A RELATIONSHIP
19) Sympathises when I cry at weddings
20) Looks great in a suit
21) Will go dance lessons with me
22) Likes bingo
23) Does not play the guitar

The next day we get ready to come home. Mum has made another one of her famous picnics to feed the 40 million for our journey home. She has even cooked us a cottage pie to have for dinner (bless her).

When I get home I put a wash on and catch up on some much-needed housework. I am just glad I don't need to do any food shopping.

I am in the middle of playing a board game with Anna when Nat messages. It reads;

'Hey, hope you had a nice week at your mum and dads. Are you back now'?

'Hey Nat, yes I got home earlier today. Everything ok?'

'Everything is fine-ish……..are you free this evening? Can we meet up?'

Now I am worrying a little

'Yes, I am free, although I have Anna tonight. Do you want to come round? If you haven't eaten dinner, mums done a cottage pie which is enough to feed an army?'

'Yes I can come to yours no problem. I might see what the others are doing as well, they may want to hear this……..no to the cottage pie but thank you. See you around 8ish'

MMMM, I wonder what that is all about.

I dish up the cottage pie, send mum a quick text thanking her for a lovely week and start getting Anna ready for bed. I have a quick shower and decide to put my pjs on. I know Nat is coming, and potentially the other girls – but they've seen me in worst. But I do ensure they are matching p.j's, not my

Confidential

unmatched, bleach covered ones I usually wear. I even get my 'nice' slippers, as opposed to the stinky ones that leave a pongy smell everywhere I go.

Just after 8 there's a knock at the door and their standing with 2 bottles of wine each is Nat and Becka. It looks like I am in for a long night!!

It appears Kerry was too busy at the gym and a film evening with her kids, and Rachel's husband is at work so she has the kids.

After Anna gives them all a hug and hands out bracelets she's made for them, I go and take her to bed, letting her play on a tablet for half hour before bed. It is the holidays still after all.

'So how is your mum dad? How was the visit?' Becka asks

'It was lovely thanks. Mum and dad are really well. I know I worried when they moved away to look after Grandma, but they seemed to have settled in really well. Dad has made himself at home at the local. And mum has made a group of lovely friends. She's a regular bingo player now, and her friends all take it in turns to go round each other houses and cook a meal. It's lovely. Although mum really needs to learn how to set a table properly. To be honest I think it is something we should do, not learn how to set a table, I meant take it in turns hosting for an evening'

'Oh, like Come Dine with me!! We could score each other on food and entertainment. Although we couldn't go poking around each other houses, we have already done that' says Becka

Confidential

I notice Nat sitting quietly in the corner, drinking her wine a little too quickly, even for a Friday night.

'Everything OK Nat?' I ask

Suddenly Nat starts crying. Becka and I immediately go over and comfort her.

'Nat, what the hell is wrong??' We both ask concerned.

'It's Adam…..I think…..I think……..I think he is having an affair'

'WHAT??' we both cry 'Surely not??'

'Come on Nat' I say. 'Tell us why you would even think that'

Nat starts telling us that over the past week or so Adam has seemed really distant. Hiding his phone or when he would get a notification he would immediately leave the room with his phone.

"When I tried to talk to him, he would just brush it off. Then last night he went out with his supposedly work friends. But I noticed he had brought a new shirt for the occasion. Which is very rare, because as you know, Adam does not buy new clothes unless forced, or they are presents. Then, before he went out I noticed he had smothered himself in his favourite aftershave, so much so I could smell it for an hour after he had gone'

'Anyway, he finally came home at about 2 O clock in the morning, stinking of perfume and booze. He got up for work this morning before I woke up'

Becka asks if she had spoken to him this evening

Confidential

'No, when he came in from work he was very quiet. Didn't give me his usual kiss on the cheek. I asked him if he had a good evening and he just shrugged. So I decided to come round here. To get your advice on how I handle this next'.

Wow, we are both lost for words. I try and handle this situation carefully

'Look Nat, I do not know Adam as well as you do, but that seems pretty out of character for him. Have you been having any marital problems?'

'No, that's the thing. Everything has been fine. I mean, we all have our ups and downs, but I thought that was just marriage life' Nat responds, looking really hopeless.

After about half an hour of comforting Nat, trying to offer her different reasons for Adam's strange behaviour I realise my phone has been left on silent. So whilst I go and check Anna is asleep I grab my phone.

Ironically I have 3 messages. Will, Aaron and Evan. For god's sake, they are like flipping buses. I text them both back quickly saying I'll message them later, have a friend crisis.

Just as I am turning my phone back to silent I get a text, from Adam.

'Emily. Is Nat with you? Please tell me the truth. I know you two are good friends, but I hope you have the decency to tell me the truth'

I immediately show the message from to Nat and Becka.

'Call him Nat' Becka says. 'In fact, video call him, show him you are here, then go into the dining room and have this out with him. It is the only way you will ever know what is going on'.

Nat video calls Adam. He answers straight away. She holds up the phone, so we wave and say 'hi' and then Nat disappears into the other room.

Whilst Nat is in the other room talking to Adam, Becka and I are pretty gobsmacked, we try and earwig at the door, wishing we could use one of those plastic cups they used to use as phones back in the olden days. Where's the plastic cups when you need them?

Becka and I catch up on her dogs and the gym/man-cave development which has now been agreed they will split the room into two. Part gym/part man-cave. A winner all-round.

Nat finally comes back and joins us. I can tell she has been crying, but now she's half crying/half laughing.

'What's happened?' We both cry in chorus

Nat pours herself a glass of wine, takes a gulp and fills us in.

It turns out, Adam accidentally came across our laptop history of the 'swingers' site, then decided to have a quick snoop on Nat's phone and found her 'fake profile'.

Adam had convinced himself Nat had joining a swinging site. He got so wound up by it that when his friends went out on Thursday he decided to try and get his own back and went out on the intention to chat up other women. But when it came to it, he just couldn't bring himself to do it. Ended up drinking himself stupid and sitting in a kebab house on his own until 2.00am. Feeling all sorry for himself and not knowing what to do.

Bless him

So after Nat told him about the Greg swinging story and how Nat came about 'joining' the swinging site suddenly everything fell into place.

Nat is in hysterics by now.

'Honestly, you could not make this up. By the end of the conversation we could not stop laughing and how silly we had been. If only Adam had asked me, it would have saved all of this heartache and all of this worry'.

We all end really laughing and are so relieved that Adam found the funny side of it all.

Nat then downs her drink, orders a taxi and announces

'Come on Becka, I am off home. Adam and I have some good make-up sex to do'

And with all that drama they leave. Well that was an unexpected night.

CHAPTER TWENTY THREE

~~Early~~ Mid-30's lady looking for a relationship. Looking for the following;

1) Loves socialising (and actually does socialise)
2) Funny
3) Kind
4) Enjoys holidays (and actually goes on holiday)
5) No d---pics
6) No pictures of your kids
7) Drives a car bigger than a mini
8) No complicated families
9) Enjoys life
10) No photo filters
11) Wouldn't mind if you had pets – but need to be house-trained
12) Doesn't turn up on a first date drunk
13) NOT into swinging
14) Celebrates Valentines night
15) Does not talk with their mouth full
16) Can challenge me to just-dance but is not that good
17) Actually turns up for a date
18) IS NOT IN A RELATIONSHIP
19) Sympathises when I cry at weddings
20) Looks great in a suit
21) Will go dance lessons with me
22) Likes bingo
23) Does not play the guitar
24) Has open/honest conversations

Confidential

The next day I realise I hadn't replied to any further messages from the guys (ha ha, I sound like a serial dater). I was so shattered after Nat and Becka had gone I got straight into bed and must have dropped off as the next thing I know Anna comes bounding into my room asking for toast for breakfast.

I send them all the standard 'sorry I did not text back last night. I hope you are ok, and ready for the weekend'.

I make Anna some toast, get us both ready and drop Anna to her dads before heading off into work. Anna has clearly missed her daddy and gives him such a massive hug.

As I get into work I catch up on my emails. It's the bottomless brunch next week, I am really looking forward to it.

Aaron has messaged me. Asking if I am ok after my friend drama crisis. He asked me if I would like to meet him for coffee at some point today. 'Interesting, no pub' I think to myself. Well that does make a nice, refreshing change.

I tell him that I either finish work around 6, or I do have some work errands to do and I could meet up for a coffee during my extended lunch break.

I can see Aaron is messaging me back….ohhh how exciting.

'Lets meet at lunch as I have plans later this evening. Shall we say meet at 'Franko's' at 2? Is that ok? Or if 2 is too late we can make it earlier?'

'2 is great' I eagerly type back. 'Although I am in my work uniform'

'Ha ha, I have seen you in your uniform before remember – it makes you look cute 😊'

I cannot remember the last time I was called cute, but either way, I was happy.

Right, I best get my head down and do some work. I shouldn't be checking my phone every 10 minutes and getting distracted.

Just after 1.00pm I start getting ready for my coffee date. Oh look at how grown up I sound! 'A Coffee Date'. My mum would be so proud. I pop on my sexy work heels, hey anything to make this uniform look nicer. I drive into town, park up and started walking towards Frankos.

I am actually quite nervous. It is probably because it's a sober date and I have not had even one glass of wine to calm my nerves. Plus, I am in my uniform and always feel more at ease when I am in my own attire. And these heels are not the easiest to walk confidently in, especially when I am now bricking myself the closer I get to the destination. At least I know if the date goes badly, I can make excuses that I have to get back to work.

As I walk in I see Aaron sitting at a table by the window. He's already got himself a drink, but as soon as he sees me he jumps up (not literally, I mean that would look abit stupid), gives me an awkward hug and asks me what I would like to drink.

Confidential

'Can I have a Vodka and Coke please………only kidding, can I have a Latte please', I say smirking. He walks off laughing. I bet he's thinking he's bagged a right comedian.

Whilst Aaron is ordering I pretend to casually look around the Café, but secretly I check him out. He looks equally as good without a suit. Aaron has short blonde hair, has a slim physique but you can tell he goes to the gym, as he has lovely biceps in his fitted jumped he is wearing. His bum is also looking very peachy in some Levi jeans. And plus he is wearing nice trainers. I do like a man in nice footwear. I can never understand when men wear those hiking shoes things. OK, so wear them when you are going mountaineering or rock climbing – is that the same thing?. Even wear them when you're going for a long walk….but not anywhere else. Especially not on a date. They just don't look nice.

'Earth to Emily. You seemed miles away there. Penny for your thoughts' Aaron says, placing my coffee down.

I tell him about my hike shoe wearing theory (well I could hardly tell him I was perving at his peachy cheeks could I?).

'Well, I need to go in a minute, I best go home and throw away my hiking shoes', and with that Aaron goes to get up

He immediately sits back down and laughs. Then we both laugh, and it seems to have lifted the nervousness in the air.

I have a great lunch hour with Aaron. Turns out he has been divorced a year now and has a daughter, Grace, who is 7 (so a year older than Anna). He is a team leader for a logistics company and in his spare time he helps out as a coach for Under 9s football team.

He has just moved into a 2-bedroom flat after moving back in with his parents for a year whilst he was going through his separation.

He seems really funny, and he had me in snitches telling me about moving back into his old childhood bedroom, that still has all his old posters and school football trophies. How his mum used to treat him like a kid and made him a lunchbox every day with work. He even said the first day he got into work, opened his lunchbox to find cheese spread sandwiches cut into triangles with cucumber and carrot sticks. His works mates still take the mickey out of him now.

I was quite sad to be going back to work. Aaron explained he had Grace for the rest of the weekend but would message me later.

He gave me a peck on the cheek as I was leaving and I hurried back to the car – well as much as I could hurry in these stupid heels. I was so lost in thought over my lovely lunch date that I completely forgot to do my errands and pick up a few bits for the christening tomorrow and drove straight back to work.

Shit. I'll have to take a last-minute trip to Celebrations in the morning.

When I get back home from work after getting pretty much everything sorted for the Christening tomorrow , except for my last minute trip to Celebrations tomorrow of course, I am happy to find a bit of leftover cottage pie in the fridge. Thank god for mum and her big portions. I decide to have a night in to myself, watch some trashy films and eat loads of nice snacks (well what limited snacks I actually have in my kitchen). I feel guilty when I'm not working in the evening and don't have Anna, but I did ring Rob earlier to say I was ok to have Anna if he wanted a night off. He laughed and said 'with a toddler, I don't get nights off anymore. And besides, I love having her around. She's my little helper when I need nappies/bottles/beer' he laughs.

By 9 0 clock I am bored senseless. It really isn't the same watching a film on your own on a Saturday night. I am already on my second bottle of wine, just to give me something to do (now, that is an excuse). I should have offered to babysit for one of my friends or something. At least then I wouldn't feel guilty for sitting around doing bugger all, just checking on the kids every now and again.

The worst thing I could have done tonight is to go on Facebook and see everyone else going out having a good time.

I feel like doing a Bridget Jones and start singing 'All by myself' through my hairbrush.

I get the odd messages from Aaron and Will. Will has been on an all-dayer after watching Ruby with the lads and seems pretty drunk. He still keeps asking me out for a drink, but I am hesitant. I don't want him not turning up again, and I do like Aaron, but it is still very early days. But they always seem nice at the beginning don't they? Unless I am that gullible.

Confidential

I decide to call it a night before I start eating the stale biscuits in the cupboard. I really do need to go food shopping.

CHAPTER TWENTY FOUR

~~Early~~ Mid-30's lady looking for a relationship. Looking for the following;

1) Loves socialising (and actually does socialise)
2) Funny
3) Kind
4) Enjoys holidays (and actually goes on holiday)
5) No d---pics
6) No pictures of your kids
7) Drives a car bigger than a mini
8) No complicated families
9) Enjoys life
10) No photo filters
11) Wouldn't mind if you had pets – but need to be house-trained
12) Doesn't turn up on a first date drunk
13) NOT into swinging
14) Celebrates Valentines night
15) Does not talk with their mouth full
16) Can challenge me to just-dance but is not that good
17) Actually turns up for a date
18) IS NOT IN A RELATIONSHIP
19) Sympathises when I cry at weddings
20) Looks great in a suit
21) Will go dance lessons with me
22) Likes bingo
23) Does not play the guitar
24) Has open/honest conversations

Confidential

25) *Enjoys stopping in on a Saturday night watching click-flicks and eating rubbish*

The next day it's the Christening party. There are only 40 guests, so quite small compared to some parties I organise.

I really wish I had taken advantage of a quieter working day and gone out last night before my weekends get completely taken up with work again. But never mind.

Before I go into work I nip into Celebrations to pick up some last-minute decorations. Sam is sitting behind the counter reading a newspaper intently.

'Reading Dear Dierdre again Sam?' I say with a huge smile on my face.

Sam nearly jumps out of his skin. Oh god, please don't tell me he was really looking at some porn and his newspaper was just a cover-up !!

'Jesus Emily, you could have knocked or something. I have you know I learnt all my sex tips from reading Dear Diedre as a kid' he responds, closing the newspaper so I don't get chance to have a look at what he was actually reading. Mmm, I am still not 100% sure it was just a newspaper afterall !!!

I laugh, it's funny, because I remember doing the exact same thing as a teenager. Perhaps I should write to Dear Deirdre and ask her some dating advice.

I reply jokingly 'How old do you actually think Dierdre is? I mean, if she was in the newspaper responding to all those

Confidential

questions since you were a kid, she must be at least 100 by now. I bet she got a telegram from the queen. I reckon it must be laugher that has kept her young. Can you imagine the type of letters she has had over the years?'.

I must be in one of those moods, because I am not usually this jokey with a 'supplier'.

Sam replies with a laugh 'God damn it, I knew I should have been a comedian. It would have given me another 20 years at least. You have obviously had a lot of laugher in your life'

'20 years? Well that would make you up to what? 80?' I say pretending to ask like it is a serious question.

'You cheeky bugger. I think I am actually around the same age as you. I have just had a hard life, and you look really, really well for your age. You must have had a good life' Sam replies giving me a cheeky wink.

Is it just me or is Sam actually flirting with me? I mean, he is married. That puts me off straight away and I immediately go into work mode, barriers right up.

'Anyway' I say, changing my tone of voice slightly 'I emailed yesterday afternoon with my order. Is it ready please as I have a Christening today to finishing organising'

'Errr, yes, right, of course'. Sam responds, completely off guard and heads to the back to collect my items.

He returns a few minutes later with my goods, all packaged up.

I pick up the box. Thank god this will fit in the car, so Sam doesn't have an excuse to bring it up in his van. I mean, what is it with guys that are in relationships thinking just because I am single, that I am desperate? I think not.

'Thank you Sam. See ya', I turn and go, walk out the door……go on, admit it, you sang it….Even better if you sang it with abit of 'go girl' attitude.

'Bye Emily, lovely to see you again. I hope I see you again soon' calls Sam.

Creep !!!

The venue is decorated all in white, with blue chair ribbons and blue runners. Yes you've guessed it – it's a boy.

There is a beautiful backdrop covering a quarter of a wall that someone from the family has designed which reads;

'Welcome to Finn's Christening.   We are so grateful to celebrating this special day with you'

In the corner of the room is a large picture of Finn and his parents, looking so happy.

I place a few balloons around the backdrop and around the room, which finishes the room nicely.

The family have decided to go for a hot-food buffet which consists of a number of different curries – Chicken Tikka Balti, Chicken Korma (for those not partial to the spicy food), Lamb Rogan Josh and Panner Balti. Accompanied with boiled rice, poppadum's and dips and naan breads. For the children who are not curry fans, and some other non-curry eating guests

Confidential

we have an array of standard pizza's – cheese and tomato, pepperoni and chicken and mushroom.

The parents have provided me with a play-list to play in the background whilst the guests are socialising.

Whilst everyone has sat down to eat I notice the mum attempting to eat her Lamb Rogan Josh whilst holding the baby. Although it's strictly not part of my job description (neither is being chatted up whilst working), I go over to the mum.

'Hey Chantelle. Would you like me to have Finn for abit whilst you can enjoy your food in peace?' I say, trying not to sound undermining, as I know some parents like to think they can do it all.

'Oh thank you so much. That would be amazing. I don't think I have ever eaten a dinner in peace since Finn was born. And plus, I have this brand-new cream dress on, which cost a fortune, and if I am honest, I am hoping to return it back to the shop afterwards. I have even left the tags on. But with curry stains all over it, I have no chance'. She replies, handing Finn over to me.

I gather Finn into my arms. He smells so lovely; I do miss that baby smell. It takes me back to when Anna was a baby. She really was a beautiful baby, those fat leg and arms rolls just made me want to melt.

I take Finn for a little walk and within 10 minutes he is screaming his head off. He clearly either wants feeding, or he is unsure of this new person looking after him. I don't blame him. I am a stranger after-all, and I have instilled in Anna 'Stranger-danger'. He is obviously a quick learner.

I try to pacify him, doing a little dance (no I did not sing 'make a little love' – how inappropriate) !!!! I rock him up and down which always seemed to work with Anna. After 15 minutes I look helplessly at Chantelle, who can see my 'help me' face. Luckily she has finished her dinner, so scoops him up in her arms and the dad suddenly appears with a bottle that has been warmed up in the kitchen.

At about 7.00pm everyone has gone home. Chantelle was forever grateful for those all 20 minutes of me looking after Finn. Bless her.

I do abit of tidying up, but the rest can wait until tomorrow. I suddenly realise its Sunday evening and I have absolutely no plans to go out. What is going on? The dating website has completely dried out (like a Gorilla's armpit my dad used to say – or an even ruder one which I cannot possibly say out-loud - no NOT Ed-Sheeran, that's 'thinking out-loud'. – but it has something to do with a nun and her private parts) – I'll let your imagine take-over !!

I realise my dating want list has gotten far too long. It's probably scared most blokes off. To be honest it would scare me off too. I must re-evaluate this list. In fact I am going to do it tonight when I get home. That is how determined I am.

Confidential

CHAPTER TWENTY FIVE

~~Early~~ *Mid-30's lady looking for a relationship. Looking for the following;*

1) *Loves socialising (and actually does socialise)*
2) *Funny*
3) *Kind*
4) *Enjoys holidays (and actually goes on holiday)*
5) *No d---pics*
6) *No pictures of your kids*
7) *Drives a car bigger than a mini*
8) *No complicated families*
9) *Enjoys life*
10) *No photo filters*
11) *Wouldn't mind if you had pets – but need to be house-trained*
12) *Doesn't turn up on a first date drunk*
13) *NOT into swinging*
14) *Celebrates Valentines night*
15) *Does not talk with their mouth full*
16) *Can challenge me to just-dance but is not that good*
17) *Actually turns up for a date*
18) *IS NOT IN A RELATIONSHIP*
19) *Sympathises when I cry at weddings*
20) *Looks great in a suit*
21) *Will go dance lessons with me*
22) *Likes bingo*
23) *Does not play the guitar*
24) *Has open/honest conversations*

Confidential

25) Enjoys stopping in on a Saturday night watching click-flicks and eating rubbish
26) Is not afraid of lists

FFS Em. What the hell is wrong with you? 26 'wants' ???? I don't mean to sound sexiest, but can men actually read lists containing anything over 5 ? Let alone 26 of the buggers!! No wonder I am not getting any new messages. This would be enough to turn anyone off. What happened to a nice short list of 4/5 'wants' and a nice picture of me with my up-lift bra and a couple of drunken selfies hiding my double chin?

I call Greg, in the desperate hope he has no plans for tonight, selfish I know but I really don't want to be alone for two nights in a row (oh please, get your violins out I hear you say).

Luckily it turns out Greg is as lonely as I am on a depressing Sunday night and invites me round for a take-away and a sleep-over. This is a blessing in disguise as I have still not been food shopping and I really have completely demolished mum's cottage pie by now.

I grab a few sleep-over items and drive over to Greg's, with wine of course. I am a guest after all and it would be far too rude to turn up empty-handed.

I enter Greg's place, drop my bags, grab 2 glasses and pour us a drink. I give Greg and big hug.

'Greg, we need to review my want list. It's got so ridiculous'

'Don't even go there' Greg says as he mooches over to grab my bottles of wine and pops them in the fridge.

'I literally have 3-things on my list – career minded, loves a great night out, loves a great night in. I thought I'd keep it nice and simple.

I laugh, surely the second two contradicts itself, but I understand exactly what he means.

We take a seat and start to review my list. Greg reads it out loudly and makes appropriate suggestions;

    1) Loves socialising (and actually does socialise)

'Keep, but take off the brackets'

    2) Funny

'Without a doubt keep'

    3) Kind

'Ditto'

    4) Enjoys holidays (and actually goes on holiday)

'Keep, but take off the brackets'

    5) No dick pics

'Delete' says Greg. 'I want to know what I am up against'.

    6) No pictures of your kids

'Delete' – men who put pictures of their kids without a filter probably do not realise the danger, and it makes you think you don't like other people's kids.

    7) Drives a car bigger than a mini

'What on Earth Emily??????? – DELETE'

    8) No complicated families

'DITTO. OMG, I AM STARTED TO SOUND LIKE THE FILM 'GHOST'.

The Capitals mean Greg is raising his voice slightly, but in a jokey, mimicking way of course.

    9) Enjoys life

'WHAT THE HELL IS THAT MEANT TO MEAN? – DELETE'

    10) No photo filters

'Who doesn't do photo filters nowadays? Keep up with the times lady – DELETE'

    11) Wouldn't mind if you had pets – but need to be house-trained

'Too picky, and WTAF – DELETE'

    12) Doesn't turn up on a first date drunk

'Sounds like coming from a bad experience, which of course you have – Delete'

    13) NOT into swinging

'As above. And why would you need to put that? Mind you, coming from experience you do have a point. Still delete'

    14) Celebrates Valentines night

'Rather than putting this direct – perhaps put 'Is a romantic at heart'

15) Does not talk with their mouth full

'OMFG – who actually does this? Does it need to go on a list? That is gross. And even if they did talk with their mouth full by you putting this on the list it's not suddenly going to make think 'oh yeah I do that, best not message her' – Delete'

16) Can challenge me to just-dance but is not that good

'Delete – sounds like you spend your evenings playing Just-dance on your lonesome'

17) Actually turns up for a date

'Delete – sounds far too bitter and from previous experience'

18) IS NOT IN A RELATIONSHIP

'MMMMM – you would have thought that would go without saying. But ok, keep. Just so they not that you really don't want to be a fling and that you want something serious'

19) Sympathises when I cry at weddings

'No, that just sounds like you're a cry baby. And no man wants that'

20) Looks great in a suit?

'FFS Em. DELTE'

21) Will go dance lessons with me

'Delete. It sounds like you are hitting retirement'

Confidential

22) Likes bingo

'Delete. Sounds like you have actually hit retirement'

23) Does not play the guitar

'There is nothing wrong with someone playing the guitar – you sound far too picky - DELETE'

24) Has open/honest conversations

'Hurray, something that is meaningful. Keep'

25) Enjoys stopping in on a Saturday night watching click-flicks and eating rubbish

'Two in a row – Keep'

26) Is not afraid of lists

'Delete. Men are generally afraid of lists. It usually means they have to do something'.

So after Greg completely tearing my list apart I have a brand new list. Here it is sports fan, here it is;

~~Early~~ Mid-30's lady looking for a relationship. Looking for the following;

1) Loves socialising
2) Funny
3) Kind
4) Enjoys holidays
5) Is a romantic at heart
6) IS NOT IN A RELATIONSHIP
7) Has open/honest conversations

Confidential

8) Enjoys stopping in on a Saturday night watching click-flicks and eating rubbish

Boom – watch those messages come flooding in….Any minute now……Im going to have the time of my life…you just wait (sorry, I was quoting a scene from Phoenix nights – one of the best scenes ever) !!!!

It almost reminds me of Valentines morning, waiting for the postman to arrive with his large sack of cards arriving through my letterbox. No not Santa, the postman !!! Who am I trying to kid? In fact do postman have sacks anymore? I can't remember. I think they have satchels. Mental note – pay more attention to my local postman and his carry-wear.

Greg and I have a great evening catching up. I fill him in on my date with Aaron, the sporadic messages from Evan, and the messages from Will asking him to give him a second date and go out with him.

'Right' says Greg, pointing a finger at me. He'd had a few by now and was on the tipsy side. 'This is what I suggest'

I pour myself another glass, ready for the lecture from Greg.

'Cave into Will. Give him another chance. He might have genuinely made a mistake by not turning up on at the cinema. If you don't, you may be missing out on someone fantastic'.

'Secondly, that Aaron sounds nice, but don't put all your eggs in one basket'

'And thirdly, message Evan and ask him outright if he is ever going to ask you out on a date. What have you got to lose?'

I ponder for a second on what Greg has suggested.

'You know, you're right' I say, wrapping myself up nice and cosy in one of Greg's blankets. 'In fact, I am going to do it right now'. I'd also had a few glasses of wine which was giving the Dutch courage I needed. That's another one – Dutch courage. What the hell does that mean?

Greg gets up from the sofa, a little unsteady on his feet 'Well before you, let me grab another bottle' and heads to the kitchen.

When I say kitchen, the kitchen is actually in the living room. Greg's flat is small but nice and modern, a white leather corner sofa that kind of sections off this room to the kitchen. In the corner of the living room is a very small glass dining table and 2 leather white chairs. Greg's main bedroom has lovely glass fitted wardrobes, and then his spare room (where I sleep) contains a single bed and a computer desk and chair. The kitchen part has a lovely breakfast counter/sink with 3 lights hanging down over the counter.

It suits Greg perfectly, very minimalist. Greg says he doesn't do little 'ornaments and candles' as it's just something else to dust. He is very clean – I do like that in a man, someone who is independent and wouldn't expect 'the woman' to do all the housework.

'OK Greg lets message Will' I say, picking up my phone.

'There done' I say. 'I have told him that I will give him a second chance and go out on another date with him'.

Next one.

'Hey Evan' I type. 'Sorry, if this seems a little forward of me, but are you ever going to ask me to go out for a drink?'

I message Aaron to tell him I am round my friends Gregs for the evening and I am looking forward to seeing him again.

I await eagerly for my phone to beep. Nothing.

We finish off the rest of the wine whilst watching Googlebox and Greg is definitely starting to flag as he is getting lower and lower in the sofa.

After feeling very deflated, we decide to go to sleep, there is always tomorrow.

'Night John Boy' I shout to Greg as I am turning off the bedside lamp

'Night Anna-Mae. Love you' I hear Greg shout

CHAPTER TWENTY SEVEN

~~Early~~ Mid-30's lady looking for a relationship. Looking for the following;

1) Loves socialising
2) Funny
3) Kind
4) Enjoys holidays
5) Is a romantic at heart
6) IS NOT IN A RELATIONSHIP
7) Has open/honest conversations
8) Enjoys stopping in on a Saturday night watching click-flicks and eating rubbish
9) Likes a clean house

Sorry, I know I am meant to be reducing my list, but the new one above is important.

Next day Greg and I go off into work together. I know its technically my 'day-off' but I have hardly worked all weekend and I could do with making up some hours. There is always something to do, at the minute I am planning events for the forthcoming calendar year, especially between now and May, when the parties are not as busy. I like to ensure the hotel has weekend entertainment evenings to fill those gaps. I also find that after booking an event I usually get at least one enquiry for a further celebration.

I like the fact that I am pretty much my own boss, and I can organise what events I like. As long as we make a profit from the events. Don't get me wrong, when I first started hosting some of the events they did not always go quite as planned.

Confidential

But I learnt from each one and I always trying to make improvements based on lessons learnt. I spend a lot of time doing research, seeing what other venues are doing, what seems to be the next popular thing etc.

Unfortunately I have had to postpone Bingo. There were difficulties with their equipment or something. So I've been trying to decide what event I could organise in its place and after abit of researching for some ideas I decide to host a speed-dating event. I figured it would not be too hard to organise, and although I would not charge for the event they would be buying drinks at the bar, and of course it also promotes the venue.

If it becomes successful I could always look at how I can make the evening even bigger. Like charging the guests but including drinks and food, but lets see how the first one goes first.

I do some further researching on the speed dating, check the bookings for the bottomless brunch and check my schedule over the next few months.

I start looking into the logistics of it all and plan a date for a Thursday night towards the end of April, just after Easter. It will be great fun, and hey, who knows, I may even join in if everything goes tits up with my current dating. And with my current dating history it's highly-likely I'll be joining in !!!

On my way to school I pop into Celebrations. I am hoping Sam 'the leech' isn't there. I have decided that is my new nickname for him. I cannot believe he had the cheek to flirt with me when he is meant to be happily married. And even worst he warns me off Mike as he has a girlfriend !!! Talk about pot kettle black – or whatever the saying is!!

Luckily Edith is behind the counter instead.

'Hey Emily. You are looking well. What can I do for you?' She says, perching her reading glasses at the end of her nose, I don't she is reading any weird looking newspapers in disguise.

'Hey Mrs Williams. I am looking for some inspiration for some upcoming events and just wondered if I can take a look around your warehouse?. You know it always helps me with ideas'

'Of course you can love', she says rising from her chair. 'Come this way, and please, how many times do I have to tell you, its Edith, not Mrs Williams'.

We head back to the warehouse. I do love looking at all the party accessories. If I had my way I would buy it all, so many different colours and sparkles.

I was thinking about some upcoming events I have. I don't think I will need anything for the speed-dating as I can use all the leftovers from the Valentines meal. I will need some Easter decorations though, especially for the outside if the weather is kind enough and we can move the egg hunt outside.

The bottomless brunch will be pretty easy to decorate with the items I have got. Although I was thinking I could have a 'selfie' corner, where I use a wedding arch we have and

Confidential

decorate it with lots of flowers. I could get some costume items for the 'selfie' corner to make it more enjoyable,

I pick up a few feather boas, a couple of silly hats and some big sunglasses. That will do for now and I head back with Mrs Williams, sorry, Edith, to pay for my purchases. I explain to Edith why I am buying a feather boa and hats.

At this point, Sam walks in.

'Oh, Hi Emily. Good to see you' (yeah I bet he is). 'Buying anything good?'

'Just bits and bobs' I reply a little short.

Anyway, got to go, thank you Edith, bye'. I say, turning and heading out towards the door.

I hope they don't think I was rude. But upon reflection, I may have been a little flirty back with Sam, and I do not want to give him the wrong impression. He may not be 'the leech', but I am not giving him the opportunity to really become one. He is the owner of one of my best suppliers after-all and I would be lost if I had to use an alternative supplier.

I collect Anna from school and after doing some light homework with her, I start cooking a lasagne. When I say cooking a lasagne, I mean cooking the mince and adding some jar brought sauces in-between the pasta sheets. But to me that's good enough.

I was thinking about my Easter bunny costume I have hired and I am pleased with my decision. Just need to talk someone into wearing it now. I am hoping that I can get Greg drunk and talk him into it.

CHAPTER TWENTY EIGHT

~~Early~~ Mid-30's lady looking for a relationship. Looking for the following;

1) Loves socialising
2) Funny
3) Kind
4) Enjoys holidays
5) Is a romantic at heart
6) IS NOT IN A RELATIONSHIP
7) Has open/honest conversations
8) Enjoys stopping in on a Saturday night watching click-flicks and eating rubbish
9) Likes a clean house
10) Would wear an easter bunny outfit (not for sexual pleasures)

The next few days go by so quickly with juggling work and looking after Anna.

Evan finally responds to my message. It turns out that is mum is currently really poorly and is having end of life care. So as you can imagine he is really struggling trying to juggle work, looking after his child and helping with his mum. She currently in a hospice, but he feels really guilty when he is not seeing her. He explains work have been amazing and have let him work from home wherever possible, but his concentration skills are lacking somewhat.

I am so shocked and feel so upset when he tells me this. I feel so terrible that I messaged him asking me to go out on a date and I almost feel like I have forced him to tell me something so private that is happening in his life.

I respond straight away, telling him that I am really sorry to hear this, and that if he ever wants to talk about it then I would listen. I also apologise for pressurising him into going out and tell him that there is absolutely no rush. That his family come first, and he must concentrate on his family.

On a lighter note, Will has also replied, asking what I am doing this weekend and whether I want to go bowling. I have agreed to go out with him on Friday night.

Aaron also asks me to go out again. He asks whether I would like to go out Sunday evening and we set a date. I feel like a right serial dater. Good job I have made my spreadsheet of what I wore to each date !!

Turns out I do have a busy weekend afterall. Two dates and a bottomless brunch on Saturday – hurray.

I have also had 2 new messages on the dating site. My shortened list must have worked, although I do feel a little guilty still looking at POF when I have so many 'potentials' going on at the minute. I cant stop thinking about Evan. I do hope he is ok. I cannot imagine what he is going through.

So I check out the messages.

One from Dan who seems normal enough. He has a 12-year-old boy. There's lots of photos of Dan with his boy, but the pictures of his boy are blurred out – which is good. He seems to do a lot with his kid, again, a big tick for me.

Other message is from Dean. Looks like he enjoys going to the gym a lot judging from his pictures. And there does seem to be a lot of photos of him posing in the gym. OK Emily, stop judging.

I send messages to both Dan and Dean. I literally have the same response; I really need to up my game with replies. Perhaps I should send a really cool upbeat message like;

'So, if you had to have your last meal what would it be?. Or what is your views on the current political situation?' Narrrrr, I'll stick with the standard 'Hey, I am good thank you. Busy working – how are you?'.

I have an end-of-life celebration today. Always something I dread. Today it is an exceptional sad one . It is a little girl that passed away during an illness she had since birth. She was only 10 years old. I cannot even bear to imagine what it must be like to lose a child so young.

I have decorated the room in sparkly pink and gold decorations, as requested by her parents. The room looks so pretty, but so sad at the same time. I have put up a memory board that the family have created, all photos of the little girl with her friends and family. I was in tears putting this up on the wall. Pictures of her in hospital, trying to put on a brave face whilst it is clear she is in a lot of pain.

The family have requested that they let off balloons at 15.00pm, which is exactly 4 weeks from when she passed. I have also managed to purchase some Chinese lanterns, although it may not be dark enough to set off at 3, I would

Confidential

give them to the family anyway. Perhaps they could let them off later or take them home for another day.

The celebration goes as well as be expected. The family were so grateful of the lanterns. The place was absolutely packed with everyone trying to put on a brave face.

At 3, just before the balloons were due to be let off, the dad made a little speech, which was so heartwarming, I had to walk away for 10 minutes, I could just not compose myself. The parents, as you could imagine were inconsolable, but were trying really hard to put on a brave face and celebrate the memories.

Everyone left around 16.30pm. I had arranged for Anna to go to her friend's house after school. Normally I would ensure I am finished work in time to pick Anna up from school and leave the bar staff to finish off any events that are on mid-week, but on this occasion I thought I would stay until the end.

I picked Anna up, she seemed to have a lovely time at her friends, took her home and hugged her really tight. I made sure I told her I loved her a million times before she got bored of me saying it.

Sometimes life really is too precious and must not be taken for granted.

CHAPTER TWENTY NINE

~~Early~~ Mid-30's lady looking for a relationship. Looking for the following;

1) Loves socialising
2) Funny
3) Kind
4) Enjoys holidays
5) Is a romantic at heart
6) IS NOT IN A RELATIONSHIP
7) Has open/honest conversations
8) Enjoys stopping in on a Saturday night watching click-flicks and eating rubbish
9) Likes a clean house
10) Would wear an easter bunny outfit (not for sexual pleasures – for a kids party)
11) Appreciates life – it is so short

Friday comes around far too soon. I spend the day checking the bookings for the Easter party, making up a few party games, as well as checking with the chief the food options for the day.

Then onto the speed dating event. As I am not taking bookings for the speed dating I spend some time promoting the event on the standard social media channels and ensure my friends share my posts. Greg has promised a few of his friends will come.

Confidential

I have 6 weddings scheduled over July and August, so it is going to be a really busy 2 months. I am also thinking of organising a family summer BBQ party early September whilst the weather is still nice. Depending on how well the Easter party goes first.

I start getting ready for my date with Will. I am still in two-minds whether to go. But hey, like Greg says give him a second chance. And after the past few days, life really is too short but he had better turn up this time.

I decide to put on my skinny jeans which make my bum look good. I also thought this would be a good move considering he'll be spending most of the night looking at my bum whilst I am bending over bowling. Luckily, you don't have to wear those horrible bowling shoes anymore. But even still, I wear some low kitten heels as I do not want to chance falling over in high heels.

I put on a nice grey jumper with my trusty leather jacket, some nice jewellery and I am ready. I am a little early so I decide to curl my hair a little as well. Well considering I wasn't keen on going I have made an effort !!

We arrange to meet at 7 at the bar within the bowling centre to have a quick drink first before bowling. I will meet him there. I have a rule that I wouldn't let anyone pick me up on a first date. I would not want them to know where I live, especially not at first. Call me paranoid, but I have watched far too many serial killer programmes.

When I arrive, Will is at the bar ordering a Cider. I ask for a Shandy. Will has ginger/strawberry blonde hair. He is about the same height as me and is wearing a tight t-shirt with a lovely designer grey cardigan. He's wearing some nice jeans and some grey suede trainers which match his cardi. Nice to know he has made the effort as well.

We have a quick chat over our drinks, then go to our bowling lane. You no longer type in your names for the game anymore. You have to tell the people on reception, and they do it in preparation ready before the game has started.. When we get to our lane I find it highly hilarious that Will has put our names to be 'S@@y Shell' and 'Wonderous Will'.

So, its official, I am terrible at bowling. I thought I was pretty good, but that is when I have realised when I play Anna we usually have the barriers down. Unfortunately, as we are adults we have no barriers, much to my disgust !!

Will is really easy to get on with. It turns out he has never been married but does have 3 kids which he doesn't spend as much time as he wants too with them. But when he does have them he enjoys taking them to football matches at the weekend. He is a big Leicester City football fan and tries to see them whenever possible.

His job is a Gas Engineer, so he travels around the UK quite a lot in the week, staying overnight at hotels which he isn't a big fan off. That is one of the reasons he doesn't see his kids as much, because of the travelling.

He really made me laugh talking about some his dating disasters. One of them made me howl and cringe at the same time. He told me about when he went on a date and ended up back at her place, they ended up doing the dirty

Confidential

deed. Then straight after, whilst lying in bed she lights up a cigarette. He was dry heaving. Nothing against smoking, each to their own. But not in the bedroom. That's a no-no. He said that fag ash was going everywhere on the bed, completely missing the ash-tray she had suddenly produced.

Now I am no Fire Marshal, but that's a fire hazard if I ever did see one !!

We decide to go for another drink after. We both drive to a local pub, and we both agree to leave the cars so we can have a few alcoholic drinks.

When we arrive at the pub it's a great atmosphere. There is a band playing so it is pretty full, and the vibe is amazing. However we are clearly both sober and on a different wavelength to everyone else. So to attempt to catch up a little we order a few shots, some Sour Snapps or something, which actually taste really nice. I order a Long Island Iced Tea which always guaranteed to get me tipsy quite quickly. Will orders the same, and a couple of Jagger bombs as well, which is always a winner for me.

We stand at the bar as there are no seats, I am so glad I wore my low-heeled boots.

Will bumps into a few people from work and introduces me. I try and act cool in front of his work colleagues, but realise I am a little drunk by now, damn those shots and an empty stomach.

Will's friends ask to join us, and as they have seats I am more than happy to tag along. There is about 6 of them, mixture of both sexes and all around the same age as me. I haven't a clue what their names were as I couldn't hear the introductions over the music.

A few more drinks arrive from the group, and I am busy having some meaningful conversation with 2 blokes (god knows there name) about whether Elf is the best Christmas film of all time. I casually glance at Will, and I swear he is getting awfully cosy with one of the other girls. Perhaps they are just really good friends, but she is clearly hanging onto his every word and seems to be abit touchy. I really do hope Will tells her I am his actual date for the evening.

On the way to the toilet I see Sam. He waves and goes to talk to me, but I manage to dodge him and speak to someone else I vaguely know. I cannot be done with the Leach tonight and besides I am on date.

I order a round of shots and as I head back to the table with my tray of shots I cannot believe my eyes. Wil is literally snogging the face off that girl.

Seriously ????? I have no idea what to do. So I gracefully put the drinks tray down, pick up one of the shots, shout 'cheers', down one and walk off.

What the hell do I do now????

I feel such a fool giving him a second chance. I thought we was having such a lovely evening. Perhaps it wasn't a coincidence I got stood up the first time. He must have got a better offer.

Confidential

I go outside to order a taxi as its far too loud to order one inside with the band playing.

Taxi is 5-minutes away, thank god. Although 5-minutes seems like an eternity when all you want to do is to get home, especially when it is freezing outside.

As I am stood waiting for the taxi I attempt to text the friends group to tell them what has happened. The text probably doesn't make any sense, but I need to tell someone.

'Hey, are you ok?'. I hear. I turn around and its Sam. Oh, this is the last thing I want.

'No I am not ok', I say turning round to face him. By now, I am really full of rage. In my head I am thinking why do men think that this is acceptable? Why can't I actually find someone decent? Why do children die at such a young age??

'It's you men that are wrong' I say, turning a little angry by now.

'I mean, why do you think that it is acceptable to be on a date and end up snogging another woman? right in front of your face. You think that's ok? And how about you, flirting with someone whilst you're married? OK, so I may have gotten carried away being a little flirty back, but at least I am not married'

Wow, that felt good getting it off my chest

'What, wait...I don't understand??' says Sam

Confidential

Luckily by now the taxi turns up. I get in, and as Sam tries to come over I close the door in his face and get the taxi driver to drive off.

I am drunk and I am done with dickheads.

CHAPTER THIRTY

~~Early~~ Mid-30's lady looking for a relationship. Looking for the following;

1) *Loves socialising*
2) *Funny*
3) *Kind*
4) *Enjoys holidays*
5) *Is a romantic at heart*
6) *IS NOT IN A RELATIONSHIP*
7) *Has open/honest conversations*
8) *Enjoys stopping in on a Saturday night watching click-flicks and eating rubbish*
9) *Likes a clean house*
10) *Would wear an easter bunny outfit (not for sexual pleasures – for a kids party)*
11) *Appreciates life – it is so short*
12) *DOES NOT SNOG ANYONE ELSE WHILST ON A DATE WITH YOU*

I wake up the next morning feeling so rough. Damn those shots and mixing my drinks. This hangover feels worst knowing I have work today.

What did I do wrong? I thought Will seemed really nice, but clearly can't keep his dick in his trousers. And then I remember how I slammed the taxi door in Sams face. Oh god, perhaps he deserved it. Although I think I did take my anger out on him. Oh dear lord, how can I face him? Perhaps I should avoid Celebrations for quite a while.

Confidential

Surprising I don't have a message from Will. I don't think I will hear from him again to be honest.

I take a quick shower and make myself an extra strong coffee and go to work.

The bottomless brunch consists of an array of Prosecco, a selection of the standard Lager and Ciders and Sex-on-the-beach cocktails. I thought we could try with the standard cheaper drinks and the quickest cocktail to make to see how successful the day goes. I looked into having more expensive cocktails and drinks, but then the brunch would seem quite costly up-front. At a price of £35, we could pitch for the lower priced drinks, and I think we would get more bookings with the cheaper option. Plus, if we had more exotic cocktails they always take a lot longer to create, and I know, from experience, that people generally want to drink as much as they can within their allocated time, so by having easier to make drinks, ensures they are always well stocked with drinks. Winner winner, chicken dinner.

The food is a mix of snacky bits. Pitta bread with humus, guacamole and spicy salsa. Spicy chicken wings, garlic bread and lots of different pizzas to cater for both vegetarians and the meat eaters. We've also got some gluten free pitta and pizzas.

We have 15 tables booked. Each different sizes ranging from tables of 10 to 4.

My friends are coming along to support me with the event. This of course is their excuse to have an afternoon off from the mundane household chores/kids.

Confidential

So there is Nat, Becka, Kerry and Rachel, and of course Greg also joins their table. I have given him the day off so he can join in, and also will be my secret investigator so he can feedback on what people really thought of the event.

I have decorated the room really low key. Just cream tablecloths and chair covers, as well as some blue runners I have over the tables. The brunch starts at 12.00pm until 3.00pm, so basically the guests have 3 hours to drink as much as they can within those that time.

I have booked a party host who will do some games and play music with them throughout. It saves me a job and I know they will do a far better job than I could ever do.

The guests start arriving and I show them all to their tables, some have already been to the bar, very keen to start drinking. At 12, I already have glasses of Prosecco lined up that I give out, as well as helping with the drink orders. I have realised that for the first hour we will be flat out with drinks orders. Luckily we have poured a few in advance saving a lot of time and people not having to wait too long, That one was Greg's idea, so I must remember to thank him for that useful tip.

The party host starts introducing themselves and going around the crowd, getting some guest interaction. Everyone seems abit timid, but give them a few more drinks and I can guarantee it will be more livelier.

After about an hour the party host has got a few willing volunteers on the dance floor playing some balloon game.

This gets the whole crowd cheering and egging their team along.

The food starts coming out now, and I go over and sit with my friends for abit, to gauge how they think it is going. They are having a great time, clearly making full use of a few child free hours.

The food seems be going down a treat, so I go and tell the kitchen staff to keep the snacks coming. Perhaps some of them were a little too eager with the 'free' drinks and need something to line their stomachs.

By now the host has announced it is time for some party music and gets as many as she can up on the dance floor. She makes them sit on the floor in 2 lines and 'oops up side your head' starts playing. Kerry is at the front of one of the lines and she clearly cannot remember the dance and keeps making things up which her line has to follow. It's hilarious.

Greg is heading the other one, and of course Greg being Greg he knows ALL the dance moves.

I make a few more cocktails, but by now the drinking seems to have slowed down a little and the guests are too busy partying. As I am walking back from the bar Becka grabs me as they are now doing the Conga around the room. I willingly join in, but I am obviously on a completely different wavelength than everyone else. Although, the amount I drank last night I am glad to be sticking to water /orange juice and coffee today.

It is nearing to 3 now and the party host finishes the party with one of my favourite songs, Tina Turner Proud Mary. By now nearly everyone is up dancing, impersonating Tina's dance moves. I realise how I must look when I am drunk dancing (obviously amazing).

Some of the guests start leaving now whilst others have decided to continue and head their way to the bar, including my friends.

When I have finished tidying up I go over and join them, getting Rachel a coffee as she is clearly flagging. There are a few pizza bits left, so I grab a few slices (that's my lunch sorted) and sit next to Kerry. They are all laughing about a story when Kerry fell over drunk with a burger in her hand, cut her face, had grazed knees and arms, but managed to salvage the burger.

Greg has gone by now as he has a hot date and needs to go home to 'moisturise and fake tan'.

Nat invites me round tonight, but I turn down the invite as my mum is coming over to stay tonight. She has been visiting a friend this afternoon, so we arranged for her to stay over with me for the night. I start telling my friends about my date with Will. They all give me reassuring messages like 'what a prat' 'you can do better than that' 'forget about him' 'you'll soon meet someone'. But I can see some of them giving me sympathetic looks which makes me feel a little disheartened. I am really hoping my next date with Aaron goes ok.

I also tell them about Sam, and how I ended up slamming the taxi door in his face.

Confidential

As all my friends are married they were in full agreement that he was flirting with me, and told me that he deserved it. Again the reassuring messages and I sympathetic looks come with the comments such as 'what a pig' and 'oh his poor wife'.

After another hour with Nat and Becka who are now on the ciders, Kerry is having another coffee. Bless her, she has the kids to deal with when she gets home and is desperately trying to sober up a little. When everyone has finished their drinks it's time for us to go home. Rachel has already been picked up by her husband as they are going to a party tonight, so I can take Nat, Becka and Kerry home. They just about fit in my car. Becka starts laughing as she is trying to get into Anna's car seat which clearly, although she has a petite bum, does not fit. I pop the child seat into the boot before she finds herself really wedged into the seat and cannot get out.

After I have dropped them all off I nip into Aldi to pick up a few bits for dinner. Then I go and collect Anna from Robs. As my mum is coming over I thought it would be nice to have Anna tonight, and plus its nice for me to have her at the weekend. I know I keep saying it, but in the next few months I won't get much time off at the weekend, so I am making the most of it going on disastrous dates and having Anna.

I am really looking forward to a nice evening tonight with mum and Anna.

CHAPTER THIRTY ONE

~~Early~~ Mid-30's lady looking for a relationship. Looking for the following;

1) Loves socialising
2) Funny
3) Kind
4) Enjoys holidays
5) Is a romantic at heart
6) IS NOT IN A RELATIONSHIP
7) Has open/honest conversations
8) Enjoys stopping in on a Saturday night watching click-flicks and eating rubbish
9) Likes a clean house
10) Would wear an easter bunny outfit (not for sexual pleasures – for a kids party)
11) Appreciates life – it is so short
12) DOES NOT SNOG ANYONE ELSE WHILST ON A DATE WITH YOU
13) Doesn't mind drunk dancing

My mum turns up about 6.00pm. She has spent the day at her friend's house including a visit to the garden centre and mum proceeds in showing me all her new plants she has for their garden.

I have no clue about plant and flowers. My garden is very minimal, with a large lawn which I have a swing and a big trampoline on the grass. That can be a pain when I am mowing the lawn. I have a few nice bushes but that's about it. Mum has tried buying me plants in the past, but I just end up killing them, so I think she has now given up.

Tonight I am cooking a leek and potato pie (shop brought of course), accompanied with mash, roast potatoes, broccoli, cauliflower and peas. It's not my usual Saturday dinner, far too healthy, but as I said before, mum does like her traditional dinners.

After dinner mum washes up and whilst she is watching strictly I give Anna a shower and get her ready for bed. We play a few games with Anna, then mum offers to get Anna to bed whilst I check on some emails and texts for the day.

Nothing from Will. I would have thought I would have got an apology or something.

Aaron has messaged to see if we are still ok for our date tomorrow, to which I reply I am really looking forward to it.

Dan has messaged to ask if I have had a nice day, and we chat abit, telling him about my brunch event. He talks about his day out shopping with his son and now they are playing some computer games together.

Dean has also messaged, saying that he's spent the day at the gym, going for a swim and a sauna after. He's just got out of the cinema with his mates, and he is going to drop them off at the pub, he doesn't drink so is going to have a soft drink at the pub and then go home.

Both seem nice enough.

I haven't got any events on tomorrow, but I do need to pop into work to sort out everything from today's brunch. I have some accounts work to do but I can easily do that from home or later in the week. I have a look on our social media page and have had some really positive feedback following some photos I had posted earlier in the day (with the guest's permission of course). I definitely need to book another Bottomless Brunch soon. My mates have also promised they will post some pictures and give some positive comments. They even do it for free – and not bribery purposes.

Mum and I watch some romantic rom-com and afterwards we both decide to go to bed. Anna is in with me tonight so mum can sleep in Anna's bed. I get into bed and spoon Anna, she's so warm and cosy.

The next morning Mum decides to make us all pancakes and afterwards once we are all ready we nip into work. I get mum and Anna a drink and they sit at the bar area whilst I sort out the room from yesterday. It doesn't take long to be honest. I check some work emails and my calendar for the rest of the week, then we go to take Anna to the soft play.

Soft plays are my idea of a nightmare. It's so loud and chaotic. Overly excited, sweaty kids running around. Parents chatting really loudly over all the noise, trying to be heard. It smells of sweaty socks, but kids do love it. So I grin and bare it – it is for Anna after-all.

I manage to grab 2 chairs for me and mum, and whilst she sorts out taking off Anna's shoes and socks I go and grab 2 coffees for us and a fruit-shoot for Anna. I know she'll be running back every 30 minutes, puffing and panting and gasping for a drink.

Mum and I are struggling to hear ourselves, so we decide to sit in silence for abit. Waving at Anna every 10 minutes who keeps stopping wherever she is looking over to check that we are still there.

I message both Aaron, Dan and Dean the exact same thing about the dreaded soft play. A little naughty I know, but it saves me having to think of 3 separate witty/funny conversations. And besides, it saves me having to remember what I have said to them all the time as well.

Aaron messages back with a funny GILF of some sweaty kids. Dan responds that he feels exactly the same about soft play areas and is grateful his son has grown out of soft play but has now gone onto trampoline parks. And I get a picture of Dean in the gym. Wow, does this bloke live in the gym? I wish I had that motivation.

After what seems like 10 hours of chaos and noise Anna is finally tired and is complaining she is hungry.

Fine by me as I am absolutely starving. We go to a pub that does the most amazing Sunday dinners. It doesn't usually get that busy so I did not have to book which I am very surprised as the food is great.

There are only a few tables occupied, so we grab a table near the window and I go buy us all a drink. When I come back mum and Anna have already decided what they want to order for dinner. I take a quick look at the specials menu.

Secretly I know exactly what I want as I have been studying the menu all week. But I like to have a look just in-case there is something that I have missed.

Surprisingly I decide on the mains I had picked all along, and I go up to the bar to order. Mum has gone for beef with all the trimmings, I have gone for lamb which extra cauliflower cheese. I absolutely love cauliflower cheese, and Anna is going for a kids beef dinner.

I would normally go for a starter as well, especially as mum is here and its lovely to be able to treat her. But as I have my date tonight with Aaron, I decide I'll be full enough with my lamb dinner.

The dinner is amazing. Luckily no-one else wanted some of my cauliflower cheese so I had it greedily all to myself. Anna ordered an ice-cream, but mum and I was absolutely stuffed and could not fit in a dessert. I am really lucky in the sense that Anna does eat really well and was never a fussy eater, even as a baby.

I wish I was a better cook. I wouldn't say I am bad, I just do not enjoy it, especially cooking a Sunday dinner. Cooking a Sunday dinner to me is just so much hard work, far too many pots and pans (especially when you don't have a dishwasher like me). I feel like I spend all day prepping the veg, cooking the meat and then takes all of 10 minutes to eat it. And then you're so stuffed the last thing you want to do is to wash up the 20 million dishes after. I have brought a slow cooker, which helps, but even still, I do all I can to avoid cooking one.

Confidential

After dinner I drop mum off at the train station. I wish she could have stopped longer, but I know she likes to go home and be with dad. I know she is already worrying what he has eaten today. 'Probably a take-away last night and beans on toast today'.

I make sure mum is on the train and Anna and I wave her off. Then I drop Anna back to Robs. I have 2 hours to get ready for my date. I definitely have time for a quick nap, this Sunday dinner has done me in.

CHAPTER THIRTY TWO

~~Early~~ Mid-30's lady looking for a relationship. Looking for the following;

1) Loves socialising
2) Funny
3) Kind
4) Enjoys holidays
5) Is a romantic at heart
6) IS NOT IN A RELATIONSHIP
7) Has open/honest conversations
8) Enjoys stopping in on a Saturday night watching click-flicks and eating rubbish
9) Likes a clean house
10) Would wear an easter bunny outfit (not for sexual pleasures – for a kids party)
11) Appreciates life – it is so short
12) DOES NOT SNOG ANYONE ELSE WHILST ON A DATE WITH YOU
13) Doesn't mind drunk dancing
14) Cooks Sunday dinners

I wake up from my nap and start getting ready for my date. I am really looking forward to seeing Aaron again. I am not sure what he has planned for us, but he did say to wrap up warm. He did want us to go for a meal, but I explained I was taking mum and Anna for Sunday dinner so would not want to eat again.

Aaron has asked if he could pick me up from my house. I hesitantly agree, but I figured I have met him before so we have arranged for him to pick me up at 7.00pm. I pop on some of my nice, tight-fitting jeans, a black long sleeved top and a soft cotton colourful scarf which gives some colour to my outfit. I decide to wear my long black flat boots, as I am not sure if we are walking, so best to be safe. Last thing I want is to wear my amazing 'meal shoes'.

By way of reference, these are shoes that are so high and uncomfortable to walk in that you can literally only pull them off when going for a meal. Which literally means, from the car to the restaurant and back. And even then, going to the toilet is a one-off for danger of falling over. You cannot wear these shoes when drinking or walking more than 200 metres.

At dead on 7.00pm I see a car pulling up and I can only assume its Aaron. I head out, lock the front door and walk towards the car. I really do hope its Aaron, as it would be a little embarrassing to get into someone else's car. I am really conscious walking over to the car as I know Aaron is watching. Thank god I opted for my flats, as if I had heels I just know I would have tripped or something.

I get in the car and thank god it is Aaron. He gives me a peck on the cheek and heads off, he still doesn't tell me where we are going. Aaron has Smooth Radio on, and I am happy it is not Radio 1....far too old for that. The car is lovely and warm, and I am thankful I managed to have a nap earlier else I think I would be asleep in the car. Aaron smells amazing, I can see he has on some navy jeans and a really nice cream thick jumper on. Our conversation seems to flow, talking about music, our weekend and the kids.

Confidential

After about 30 minutes we arrive at the chosen destination. We are going ice-skating. I am pleasantly surprised and grateful I popped my gloves into my coat as I was leaving. I have been ice-skating a handful of times, and whilst I am not quite ready to star on 'Dancing on Ice', I can let go of the rail for at least a lap of the ring. I have taken Anna once, and she looked so cute holding onto the penguin they give to the kids to help them.

Aaron informs me he has never been skating before, but 'how hard can it be?' he says.

I laughingly joke about getting him a penguin and he gives me a playful push.

Well, we get onto the ring and immediately Aaron starts wobbling and grabs the side. I grab the side as well, until I get the confidence to skate a little, grabbing the sides every 30 seconds to gain my posture. I turn around and see Aaron has managed to move about 2 metres, only moving by dragging himself along the side. Oh bless him. I wait for him to finally catch up and then take him by the arm and try and help him skate abit. He manages a few strides before he completely loses his balance and falls over. We manage this about 5 times, Aaron going down each time. At one point he even dragged me down on the floor as well.

Aaron is really trying hard and I can see he is really embarrassed and probably wants to give up but is putting on a brave face for me. How sweet !

In the end I manage to locate a penguin and hand it over to Aaron. He is hesitant at first, but reluctantly takes it and all of

Confidential

a sudden he can skate. I cannot stop laughing. Aaron is quite tall and is bending down so much to grab the penguin's handles. But he is skating around with a massive smile on his face, ignoring all the sympathetic looks from the adults and the sneers from the teenagers.

We skate around for another half hour before we admit defeat. I forgot how exhausting ice-skating was. We go and exchange our ice-skating boots and tease Aaron that he will not be rushing to do this again.

We go for a drink near to the ice-skating centre. I order a glass of wine and Aaron has a pint of shandy. We both have a lovely colour in our cheeks. We cannot stop laughing and talking.

Aaron tells me about his job as an Operations manager and some difficulties he is having with 2 of his staff who are not getting on as one of them ran off with the other person's wife.

Every now and again I start laughing about the image of Aaron happily skating around with the penguin, and we both stop mid-conversation and start laughing. I even think I snorted at one point which made us laugh even more. After 2 more drinks Aaron takes me home.

When I go out on a date I always dread the 'bye' scene. Its fine when you've had a rubbish date, but when you like someone there seems to be an awkwardness in the air. Like you are not quite sure what you are meant to do to show them that you enjoyed the date without seeming too forward. I mean, snogging someone's face off seems far too eager (unless your drunk of course and you can blame it on the drink). So do you go in for an awkward hug, a kiss on the cheek or just leave? Play hard to get?

I definitely want to see Aaron again, we had such a laugh and our conversations just flowed. So I definitely want to do more than a high-five when I leave. Aaron pulls up outside my house. I am not inviting him back for a coffee, it's far too early for that, and besides I want to make sure my house is thoroughly tidy beforehand, no skids left in the toilet (Anna of course, not me) !!!!

We chat and laugh a little more, and I thank Aaron for a great date and before I have decided what to do, Aaron leans over and gives me a kiss. Nothing too full-on, no tongues or anything, but definitely a indication that he wants to see me again.

Aaron pulls away and grabs my hand. Thanks me for a lovely night and tells me he will text me soon. He watches me unlock my door and I give him a wave and tell him to 'give me 3 rings when he gets home'.

I can hear him laughing as he pulls off.

I am proper smitten and feel like I am floating on a cloud. Of course I text Greg straight away to tell him and I ask him how his date last night went.

I start doing my bed-time routine and decide to get into bed and watch some TV. I check my phone and I haven't had a response from Greg. Hopefully he is busy out on another date. I do realise I have had a missed call from Aaron, he has messaged to say

'I gave you 3 rings'. I smile and message back immediately, thanking him for a great evening.

He replies and says he is looking forward to seeing me again soon.

So cute. I had a great evening. I don't even bother checking for any other messages, tonight was great enough.

Before going to sleep I text the girls Chat to update them about my date with Aaron. I know they'll be keen to hear the low-down.

CHAPTER THIRTY THREE

~~Early~~ Mid-30's lady looking for a relationship. Looking for the following;

1) Loves socialising
2) Funny
3) Kind
4) Enjoys holidays
5) Is a romantic at heart
6) IS NOT IN A RELATIONSHIP
7) Has open/honest conversations
8) Enjoys stopping in on a Saturday night watching click-flicks and eating rubbish
9) Likes a clean house
10) Would wear an easter bunny outfit (not for sexual pleasures – for a kids party)
11) Appreciates life – it is so short
12) DOES NOT SNOG ANYONE ELSE WHILST ON A DATE WITH YOU
13) Doesn't mind drunk dancing
14) Cooks Sunday dinners
15) Enjoys ice-skating

The next few weeks go by so fast. I take Anna to her swimming lessons; I have the girls round one night for a catch up and I even manage to cook them all a Chilli.

Greg has gone off the radar a little as he has started seeing someone named Simon, who he seems pretty smitten with. We still catch up at work and send the odd messages, but

Confidential

every spare moment he has he is seeing Simon. I am so pleased for him.

I on the other hand have been seeing Aaron quite a lot. We have been to the cinema, a meal and met up for coffee a few times during his lunch hour when he can.

I have decided to come off the dating site for abit (so no more every growing list). Evan still sends me the odd messages, but it is more of a friend zone. He doesn't tell me anymore about how his mum and I don't divulge. I'll be there if he ever feels ready to talk about it.

I feel a little bad about Dean and Dan, so I send them both a quick message to tell them I am currently 'dating' someone so do not feel right continuing messaging. I wish them well in their dating conquest. I felt like it was the right thing to do rather than just ghost them. And hey, if it goes tits up with Arron then I have a back-up plan. That's if they are still single of course.

Work has really picked up. I have managed to arrange another bottomless brunch and now have a date for the bongo bingo event which I am currently advertising.

I have taken a few wedding bookings for next year, one on Valentines day, 3 in the summer and some other potential bookings.

This weekend its Mother's day celebrations. With Mother's day in March and Easter has fallen earlier this year the Easter party falls he week after. So the next 2 weeks are really busy.

Confidential

Aaron has asked to see me this weekend, but I am so busy with Mother's day and a party on Friday night I simply cannot fit in the time. So he suggests a meeting at the park with the kids.

'We won't make it a big deal; we'll just both take the kids to the park and happen to 'bump' into one another' Aaron says

As the weather is finally starting to brighten up, I'll be glad to take Anna out to the park to get some fresh air and some sun on our Paley white cheeks.

This year for mother's day I have gone all out. On the Saturday I have arranged a flower arranging session. I know it's not on a Sunday but I thought it would be something different to the usual meal. Then on the Sunday I have an afternoon tea booked and in evening a mother's day Sunday dinner. They are all fully booked.

I have managed to avoid Sam 'the leech' by sending someone else to Celebrations. He must have got the hint by now that I am not interested in dating married men!!

I pick Anna up from school and she is so excited we are going to the park. I take a change of clothes for her, so she doesn't ruin her uniform and she gets changed in the car with me using a blanket I have in the car so 'no-one peeks'.

Anna skips off to play on the playground and I find a bench nearby so I can see her. There appears to be a few other parents who have had exactly the same idea and making the most of afternoon with no rain and actually seeing some sun.

Confidential

Although there is still a nip in the air, and we still need our winter coats and boots, it's nice to be outside.

I see Aaron and Grace after about 10 minutes. She is skipping as well, holding her dads hand. When she sees the park she runs off and upon Aaron seeing me, he comes and sits on the bench next to me. Not too close, and it feels weird that he doesn't give me a hug or a kiss.

When I say Aaron and I have been seeing each other for a few weeks, we still haven't done the dirty deed. He has cooked me dinner at his place, but I had work really early the next day so I went home. He has also come back to mine after a night out, and although he did actually stop over, we didn't do anything. Apparently I was really drunk and he didn't want to be seen as taking advantage, although apparently I was 'begging him' and trying to seduce him in my drunken state. That was very embarrassing, and I have vowed not to get into that state again with him for a while.

Luckily he did see the funny side of it and doesn't seem to be in any rush. Which is fine by me, although I do make sure I shave everywhere and wear my best matching underwear, and clean my house top to bottom, just in case. Its flipping hard work this dating business. I can't wait to settle down with someone and can wear my manky comfy pants, my white/grey bra, have stubbly legs and not have to bleach my toilet every 5 minutes !!!

I have brought a flask of coffee as it does seem abit chilly sitting still on the bench and I share a coffee with Aaron. I can see Anna and Grace playing but they haven't spoken to each other yet.

Anna does her usual and keeps looking over and waving to me, I ensure I wave back. Grace comes over.

'Daddy, I am really thirsty, can I have a drink please?' she says panting from all the running around she is doing.

'Of course, Grace, here you go' he replies handing her a fruit shoot.

'Grace, I want you to meet my friend Emily. Emily this is my daughter Grace'.

Grace glances over at me, looking at me curiously.

'Hi Grace. I have given shared some coffee with your daddy as he is getting abit cold'

She doesn't reply so I try abit more

'My daughter is over there at the park in the red coat. She is nearly same age as you. Her name is Anna. I am sure if you said hello she would speak to you'.

Grace doesn't reply, but I can see her looking in the direction of the park, scanning for someone with a red coat.

Grace finishes her drink and goes back to the park, and within a few minutes I can see her and Anna running around playing

Result

After about 10 minutes we have drank all the coffee and my bum is definitely going numb, but I don't mind as it's nice to spend some time with Aaron. I am telling him about the mother's day weekend and how he should come along to the Easter party with Grace.

Confidential

At that point I hear someone crying and mothers instinct kicks in and I know instantly its Anna. I get up and go over to her.

Anna is there, rubbing her face, tears streaming down her face.

'Oh Anna, whatever is wrong?' I say pulling her in for a hug.

She is sobbing by now

'That girl has just hit me mummy. It really hurts'

I suddenly feel raged. What kid would hit my baby girl?

'Which girl was it Anna?' I say, ready to go over and give this girl a peace of my mind

Anna points over, and I realise its Grace. Oh for god's sake, it would be wouldn't it !!

At this point, Aaron has come over asking if everything is ok. I explain that Anna says Grace has hit hurt. Aaron immediately goes over to speak to Grace, whilst I continue hugging Anna to try and calm her down and comfort her.

Aaron comes back and says he has spoken to Grace and apparently it was an accident.

'Grace has never done anything like this before, so perhaps it was an accident. Do you want me to get her to apologise?'.

Aaron bends down to speak to Anna.

'Hi Anna, I am your mummy's friend Aaron. The little girl that you said hit you is my daughter, Grace. But Grace says it was an accident and she didn't mean too. She feels very sorry and did not mean to make you cry'.

Anna's crying seems to have slowed down by now. She looks up at Aaron

'OK, as long as Grace did not mean too as that would be mean. Mummy, my face hurts, can we go home now?' Anna says looking at me.

'Of course sweetheart. Let's get you home and I can make you a lovely hot chocolate'. I reply, picking Anna up.

I say my goodbyes to Aaron, and I see him mouth 'I am sorry. I will text you later'

Aaron then calls out to Anna 'Goodbye Anna. Nice to meet you. I hope your face feels better soon. I am sure your mummy can find you some marshmallows with your hot chocolate as I have heard that helps with poorly faces'.

Anna grins then says 'Mummy do we have any marshmallows?'

I grin back at Anna. 'Yes of course I do sweetheart. Let's get you home. Bye Aaron'.

I also shout bye to Grace, but I don't think she hears me, too busy playing on the slide.

We head off home and I make sure I give Anna extra marshmallows with her hot chocolate. Her face is still a little red, she must have had a good wallop, but hey, these accidents do happen. I am just hoping Aaron doesn't feel guilty.

CHAPTER THIRTY FOUR

The next day I get Anna ready for school, I check her face and luckily the redness seems to have disappeared. There is a slight bump, but not really noticeable. I tell the teacher what has happened and message Rob as well so he doesn't think she has done it at school and starts interrogating the teacher.

At work I start getting the room prepared for the flower arranging event. I decorate the tables with pale pink table cloths and chairs. I have placed cream vases in the middle of each table which will be decorated with flowers.

The florist, Elizabeth will be arriving with fresh flowers and she will be delivering the class. The guests will be learning how to decorate a wreath which can be used for decoration purposes such as a centre piece, hung on a front door or could also be used as a memorial wreath for those mums/nans that have passed away.

Elizabeth will be bringing all the materials. She is a friend of my mums and has a small florist not far from the hotel. She was really pleased when I started using her as a regular supplier. I just felt she gives me a more personal touch, and she does give me a good price as well. Elizabeth treats her florist as more of a hobby as opposed to a business and no way does she make hardly any profit. But she certainly takes pride in her work. She has already dropped off the hoops and some other decorations, so I start placing those equally on the tables.

There are 26 guests in total, so I have arranged smaller tables of 4. With the remainder decorations I spread them out on one of our spare tables at the side of the room. On another table I place cups and saucers and condiments. There is going to be unlimited tea/coffee and orange juice, and of course the bar is open if anyone wants an alcoholic drink.

Elizabeth turns up with the fresh carnations for the wreaths. Elizabeth informs me that these are regarded as a symbol of the eternal love that a mother has for her children. Each colour carnation represents a meaning. Pink symbolises a mothers undying love and white is often used in memory of their mother. Light red symbolises admiration and dark red is love and admiration. I thought this was really touching for mothers day. She has also brought some pink carnations to go in the vases for the centrepiece.

The guests are due to arrive at 2.00pm, with the lesson starting at 2.30pm. This should give everyone time to arrive, find a seat and help themselves to a drink. I take some photos of the room set-up that I can use for promotional purposes. The wreath making should last about an hour to an hour and half, depending on how fast the 'students' are. Then we will be serving jacket potatoes with a choice of fillings such as cheese, beans, chilli con carne or coleslaw accompanied with some salad for each table.

For dessert we have a choice of apple pie and ice-cream, strawberry cheesecake or toffee sticky pudding and custard.

I did a similar wreath making event for Christmas, and it was so popular I plan to run these events a few times a year with different themes. At Christmas though we had 50 guests, which was far too many, and Elizabeth struggled with such a large group, so I have halved the total this time so it seems

Confidential

more personal. It also allows Elizabeth chance to chat to each of the guests.

The event is a success. There is a mixture of ages, some younger adults that have clearly been dragged along by their mums and have no interest in flowers, but come along to please their mums.

The grandmas seem to absolutely love it. Some of them were struggling attaching the tiny stems into the nests, but luckily either Elizabeth or I, or even some of the other guests would help. That is one to bear in mind for the next event.

Everyone seems really pleased with their finished wreath. I take some photos of the groups holding up their completed decoration and promise I will email the photos to them. They have all granted permission for me to add the photos to social media which I will do later.

After they have all left I start getting the rooms ready for tomorrow. The afternoon tea starts at 1.00pm, with guests arriving from 12.00pm. Then the mother's day dinner starts at 5.00pm, so it is going to be a really busy day tomorrow. I am just sad that I will be too busy to see my own mum, or even spending some quality time with Anna.

I have ordered 2 bouquets of flowers from Elizabeth. One for mum which should arrive at her house tomorrow morning and one for Anna's step mum. I know Rob has probably got her something, but I still wanted to get something from me (well Anna really). And besides it's a good excuse to see Anna when I drop the bouquet off in the morning before work.

Confidential

I get back home around 7.00pm, I make some cheese on toast as I really do not feel up to proper cooking. I take a shower and get ready for bed. Once I am settled I give my mum a call, making sure strictly has finished beforehand. We have a quick catch up. Mum telling me how she won a bottle of wine at bingo and that she'll save it for when I next go and visit. She tells me about dad going to the cinema with his mate and he could not believe the chairs have footrests that actually lift up from the floor. He also could not believe the cost of the popcorn and was grateful mum had given him a bag of wine gums that he snuck in his coat pocket.

Although thinking about it, I am not sure if taking food into the cinema is actually illegal. I certainly don't think the employers at the cinema stamping your ticket really care if you've brought in some strawberry laces. I am sure the cinema sweet police will not ban you from the cinema. But somehow, people always seem to sneak them in as if it's a crime !!

I feel really guilty that I am not seeing mum tomorrow. I should be cooking her a dinner, but instead she is cooking her own. Although Mum doesn't really like a fuss and she says she understands it's one of my busiest weekends and to her it is 'just like any other day'.

When I finish speaking to mum I see I have got a missed call from Aaron. I give him a call back and we have a general chat about our day. I end up telling him how I am missing my mum and wish I could see her on mother's day tomorrow. Aaron gives a sympathetic ear; he tells me him and his brothers are going to see their mum tomorrow – but she is cooking as she is a great cook and insists on cooking herself. Apparently they'll be about 10 of them there and its manic like Christmas day dinner, but his mum wouldn't have it any other way. She loves having all her family round.

Aaron once again apologises about Grace. I can tell he feels terrible for Anna. I reassure him that Anna is absolutely fine, and kids are just being kids. He asks if I would mind if he brought Grace along to the Easter party. I am delighted he wants to come. Although I have warned him that most of my friends will be there and they will be interrogating him. I also told him that Greg will also be hanging around him as Greg is a sucker for a good-looking bloke. Aaron really laughs at this and starts teasing me that I have called him 'a good looking bloke'.

After about 2 hours of talking about absolutely anything but nothing we hang up. Our conversation has definitely cheered me up.

I message Greg again. He must be totally in love as I have not properly spoke to him for a couple of weeks now. Although thinking about it, he has been quiet with me at work as well. I must have a chat with him tomorrow. I hope I haven't done anything to upset him, although I cannot for the life of me think what it could be.

CHAPTER THIRTY FIVE

On my way to work I nip and give the flowers to Anna's stepmum. She comes to the door with the toddler in her arms, who is so cute. Anna also comes running out with a box of chocolates and a lovely card she had made at school for me. It was perfect, and I hug her so tightly. Rob is busy cooking dinner for them all including his parents but invites me in anyway. I head into the kitchen and there is pots and pans everywhere. Rob looks so stressed bless him. He is wearing one of those aprons that makes you look like you've got a 6-pack, I think 'Anna' brought that for him one Christmas. I spend about 10 minutes having a chat and Anna showing me some of her drawings and leave them to it, blowing kisses to Anna as I walk to the car.

The afternoon tea set up is very traditional. I have purchased a selection of matching cups, saucers and teapots. Some are white and blue; some white and light pink and the others are white with gold. I also have matching 3-tired cake-stands. On the bottom tier is an array of brown, white or granary sandwiches with a choice of salmon and cream cheese, coronation chicken, cheese and pickle or turkey and stuffing wraps. The next tier has some caramelised onion and thyme sausage rolls, ham and mushroom mini-quiche, prawn vol au vonts and mini pork pies.

Top tier we have some coconut macaroons, mini strawberry gateau, chocolate eclairs and of course the traditional scones with clotted cream and jam. My mouth is watering just looking at them. I hope Alberto has made a few extras.

We have a selection of teas such as Earl Grey, Camomile, herbal and the most popular of choice, English breakfast. Some people have also chosen to add a glass of champagne, so I add the champagne glasses according to the table plan.

I have re-used my seating blackboard I use for weddings and have organised the tables in group sizes, depending on booking numbers.

I am using the flowers I had yesterday, but this time I change the vases to a nice gold colour. I have got some light music playing in the background. There are no activities or games, just an afternoon tea, although I have designed a small quiz for each table that the guests may want to do. Jut some general trivia questions following by…..'guess the famous baby'. I place the sheets and a pen down on the tables.

Greg turned up about an hour ago and he is in the kitchen helping with the afternoon tea. He really is avoiding me and cannot look me in the eye. Perhaps after this tea I will try and talk to him, find out what is wrong.

The guests start to arrive, and I show them the seating plan and they make their way to their respective table. Rachel and Nat are bringing their mums along as well, and Rachel has booked another 2 places which I am presuming must be for her mums friends. They are all sitting together so they have a table of 6.

I can hear Nat's laugh from miles away, so their party has arrived. But wait, I also recognise another voice.

Surely it can't be who I think it is? Can it? It is…..

At this point my mum walks in. Beaming from ear to ear. I run over and give her the biggest hug ever, tears streaming down my face with joy.

'Mum, what on earth are you doing here?' I say once I have regained my composure.

'Surprise love. Nat, Rachel and Greg have arranged it. I got the train down first thing this morning and your dad is coming to pick me up later' She says very delighted she has managed to keep a secret from me.

'Well thank you for organising this. Go and sit down and make a cup of tea and I'll come and join you later when I can' I reply, I simply cannot hold in the tears and start wiping my face. I may have to reapply my mascara.

Greg suddenly appears 'No Emily, that extra seat is for you. You are having afternoon tea with your mum'

'But I can't ! I have to work !' I say, although grateful for the kind gesture

Greg starts walking me to my seat 'No Emily, I am covering today. I have it all under control. Now go, and don't you dare start working. I am just pleased the secret is out now'

Oh, I get it now, so that was why Greg was 'off' with me. He wasn't off with me at all; he is just hopeless at keeping secrets and so the easiest thing was to avoid me. Bless him, I bet he is relieved.

The afternoon tea is lovely – even if I do say so myself. I wish I could have had more champagne, but after all the sandwiches and cakes I ate if I did another glass I would be wanting a lie-down and unfortunately that is something I definitely cannot do today.

There are loads of left-over food, but I had brought some little fancy takeaway boxes which seem to go down a storm. The guests must not appreciate food-waste just like me.

Mum and friends are the last to leave. Mum is going back to Nat's house for a couple of hours with Nat's mum and dad will pick her up later on from there. I give them all a big hug and thank them again for a lovely surprise. Mum thanks me for the flowers which arrived just before she left here. I could have given them her today if I had known, saved on the delivery fee !!!!!!

After they had all gone I start re-arranging the tables ready for the mother's day Sunday dinner. Guests are due to arrive at 5.00pm, so I need to have everything ready for 4.30pm just in case we have any keen early arrivals. This means I have an hour and half to get it all done, plenty of time.

I shout Greg into help me and he fills me in on his latest love life.

'Well, as you know his name is Simon, a couple of years older than me. Does something with computers for a living. He goes Yoga in his spare time and wants me to join him one time for a session'. Greg says, sitting down for 5 minutes whilst I start rearranging the chairs.

'I mean, Emily, I am all for watching men in tight Lycra shorts, especially bending down doing the downward dog or whatever you call it. But I am about as bendy as a stick. And I don't think my knees could hack it anymore' !!!

I do laugh, Greg does have a way with words.

I fill him in on Aaron and the fact I have come off the dating site. I still text Evan, but the others are on a backburner for the time being. I tell him about Grace and the incident, but only lightly as I don't want to make a big deal about it.

There are about 50 coming for dinner tonight. I have arranged a special deal at the hotel. So you can book a 3-course mother's day dinner with entertainment in the evening. This also includes a night at our hotel and breakfast in the morning. Not all the guests that are coming for dinner have chosen this option, but it has helped to fill the hotel rooms on a Sunday night which is great for business.

Once the room is all ready and the singer has set up I go for a quick break at the bar. I check the hotel's social media post and I am pleased to see some people have posted pictures of the afternoon tea and the wreath making event with beaming, positive comments. That's what I like to see.

By 5.30pm everyone is seated, and the starters begin arriving. There is some confusion where someone forgot to say they were gluten free, and another forgot to cancel a seat booking, but it's all sorted now after abit of juggling.

By 6.30pm their isn't really much more I can do, the waitresses are getting ready to serve the puddings, the singer is all set up and will start at 7. I can help clean up tomorrow as we have nothing on tomorrow, thank god.

Greg is serving behind the bar until 8.00pm but he manages to talk me into going out for a few drinks when he finishes work. I am shattered, but I have missed Greg's company so would be great to have a catch up.

'I'll pick you up at 8.15pm – be ready' Greg calls as I am grabbing my coat and heading out of the door.

On my way back home I call mum to check she is home ok. When I get in, I send Evan a quick message telling him I am thinking of him today and face time Anna. Then I start getting ready.

I decide to go for my black jumper dress, tights and my kitten heeled boots, finished with some nice jewellery to complete my outfit. Not bad for someone who is absolutely shattered – even if I do say so myself. I straighten my hair, put some make up on which to be fair, I have been applying it exactly the same since I was 18 years old. Apart from I no longer have the sparkly glittery silver eyes and heather shimmer lipstick. My make-up has gone up a little in price, but I still slap it on the same. Mental note - I really need to watch more beauty make-up sessions on you-tube.

Greg turns up just before 8.30pm. He has even managed to get changed (mmm, someone tells me he must have planned this and brought an outfit into work). Tonight he is going quite low-key with bright blue jeans and a paisley shirt completed with a blue trilby hat.

We head off to the new cocktail bar which appears to be our new local. Apparently there is a male vocalist on, and I am grateful it's not karaoke as I can't sing for shit. However Greg always manages me to talk me into joining in with him. Usually it is something like 'All the Single Ladies', or a Katy Perry tune that Greg has chosen.

I go to the bar whilst Greg tries to find us a table. It's pretty busy considering it's a Sunday and its mother's day. I thought it would be quiet. Perhaps Sunday evening is the new Saturday. I order a vodka and coke, Greg a martini and lemonade and having no success finding a table we grab a few stools and sit at the bar.

Greg and I are having a general catch up when two of the blokes I recognise from the night we met from the pool team come over and say hello. I think its Craig and Greeny (or something like that). We exchange pleasantries although Greg must have talked to them much more than I thought and was asking one of them about a weekend away they recently had and how the other one's dates had gone. They ask us to join them as they have a table, so we agree and follow them to where they are sitting. There is another 2 people at the table who introduces themselves as Morgan and Joanne.

I think back to the last time I was in a bar with a group of people was when I watching Will snogging someone's face off whilst I was on a date with him. Thinking of Will, I never did get that apology.

After an hour or so I am suddenly flagging. The drinks seem to have gone straight to my head, probably as I am both tired and haven't eaten since lunch.

Confidential

As I am finishing off my last drink Sam comes and join us. I am happy I was just about to leave. I say hello, then hug everyone goodbye, including Greg who seems to be there for a late night.

'Emily, are you ok'? Sam asks as I am heading outside to a taxi.

'Hey Sam. Yeah I am fine. I am tired, a long day'. I reply, putting on my 'tired face'.

'Perhaps it is just my imagination but I thought you have been off with me. And then when you was drunk the other night you started having a go at me which confused me even more. But never mine. Goodnight Emily' Sam calls as I am getting in a taxi.

I start to get back out the taxi to explain, but Sam is already walking off. I am so tired I cannot be bothered to follow him and then have to wait again for another taxi.

Just as I am about the close the taxi door Sam suddenly turns around and shouts 'Emily, check your dating messages' and walks off.

I sit back in the taxi a little confused. I have paused my dating app, so I haven't been on it for a while now. I realise I don't have the dating app anymore on my phone. So I will have to log in on my laptop later.

I get ready for bed, not even bothering with taking my make-up off because quite frankly I cannot be bothered. What a bugger I am.

Confidential

I think about Sam's last conversation with me. I am so tired it's even a struggle to get my laptop; my eyes are too sleepy I won't be able to see the screen properly anyway.

I will have a look tomorrow.

CHAPTER THIRTY SIX

OMG, OMG, OMG.

Sam is on the dating site.

OMG

So in the morning I manage to re-log into my dating site. I have a few messages, scroll through them and then I see someone I recognise

Only flipping Sam.

His profile isn't too bad to be fair, workable with a few general tweaks, but overall not too bad.

Hi, my name's Sam. Not short for anything, just Sam. Although I guess it would only be short for Samuel !!

Recently divorced after a long marriage that was mostly happy. Looking to meet my new soul mate, would like to eventually settle down. I have no kids of my own, but I love my families kids and would not object to dating someone with kids – just not more than 3.

Got a pretty decent job, enjoy playing pool and currently learning how to speak Italian but not very good at it. I play pool at my local club, and really need some new hobbies.

If you have got this far and enjoy reading this profile then drop me a message. I think I'm a pretty decent bloke (or so my mum tells me anyway)

So, he wasn't flirting with me !!! And he wasn't married after all. I feel awful. I was so mean to him.

Then I remember he had sent me a message

'Hey Emily. Fancy seeing you on this site. I hope it is going well for you. Early days for me, and I have come across a few wierdos. Anyway, probably see you around soon'.

Ahhh, what a nice message. Nice and simple and would have made it not awkward next time I see him – except the fact that I was a total cow to him.

I decide I will apologise in person next time I see him. It doesn't feel right messaging him back on here to apologise.

So for the remainder of the week I am really busy organising the easter party. I take Anna on her weekly swimming lessons. She is very slowly getting better, no diving off the boards yet so I think I have a few more visits before I can quit. Bad mum or what ???

I am organising another date for a flower making session. I am thinking of a doing one at the beginning of summer as Elizabeth informs me there will be many new choices of flowers to choose from.

I make a few more party bookings for later in the year. And start making more plans for the upcoming weddings. I have a few meetings with the brides-to-be, going over the meal choices and room arrangements.

I also have another lunch date with Aaron. I am finding it difficult to find time to see him at the minute. With me

Confidential

having Anna most nights in the week and he seems to have Grace on the weekends I am not actually working, or when work finishes at a reasonable time. Typical. Hopefully once he has meet Anna a few times he will be able to come round in the week once she has gone to bed.

Aaron and I meet near his place of work as he is really busy with work and can only half an hour. We order a ready-made sandwich meal deal and take a seat.

We have a catch up on our day, he says he is looking forward to the easter party on Saturday, although is not looking forward to meeting my friends.

Aaron asks if I would like to go round on Saturday evening after the Easter party. He would cook me some dinner

'And perhaps it would be nice if we could have a drink together' Aaron says, leaning closer to me. 'Rather than get a taxi would you like to stay over? I am dropping Grace to her mums after the Easter party, so I have Saturday evening and all-day Sunday free if you are?'

I reply 'OK, that sounds lovely. I'll come round on Saturday when I have finished with the party. I won't need to drop Anna off to her dads as Kerry is doing that for me as I'll be tidying up and that after'.

'And yes, I can stop over. But could I be cheeky and ask to have a shower when I get to yours as I'll have been working all day?'

Confidential

Aaron laughs 'Of course you can have a shower. In fact, if you want I can run a bath ready for you when you get in from work. Have some candles, or whatever you ladies do'

I return the laugh 'Hey, I could get used to that pampering. No its fine, I am not a fan of baths. I'll take a shower. I'm not sure if I have anything on work-wise Sunday. Perhaps just tidying up after Saturday, and some socials, but I can do that on Monday if needs be'.

We finish our lunch and I walk Aaron back to his office. We have a sneaky kiss before Aaron heads back to work and then I head back to the hotel.

I am looking forward to my sleepover at Aarons. Although I a little nervous.

Operation shaving will be required. It's been a while

'Oh cobwebs' – Drop dead Fred would say

CHAPTER THIRTY SEVEN

It's the day of the easter party and thank god the weather looks ok. It hasn't rained all weekend, so I plan on hiding some of the easter eggs in the garden as well, get the kids doing some running around, let off some steam.

The party starts at 12.00pm until 300pm. I've decorated the large room in easter décor, so pictures of bunnies and easter chicks fill the room. Every child that attends will be gifted an easter basket, which they can use on the hunt. I have also got some easter creative bits that the kids can use to decorate their basket. I've got some glue sticks, shiny paper, pictures of eggs and chicks that they can colour and lots more shiny bits.

I have also got some crayons and pictures of easter eggs that they can colour in. And some bubbles, I always think you can't go wrong with kids and bubbles, and of course some balloons.

We have an easter bonnet competition, so I have spent the week helping Anna make a bonnet. Being creative is definitely one of my greatest gifts, but in all fairness I made it fare and let her do most of it. I just guided her a little (and re-stuck some wonky bits when she wasn't looking).

We have a disco playing and I am arranging to do some party games, musical statues, some disco dancing and passing the balloon game down the line for the older kids.

The room looks great, and I am really hoping it will be a successful party and it is something I can do every year. Sam called me in the week to say he was coming to the party and that he'd drop the easter bunny costume off to me. Luckily, the conversation was fine, no awkwardness which I was really grateful for.

Everything was going to plan until Greg calls me, he has 'man-flu' and can't come into work. But who is going to be the easter bunny now? Sam has dropped the costume off in my office so the kids wouldn't see it and I head off into the kitchen where most of the staff are

'Right guys, I have an emergency' I shout, so they all stop what they are doing

'Greg has called in sick. So, I'll need someone to come out front every now and again whilst I'm organising the games to check I am coping. And secondly, I need someone to dress up as the easter bunny. This will be about 12.30, so I don't care who does it, but I need someone please'

I head out back to the venue. I have great staff, so I know someone will be willing to step up and help me.

We are having a great party. Anna has turned up with Kerry and her kids and I manage to help her do some colouring for a little while, but she's enjoying playing with Flo and Tilley and some other friends she's made.

Kerry's kids are far too 'old' to do any colouring so they wait patiently for the games to start.

Aaron also turns up with Grace who is looking a little shy. I go over to where they are.

'Hello Grace, I am Emily. You met me at the park a few weeks ago and you played with my daughter Anna. Would you like to go and sit with Anna?'

Grace nods and surprisingly she takes my hand and we walk over. Grace immediately picks up some crayons and starts colouring an easter egg.

I go back over to Aaron and introduce him to my friends; I can tell Aaron is a little nervous. I wish I could give him a reassuring kiss but decide against it.

'Sorry to leave you Aaron, but I know you'll be in great hands with my friends, and worst case, there's a bar over there' I give him a big smile and head in the kitchen

As I enter the kitchen, I am pleased to see someone has volunteered to be the Easter bunny, so I shout over 'Thanks Easter bunny, I'm going to make an announcement that you'll be coming out soon. Here is a basket full of chocolates and I want you to hand them out to the kids, have some pictures taken and generally just be around for abit. And thank you'

I head back out, I couldn't hear the response as the kitchen was far too noisy, and plus the costume would have blocked out their voice.

I make an announcement and the easter bunny comes out skipping, waving to the kids. I see Anna scream with delight and goes running over waving.

The kids seemed to enjoy the party, although the egg hunt was a little challenging as the older kids seemed to find the eggs a lot quicker. I manage to sneak a few more chocolates

Confidential

into the younger kids basket. I even manage a few cuddles with Rachel's triplets, although that was tricky juggling holding them. They are absolutely adorable, with those fat roll legs that I love. I could just eat them, not literally of course.

We do the easter bonnet competition, and of course I am not able to be judge so I get the easter bunny to select the top 3. The winners seemed delighted to receive an Easter egg each.

The kids have a buffet selection of chicken nuggets, chips and pizzas, although I think some may have eaten far too chocolate. Some of the adults have been making most of the bar, so hopefully that would have made us a profit as well. The party games are really fun, although Anna is so busy dancing she forgets to stop when doing musical statues.

I cannot believe how great the easter bunny is, I try and figure it out (I feel like I am a judge on the Masked Singer). I am convinced it must be one of the new waiters we've hired. They have been dancing with Anna and some other girls for about half hour by now. I go over to tempt Anna away so the Easter bunny can finish and finally take their outfit off. They must be sweating in the costume, but I end up having to do the hockey cokey with Anna, Grace, the Easter bunny and some of the other kids. What a sight that must have been.

After the hockey cokey I manage to sneak away and talk to Aaron. He tells me he thinks my friends have given him the 'third degree', but other than that are a really great bunch of friends. I am so happy.

As the party starts coming to an end, Anna comes running over to me crying.

'Whatever is the matter darling?' I say, crouching down to give her a big hug

'It's that girl again from the park, she has hit me again'. Anna shows me her arm, and yes its bright red.

'Oh Anna, it might have been an accident. Do not let it ruin the great party. And look at all the chocolates you have had' I say, trying to hide my annoyance and diffusing the attention from looking at her red arm.

At this point, Kerry comes over with her kids who look exhausted from all the disco dancing.

'Are you ready to go now Anna?. Let's take you to your daddy to show him all the chocolate you have got' Kerry says, giving me a look to indicate she knows what has happened.

I give Anna and all my friends a hug. They all whisper in my ear that Aaron is a 'delight/hot/amazing'.

Nat whispers me 'good luck for tonight, I hope you've brought you're sexy pants' and gives me a sneaky wink.

Everyone starts to leave by now. I say goodbye to Aaron and Grace, and he says, 'see you soon', as he leaves.

I can't wait to see Aaron tonight, but equally I am so angry with Grace. This cannot be coincidental that she has hit Anna twice, on the only two times she has actually met her.

Confidential

I try not to dwell on it too much, I really want to enjoy my evening with Aaron. I can talk to him about it later on.

CHAPTER THIRTY EIGHT

Its sleepover night. I am so excited, but equally so nervous.

I finish work around 4.30pm after tidying all the bits away. With all these new decorations I am purchasing I really need some more storage space.

There are a few families still in the bar area who thank me as I am leaving. I grab my overnight bag and head over to Aarons.

Aarons flat is pretty basic but nice and clean. He did apologise for the lack of furniture and paint everywhere, as he explains he is currently decorating his bedroom. He also laughed and said he has no style when it comes to house décor, he left that all to his ex.

In his living room there is a 2-seater black leather sofa, with a matching 1-seater chair, a flowery rug (which apparently came from his mum) and a black coffee table. He has a cabinet in the corner which has a few drawings that Grace must have done for him, and a few toy boxes in the corner. Above the fireplace is a large TV which seems the size of a cinema screen. There is a random picture on the wall of some flowers (curtesy of his mum again).

Grace's room is decorated beautifully with light blues and yellows. She has one of those cabin beds with a ladder to climb into her bed and a tent underneath which one side is full of books and toys and the other is a little space which apparently Aaron calls it her quiet, reading corner. But really he explains it's for when he needs some quiet time and it's an excuse for him to have 10 minutes of peace !!!

The remainder of the flat is Aaron's bedroom, or his 'love den' as he informed me whilst laughing. A kitchen which is a little outdated, but full of the latest gadgets, coffee machine, smoothie maker, air-fryer, slow-cooker, soup maker. I can see a few pots and pans steaming away and whatever he is cooking smells lovely. And then of course, the bathroom, which Aaron tells me is his next project to sort.

'When I moved into the flat' Aaron starts telling me 'My mum came round armed with stuff. Most of it was horrid and I swear it was stuff she'd had since her and dad was married in the 60's. She even tried to put one of those doll doolies on the toilet roll holder'.

'I have been slowly getting rid of the stuff she brought round without hurting her feelings'. He continues.

I start chuckling and Aaron pulls me in for a kiss and a hug. I am conscious of my breath, and I am grateful for the chewing gum I found in my car. He smells amazing again. Tonight he is wearing some casual black joggers, a navy fitted polo shirt and these great big pink flamingo slippers which for some reason I only noticed after I accidentally stood on one of them when he pulled me in for a kiss. Grace had brought them for him at Christmas and he has to wear them everytime she comes round. Although I secretly think that's just an excuse and he actually loves them.

Confidential

'Is it ok if I go and grab and shower please and get out of my work clothes?' I ask, pulling away from his hug. 'I feel like a smell of easter egg chocolate'

'Of course' responds Aaron, heading towards the bathroom. 'Let me grab you a clean towel. Please help yourself to any toiletries, although they may smell abit manly'.

Aaron heads back to the kitchen to continue cooking and I go and take a shower. It felt abit weird having a shower in someone else's house. Like I was invading their privacy or something. But nevertheless, I quickly get changed into a jumper dress and tights. It's quite a baggy dress as I figured my belly will bloat after our dinner. I re-do my make-up and attempt to tidy up my hair. Damn, I wish I had brought my straighteners as it has gone proper frizzy.

I have my matching underwear on, just in case. And I have brought my best silk pj's that feel so nice to wear. As I drop my bag into Aaron's room as he suggested I notice a note on the bed addressed to me.

'For you' – it reads. And on the bed are some matching flamingo slippers. I laugh out loud and quickly slip them on.

As I head into the kitchen I do a grand entrance by doing a truffle shuffle dance, highlighting my slippers. Aaron copies me and grabs me by the hand and twirls me round. I nearly fall into the oven, and we quickly decide that this kitchen is not big enough for dancing, especially wearing great big matching flamingo slippers.

Confidential

Aaron hands me a glass of wine and tells me to go and make myself comfortable in the living room. He has put the TV on for me - or should I say the cinema screen.

I banish myself into the living room, I would normally have a nosey around but there isn't really anything to be nosey about. Although I do notice a few holiday brochures on the table, Centre Parcs, Butlins, Pontins – looks like he is planning a break away with Grace.

As I flick through the channels I give Greg a quick text to see if he is feeling any better. I have had a text from Kerry 'Dropped Anna off at Robs OK. Aaron seems amazing – enjoy your night 😊 😊'

I am still messaging Evan; just friends of course which obviously I am happy about given the circumstances. We normally just have a chit-chat about how our week has been, what we have been watching on the TV. Nothing serious, just friendly banter.

At that point Aaron comes in to top up my wine and brings some olives and breads.

'Just some little bits to munch on whilst we wait for dinner' he says, pouring a pint of beer for himself. 'Sorry Emily, but I am not a wine drinker, I can't understand how you can drink that – its vile'.

We sit for a while, I eat the bread as I am like Anna and cannot stand olives. We have a catch up about the party. I decide not the mention the hitting scene, it can wait until tomorrow, I don't want to ruin our night, especially how it seems Aaron has put in a lot of effort for the evening.

'You did a really good job today Emily. It was lovely to see you at your place of work again and watching you work. You seem to glow when you are working, you can see how much you enjoy it'.

I thank him for the compliment.

'I best go and serve up dinner' Aaron says, jumping off the settee 'I am sorry I don't have a dining table and I am afraid we will have to eat it on our laps'.

'Dinners served' announced Aaron, bringing in 2 trays. He has cooked us a chilli and rice with garlic bread (I best brush my teeth after).

The dinner is lovely, and I do really well not to spill any down my dress.

After dinner I insist on washing up, but Aaron is adamant and pours me another glass of wine before heading back into the kitchen – anyone would think he is trying to get me drunk !!

I was impressed, the dinner was lovely. It is very appealing dating someone that can cook, especially when I dislike doing it myself. I could definitely get used to being wined and dined on.

After Aaron has finished cleaning up, we settle down to watch a film. He pulls me in close to snuggle up on the settee and he grabs a blanket to make it even cosier.

Confidential

The next thing we know I wake up. I open my eyes and try and figure out where I am. Damn, I fell to sleep watching the film. I lift up my head off Aarons arm and realise he too had fallen to sleep and starts stirring. When he realises what we have done we both start laughing

'Well, so much for a night of passion eh'. Aaron says. 'Come on, let's go brush our teeth and get ready for bed. I've even got some pjs especially for the occasion'.

'Oh Aaron' I say teasingly 'you do know how to seduce a woman'.

We both get up and whilst Aaron brushes his teeth I change into my pjs. I'm in two minds whether to take my bra off and let it all hang down or keep it on. Sod it. He can take me as I am.

After I have brushed my teeth I come back to find Aaron already in bed wearing a Christmas onesie.

'Sorry Emily, Grace made me buy us matching onesies to wear at Christmas. I usually just wear my boxer shorts but thought this would be more appropriate'. He laughs and opens up his arms. I am starting to think he uses Grace as an excuse for him to wear comical things !!

I get into bed and into his arms. We have a chat, and he turns off the light. We have abit of a kiss and then we fall to sleep with Aaron spooning me. It's a perfect date, and although I am gagging for some 'action', it couldn't have gone any better and I am secretly pleased we haven't rushed

Confidential

anything, although the throb on I currently have is telling me different.

CHAPTER THIRTY NINE

The next morning I wake up early realising I am not in my own bed. Aaron has set his alarm as unfortunately last minute plans means he had to do some football coaching late morning. Although we didn't have to get up early, he will still need to leave at 11.00am. I think he was hoping for a full night of passion, and of course so was I. Well that certainly didn't happen !!

I realise Aaron must have been abit hot in the night with the full-on winter onesie and it appears something is poking in my back. I hope hes not lying there completely naked.

I am wondering whether I should go and brush my teeth and sort out my hair, put a little mascara on or something. Then climb back into bed before he wakes up and he'll think I look amazing first thing in the morning.

Then I realise if this become a regular thing then I'll have to continue with the routine and set up an alarm 30 minutes before Aaron wakes up every morning. What a ball ache ! Narr, sod that.

Aaron suddenly starts stirring and I think he realises the action he has down-below and casually moves away. Bless him, he must be conscious of it.

'Morning you' Aaron says. 'Did you sleep well? I got a bit hot and itchy in the night so I had to take that onsie off'.

'Morning you. I slept really well thank you, I hope I didn't snore'. I say leaning in for a kiss. 'Excuse the breath'.

Confidential

Aaron laughs. "Yeah, I was debating whether I should have served up garlic bread for dinner, I know my breath is rank'

We cuddle for abit longer before Aaron gets out of bed (his poking stick must have gone down by now). He pops on some joggers but leaves his top off, the tease!!

'Right, would you like tea/coffee/orange juice. I am going to cook you a sausage and bacon sandwich. Is that ok?' Aaron asks

'That would be lovely thank you. And coffee would be great' I reply, waiting for him to leave before getting out of bed.

Whilst I hear Aaron scrambling around in the kitchen I start getting dressed and ready. I am dying to fart and manage a quick sneaky one in the bathroom. To try and hide the noise I flush the toilet as I am doing it – genius. Please come back later for more tips!!

I have a quick wash, brush my teeth and put on some basic make-up. My hair has gone completely wild by now, so I tie it back to make it as neat as possible. I also pop on some perfume incase my fart smells.

I join Aaron in the kitchen

'Can I help?' I say. 'Where's the mugs?'. Aaron points at the cupboard and I start making a coffee for me and a cuppa for Aaron. He still has his top off and I am so tempting to give him a quick feel, but don't want to come across as a leech !!!! But these fanny flutters I have are driving me crazy, if he is not careful I will end up jumping him !

We eat the sandwich and have another proper coffee this time using one of Aaron's many gadgets. Aaron needs to leave soon so I decide I might as well pop into work.

'Aaron, I have had a lovely evening and morning. So thank you. However, I do need to have a quick chat with you about something' I decide I do actually need to talk to him about Grace. I really don't want to ruin our sleepover but I can't leave it any longer.

So I tell him about Anna crying at the Easter party, how she said Grace had hit her again. Aaron listened, but questioned whether he was sure Anna wasn't making it up.

'I saw the red mark Aaron, so I know she wasn't lying. And Anna definitely did say it was Grace that did it. But she didn't know why'. I respond, feeling abit uneasy having this conversation, as no-one likes to hear someone dissing their child.

'I am sorry I had to mention it Aaron, especially after a lovely time we have spent together. But I felt I needed to say something'.

He reassures me he is glad I have said something, which makes me feel relieved. 'I'll try and talk to Grace. I don't think she has ever hit anyone before, but I will talk to her mum about this'.

Shortly after we both leave. Aaron gives me a lovely, lasting kiss that could have easily lead to other things. Damn it this going to work and football coaching business !!

I go into work, very smiley and happy. I stick the radio on full-blast and sing my heart away to Whitney Houston 'I'm every woman'.

Today is going to be a great day.

CHAPTER FORTY

The next week goes really quickly. Rob and I have a parents evening for Anna. She seems to be getting on well at school and has made some lovely friends. Greg is feeling better, and we have a catch up over coffee one lunch.

I haven't managed to see Aaron this week, he's been really busy with work. But we are going to see each other Saturday evening after work. He does have Grace that evening, but I am going to go round after she has gone to bed to watch a film (but this time, not to fall asleep, and definitely no sleepovers).

I have a wake on Friday afternoon/evening and the speed dating event on Saturday night. On Sunday I have a meeting booked with the bride's parents about the room set-up for a wedding I have scheduled. So a very busy weekend.

It is really strange organising a wake. I never know whether I should be sad, smiley or happy. I tend to try and gauge it by how the guests are when they arrive, but usually by the time the guests do arrive at the wake they are ready to celebrate the person's life. But I can never be too sure, and I am still cautious. The last thing they want is me being all happy chappy around them when they are grieving.

The wake is celebrating a 60-year-old lady who had lost her battle from cancer. The husband does a really heart-felt speech about how she tried too hard to fight the virus, but at the end her body became so weak. He spoke about how much him and his family loved her and what a beautiful, kind lady she was. It was a really emotional speech which left

Confidential

everyone in tears. But after the speech the music was turned up, the food buffet was opened and quite a few people got up to dance. I believe she had a great send-off.

After work I head over to Aarons. I'm really excited to see him, although I'm really gutted I can't stay over. I am so ready to take things further. In fact, I am so ready it's all I can actually think about ! Everything reminds me of it. Cutting up some cucumber for Anna's lunch, every programme I watch someone is having it off and I swear I even heard my neighbours at it one night !!

As I go into the flat, Aaron indicates me to be quiet 'I have just put Grace to bed' he says, with his finger on his lips. I gently take off my shoes and go into the living room. Luckily I have managed to grab a leftover sandwich and a couple of buffet bits for dinner, so I am not hungry. Which is a good job as it looks like Aaron and Grace have already eaten.

We sit watching a film whilst having a cuddle and talking quietly. About half-way through the film, we hear little footsteps come into the living room

'Daddy, I cannot sleep. Who is that?' says Grace, rubbing her eyes sleepily and pointing at me. It's obvious she has been asleep already, perhaps she has had a bad dream, or whether we woke her up talking abit too loudly.

'Gracey, this is Emily. I told you I was having a friend coming round tonight. Remember Emily, she was at the Easter party with her daughter Anna?' Aaron says, getting up to give Grace a hug. I give Grace a little wave.

'Come on Grace, let's get you back to bed'. He walks Grace back to room whilst mouthing a 'sorry' at me. I give him a reassuring smile. I was lucky that Anna is a really good sleeper, the minute I put her down, she is fast on, and she is usually there for the rest of the night. Although now I've said that I bet she doesn't now and keeps me up all night!!!

After about an hour of me sitting alone watching TV and scrolling through facebook, Aaron comes in.

'I am really sorry Emily, but she's not settling' he says, looking really sad.

'Don't worry' I respond, starting to get up and grabbing my shoes. 'I'll leave you to it. I hope she manages to settle soon'.

I start heading towards the door. I can see how disappointed he looks, and I am not going to lie, I am disappointed too, especially when I really wanted to know how the film ended !!!

'I am really sorry; I'll text you later' he says and gives me a peck on the cheek.

'Honestly, do not worry. Kids come first' I say and gently I close the front door behind me.

I do completely understand, and I feel so sorry for him. Bless him, but as I have said, kids do come first, and I would be exactly the same if I was in his situation.

As I get home I have a quick shower and do my beauty regime, which has definitely been neglected over the past few weeks. Come to think of it, so has my exercise, damn that Joe Wickes. I really do need to get back into it. These bingo wings won't fix themselves. Especially when, hopefully soon, I will be getting naked with Aaron who, as I have seen (obviously not because I perved, but because he made me breakfast without his top on) is not shy of going to the gym, and although does not have pecs, definitely has some definition.

I receive a message from Aaron apologising and I respond back, reassuring him yet again. He messages to say he will make it up to me soon.

I hope he makes it up to me in a more physical way !!! God, I am like a dog on heat.

CHAPTER FORTY ONE

I get up early feeling fresh as a daisy. I even manage a quick 10-minute Joe Wickes work-out before work. Let's see how long that will actually last – again. I can almost feel the bingo wings disappearing as we speak.

It's the day of the speed dating event. I am a little nervous of how many people will actually attend. I have been promoting it like mad on the social media channels, which I can see on Facebook this has gained quite abit of interest. A few people have confirming they are attending and a few saying they are 'interested', so I really have no idea.

I have aimed it to be for age 30 plus event. Not sure if that was the right thing to do, but upon researching it seemed like there was a lower count for people attending speed dating events for people under 30. And plus I need to narrow the age somehow.

I couldn't exactly narrow the age to 'no over 80s' as I didn't want to get the ageist police on me. Who knows who will actually turn up, I guest it's just a case of wait and see.

The aim of the evening is upon arrival there will be a meet and greet and I will the guests to the bar, where a courtesy free drink will be available with a chance to do some socialising. Then it will be onto the venue room where the main event will be held. I am planning on each couple having 5-minutes to chat before moving onto the next. Then after the event, they have a chance to move back into the bar, should they wish, to socialise even more, and hopefully form some successful matches.

Confidential

Each person will have a name tag and given a piece of paper to write their top 3 favourites on. At the end of the networking rounds, I will collect the papers in, and anyone with a match on their top 3 I will give the person their results. I will try and do this quite secretly to save grace and embarrassment If anyone is unfortunate to not have a match.

I have also arranged for a two-piece band to play in the bar. I am thinking that if there is no match, then at least they can have fun, and if there is a match then it's an excuse to stay and listen to the music whilst having a drink at the bar – everyone's a winner. The band is a local start-up and is trying to book more business, I have not used them before but I am more than willing to give them a try.

I arrange the tables in two's, with a decent gap in-between so no-one can overhear the other couple's conversation. As I have no idea how many people will arrive I guess and arrange for 15 tables, meaning 30 people attending. That may be over-estimating, but I will have more of an idea once the guests arrive, hence another reason they are having a drink at the bar first. I re-use the red tablecloths from Valentines and have a few leftover balloons that I place around the room.

I am hoping that by luck there will be an equal ratio of men/women, but what are the chances that will happen? So a back-up plan that if there are a few people who are not currently talking to someone, either I or Greg can step in, or they can use this as a toilet break/go to the bar.

By 7.15pm the guests start arriving. I have arranged everyone to arrive by 7.30pm at the latest, with the networking to start at 8 prompt. Some female guests have come with friends, some are which are not joining in but have asked if they can have a drink at the bar, obviously giving their friends morale support which is lovely to see.

I see a few males hesitant whether to enter or not, and I go over and encourage them to join, ensuring them it is not something to be worried about. I tell them to think of it as a night out socialising, just abit of fun and they will enjoy it.

A couple of Gregs friends have come as promised, which is great as they are like an older version of Greg, full of confidence. Which is something we really need tonight to help with the nerves from some of the guests that have arrived.

There seems to be a range of different ages, at a guess we are looking at 30-60, where one lady at the age of 60 is looking very uncomfortable after realising that some people are twice her age and could actually be her siblings.

I go over to her and I can see she is looking really uncomfortable.

'Oh, I didn't know whether to come or not. I have been separated from my husband 10 years now, and thought it was about time I moved on. I can't be done with those dating websites. Too much faff, so my friends encouraged me to come here. I wish I hadn't. Look at them, I am 60 years old. Who would look at me?' she says.

Confidential

I manage to convince her to stays, saying that if anything it would be good experience for her. That it would be a great laugh, and an opportunity to meet new friends.

She reluctantly agrees, although it may be down to the glass of wine I get her to calm her nerves.

I quickly count the people that have badges. It seems like there are about 19 people, not ideal, but it's a start. There's another 10 at the bar though which are clearly here either for morale support or just for the laugh.

By 7.30pm I start encouraging the guests to make their way to the venue room and take a seat. I explain the rules to everyone, telling them they have 5 minutes to chat and to make notes on the paper provided. I have a stopwatch and will blow a whistle at the start and end of each session. As there is an odd number I am encouraged by the guests to go and join in, although they know I am not really playing the game. However I think it helps them, as they know they will have 5-minutes of gaining their composure when speaking to me, and maybe I can give them a few tips. But really I just want the gossip!!

At 7.40pm I blow the whistle, and everyone begins. So we have 10 tables, at 5 minutes a round with approximately 2-minutes to end the conversation and swap over. So quick maths I am guessing it will take an hour. Hopefully that is plenty of time for talking and everyone will be fed up with talking by then. I also decide to take a break halfway through. Time to grab and drink and have a toilet break.

So, first person, it is a 45-year-old man. Recently divorced, 3 kids, 1 grandkid. It's really nice chatting to him, as I love finding out about new people, but equally weird as I am not exactly 'on the dating scene'. He seems glad to have me first as he says I am breaking him in nicely for the 'proper quick conversations'.

After 5 minutes I blow the whistle and move onto the next. The next guy is great. Really funny and has me in stiches telling me joke after joke. I am laughing that much I almost forget about my stopwatch going off.

And onto the next. Bloke in his 30s. Clearly really nervous. I try and encourage some conversation, he seems lovely, but his nerves are taking over. When I remind him that I am the organiser and not actually doing this for real and just making up numbers he seems to relax. I give him some pointers, some conversational starters, which he appears to be grateful for.

I blow the whistle; I am actually feeling really sorry for this one. And really hopes he gain the courage to be abit chattier, and I hope that my pep talks helps. Although I don't know why I am giving him dating advice, it's not like I am the expert or anything.

Next person – bloke in his mid-30s. Can chat for England, so I let him talk. Complete opposite to the previous person. It really makes me realise how different we all are. How we come from different backgrounds, experience different things.

I blow my whistle and Nick thanks me for 'listening' – geez, I don't think I had any other choice.

And onto the next. Oh my days this feels like hard work, and I am not even doing this properly. I feel sorry for the women in this group.

Whilst I move onto the next and make some polite conversation I notice someone on the next table shifting really uncomfortable in their seat. I look over and realise its Sam. Oh no !! How awkward is this going to be? I try not to think about it and put all my energy into really listening to the current bloke. He is asking me questions and taking it really seriously. I don't think he realises I am the host. I answer his questions, trying to keep them short and I ask him a few questions as well, trying really hard to concentrate to listen to his responses.

I realise it's not even time for a break and I will have to sit with Sam beforehand. 1 minute to go. ...Right, that's it, I blow the whistle. The guy thanks me for a nice chat and shakes my hand. I try and take my time moving onto the next seat, but I cannot slow down anymore without making it really obvious or looking like I have turned into a sloth.

I blow my whistle again whilst sitting to opposite Sam. I think we both go bright red and Sam is looking almost as uncomfortable as me. He finally breaks the ice

'Hi, I am Sam. Or at the weekend I can be otherwise known as the Easter bunny' he says, reaching out to shake my hand.

I take his hand, it's a little sweaty, he really is nervous.

Confidential

'What???' I reply, suddenly dawning on me what he is referring too.

'Oh, so you were the Easter Bunny? Well you were my saviour for the afternoon, and you did a great job. Anna didn't stop talking about you all weekend' I say laughing

'Well thank you Emily. I got to admit, I had a great time, although I was sweating like a trooper in that costume. And I would like to compliment you on your hockey cokey skills' he responds sitting back now in his seat looking more at ease.

'You bugger. I completely forgot about that. I don't think your dance moves were quite as bad either, considering your attire' I say returning the compliment.

We both start chatting away now, him telling me about his break-up and some dating disasters he has had since being on the dating site. One story he told me that he went on a date, and she brought her baby along. She sat in the pushchair the whole time and the mum kept feeding her crisps to shut her up. I tell him about some of my disasters, the Zombie guy, the guy who loved himself and remind him of Will who actually kissed someone else during our date. I do also point out that I am currently 'dating' someone. He laughs and says he understands why I had a big 'want' list on my profile (wow, he really must have stalked me on that). He also tells me he has a date next weekend and he is really looking forward to it but thought he would come along tonight to see what it was about. He was also hoping to bump into me so we could have a chat. I am pleased for him and this conversation really seems to have broken the ice.

Confidential

I didn't realise how attractive Sam was. I guess I never looked at him like that before. He's not one of those obvious 'corrr, look at him' attractive, like Aaron is. But he has a soft face with stunning bright green eyes. And his banter is so 'on-point'. Check me out with the hip sayings – that's hanging around with Greg teaching me to get down with the kids.

I suddenly realise that we have been talking way past the allotted 5-minutes and people are starting to fidget in their seats – I must have turned off the beeper subconsciously.

'Halfway everyone, let's take a 20-minute break to freshen up and get a drink' I suddenly shout

Sam thanks me for listening and for the company. He admits I have been the best so far, but it really is slim pickings. He does laugh as he says this and offers to buy me a dink as a peace offering and I graciously except.

As Sam brings me back my drink we stand a chat for a minute or two but then I make my excuses as I really should mingle with the other guests, check they are all OK. As I go to walk away Sam suddenly grabs me by the arm.

'I really did like you Emily and I was really upset and confused when you were off with me. I was really hoping you would message me back once you saw my message on the dating site and you realised I was actually single. I did the Easter bunny thing for you, to try and impress you and Anna. But then I saw you with that good looking bloke and it dawned on me why you had come off the dating site in the first place. I hope it goes well for you; I really do. And at least the

Confidential

costume worked on Anna. Who by the way really is an absolute credit to you. I am gutted'

And with that he walks off and stands with some other guests. I stand there, open-mouthed like a goldfish, face all flushed not knowing what how to take that all in. I knew he liked me, but not in that way. Just as a friends way. And dressing up to impress me, abit of a strange way to impress me, but sweet at the same time, especially with the Anna thing.

The guests are now starting to come back in and taking their seats. I have a chat with a few of them whilst we wait for everyone for return. I look round and realise Sam had gone. He must have been too embarrassed to come back after his revelation. I feel terrible I didn't say anything back and just stood there like a lemon.

On the plus note, at least this means I don't have to stand-in anymore.

The rest of the event goes ok, it's a shame their wasn't more people but I gave it a try. I can't stop thinking about Sam. I will talk to him when I see him next and thank him for his honesty. But I want to explain that I am dating someone that I really like although it is still early days.

After I blow the whistle for the last time, I collect in the papers and see if there are any matches. There are a few which I discreetly let them know, and surprisingly Sam was a firm favourite by the ladies.

I suggest going into the bar to get to know everyone further and listen to the band. A few thank me but decide to leave, but we have a few that decide to stay. The bar has a quite a few moral supporters for the band and the group of friends from one of the speed dating guests, so there are quite a few having a drink. I am not sure if 'love is in the air' for anyone, but if anything, at least they have made new friends. The 60-year-old lady comes over and says she has had such a laugh, and although has not met the man of her dreams she has exchanged numbers with a few and are going out for a coffee, just as friends of course.

I stay for another drink doing some networking and getting some feedback when Nick collars me and chats non-stop for about 10 minutes. Luckily Greg, who is currently working behind the bar for the evening sees my 'cry for help' face and rescues me and pretending they need me for an emergency.

The friends who came for morale support seem abit drunk by now and are having a little dance. They seem to be enjoying the band at least.

I make my excuses, thank everyone for coming, go and give Greg a hug and tell him we really need to catch up soon, then I head off home.

Confidential

CHAPTER FORTY TWO

The next day I get into work for 9.00am. The wedding meeting starts at 11, so I have plenty of time to rearrange the tables and prepare everything. They have booked a food trail, where they will get to sample all of the dishes that can be served at the wedding lunch.

I check with Alberto all is going to plan. He is a little flustered as he is prepping all the meats ready for Sunday dinner bookings at the hotel and hasn't long finished doing the breakfasts. So I leave him to it and do some social media posts of last night's event (of course, I do not add anyone's face). I notice Sam and I in one of the photos Greg kindly took for me and we are both really laughing. I can't help but feel a little cringy now after what he said to me last night. I really do hope his date goes well.

Greg turns up abit later. He had been nightclubbing with Simon after the speed-dating event last night and was hungover – I have no sympathy, all self-inflicted. I was going to ask Greg if he fancied going out for a drink after work, but I take one look at him and realise when he finishes his shift he'll be going home and straight to bed.

When I get home I do another Joe Wickes work-out – geez, I must be getting some big guns by now, I mean it's been twice in a week. I call Kerry for a catch-up as she is wanting to book the venue for her daughter's birthday and wants to check availability.

Aaron has messaged me asking if we could meet up for coffee after work later in the week. I do have Anna, so I check to see if she could go to Kerry's for dinner after school for a couple of hours, which Kerry is more than delighted to do.

The rest of the week is the usual mundane week, battling car park spaces at the school, attempting to look remotely interested at swimming lessons and trying not to engage with the mums at Anna's dancing without looking really rude.

I have a small wedding on Friday that I have organised but that's all for events this weekend. I am hoping that Aaron and I could do something together on Saturday evening that rolls into Sunday (if you catch my drift). I don't need to go into work on Sunday, just as long as I can do my emails and some further event planning for a few hours. I can make up the rest of my time on Monday.

On Thursday I pick Anna up from school, take her home for an hour and we do some homework together. Then I quickly get changed and drop her off to Kerry's.

'Thank you Kerry, I owe you one' I say, passing her Anna's bear rucksack with all her essentials inside. When I say essentials, it's a cup that she likes to use for her juice, her teddy and some random rubbish she has put in. Oh, and some wipes. I can't leave the house without some wipes.

Anna has already run inside to see Kerry's kids so I get back in the car and drive to Starbucks where I have arranged to meet Aaron. Aaron is already there, smelling wonderful as usual. He seems a little on-edge, fidgeting in his chair and doesn't get up to hug me like he would normally do.

He has ordered me a coffee already so I sit straight down.

'Hey Emily, I hope you are ok?' he says, not waiting for me to answer

'I am really struggling with this and I am going to get straight to the point. But this isn't going to work between us. I really am sorry'. He hangs his head down and can't quite face me.

I am a little taken-aback. I was not expecting this in a million years.

'OK, may I ask why? Have I done something wrong? Have I upset you in anyway' I respond, starting to feel a little teary.

'There is no easy way to put this. But its Grace. She has been wetting the bed the past few weeks, been hitting kids at school' He replies, 'The school even called us up as they were worrying about her behaviour all of a sudden'.

He looks up now, and I encourage him to continue.

'So, her mum and I spoke to Grace, and she admitted it is because 'daddy has a new lady friend' and she doesn't like it. Her mum and I have really tried to talk to her, telling her it's natural that mummy and daddy will have new friends. But she kept crying. It was horrible Emily'.

I grab Aaron's hand as I can see he is visibly upset.

Aaron continues 'I have been mulling over this for days. As I really do like you. But it really isn't fare on Grace. I think it's just too soon. And the last thing I want is for her to hit poor Anna again. I was even wondering if we could just date without getting the kids involved, but I don't see how that could possibly work in the future.'

By now, I am filling up. I can clearly see how much he has debated over this.

I try and reassure him 'Don't worry Aaron. I completely understand. I have always said that kids come first. And hey who knows, one day when Grace is more accepting we could meet up again'.

At this point I quickly finish my coffee and stand up.

'Thank you Aaron for your honesty. I am gutted this hasn't worked out, but I wish you all the best'.

And with that I give him a peck on the cheek, a really big hug and walk out.

I am absolutely gutted. I thought for sure he was a lasting thing. He was such a great bloke and ticked so much off my list. But I do completely understand, I try and think what I would do if I was in that situation, and he has done the right thing.

I pick Anna up from Kerry's, thank her and tell her I will text her later. She could see I was hiding something. I didn't want to mention it with Anna there incase I started getting upset.

I get home, get Anna ready for bed and we read a few stories together. I always find it hard when you have children you have to hide your emotions when you are upset. They do tend to pick up on things. So I try my hardest to hide my sadness from Anna and we start laughing at the horrendous accents I am doing whilst reading.

Once Anna has settled down ready for bed I pour myself a glass of wine and send a picture message to my friends group-chat with a picture of my hand holding out the glass of wine with a caption saying

'Just been dumped. Cheers'.

The texts come flooded in. So I have to explain the situation. Then Rachel sends a picture back of her drinking a glass of wine with the caption

'Survived the day without killing anyone – cheers'.

Becka soon follows with a picture of a glass wine, in the background there appears to be some holes in the garden

'I may kill my dogs – cheers'.

The pictures continue like that for a good hour. I am proper belly laughing and try and find the most random things to hold to send a photo.

Nat even took one of her dildo with the caption

'Batteries ran out – cheers'.

I can't believe how lucky I am having a great bunch of friends that are there for me when the going gets tough (go on...sing it....the tough gets going)....

CHAPTER FORTY THREE

Mid-30's lady looking for a relationship. Looking for the following;

    1) *Loves socialising*
    2) *Funny*
    3) *Kind*
    4) *Enjoys holidays*

Yep, so I have deactivated my dating site account. I know its probably too soon, but I need a pick-me-up.

It's the day of the wedding event. There are only about 50 people coming all day. They are due to arrive at 14.00pm after their church ceremony, so it's a low-key event, with a 3-course meal being served at 15.00pm followed by an evening buffet at 19.00pm. It's a gothic themed wedding, so all the tables and chairs are black, with red drapes. The table centre pieces are skulls and even the wedding cake is black with a skeleton bride and groom placed on the top. All of the dishes and cutlery are black, and the table names are painted black onto red paper. It looks really good (even if I do say so myself) and I take a few pictures that I can use to promote.

I am only due to be working until 20.00pm, one of the bar staff says they would clear away the remainder of the buffet food. The rest can wait until Monday. Although as my weekend plans have been completely ruined I might end up coming into work.

As I am taking a break I get a message from the girls group chat.

'Emily, we are coming round tonight to cheer you up. What time do you get home?'

I immediately text back 'Oh thank you. I really could do with a girly night. I'll be home at 20.15pm. House is a mess and I have no food in (no surprise there), so if you wanna eat, it will have to be a takeaway'

I am made up. Here's me thinking I was going to have a boring night on my own, but the girls have stepped up. I am sooo looking forward to having a girly night.

At 20.30pm on the dot there's a knock on the door, I open it and in come Nat, Becka, Rachel and Kerry. Each carrying bottles of wines, crisps, cakes and Kerry has brought olives (being the gym queen and all that).

We start taking the mickey out of Kerry for attempting to be healthy with her olives. I must admit, I pretty much like most food, I just don't get olives. I have always liked the thought of sitting at a posh bar, sipping my posh cocktail and eating olives with my cocktail stick. But unfortunately its all I can do, just imagine it. Give me a peanuts any day. Although I have been warned about blokes who go to toilet and don't wash their hands and start dipping into the nuts !!! (that's peanuts obviously).

Rachel starts telling us about her week from hell that the triples have had diahorrea so she's spent all week covered in nappies and shit. Becka tells us about when one of her dogs nearly attacked the vet when she took them for a jab. Nat is moaning about her dad who refuses to throw anything away

Confidential

and Kerry is telling us about her daughter who is starting to get an attitude and keeps back-chatting.

We all try and sympathise and give each other advice. That is what I love about 'my girls'. We don't judge, we just try our best to listen. We realise we all have our own problems, and as trivial as they may seem to some of us, they obviously mean a lot to someone else. When we're not giving each other advice we are taking the mickey out of each other, just friendly banter of course.

We get on the conversation of Aaron and what has happened with the Grace situation.

'I have a confession' Kerry says 'I thought I saw Grace hit Anna, but I wasn't 100% sure, so I never said anything. And plus, I saw how happy you looked in his company'.

They all agree with how happy I looked.

'And he smelled sooo good' says Rachel looking like she is trying to remember the smell.

I start chipping in 'I must admit, I am gutted. He was really nice, we got on so well and he was proper fit. But, if his daughter is not going to like it and will cause problems, then it is not going to work. I get it'

We all have a group hug, and Nat chips in

'Bugger this, you have found your Prince Charming once, you will find another one again. At least you know there are good ones out there. And plus, you didn't know him that well, perhaps he had some hidden secrets – like his feet smelt'

'Or he only had one Ball' chips in Rachel

'Or he only lasted 3 minutes' pipes up Becka

'Anyway' Kerry interrupts 'let's get some music on do some dancing'

Yeah we all shout, but instead of jumping up, we all pour ourselves a glass of wine (priorities and all that), then we get up to dance. I stick on You-tube on the TV and type in 'old school party tunes'.

After having a good old dance, I am literally sweating. I didn't realise how much exercise dancing can be. Sod Joe Wickes, this is so much more fun. Although it helps that wine is involved and probably counter acts the calories I am burning.

'Right, I have a confession' says Becka disappearing into the kitchen and bringing out the cakes.

'These cakes are not just any old cakes. They are 'funny' cakes' (such a better cliché than these are not just any old cakes, they are M&S cakes I think in my head).

'Oooohhhhh' we all sound in chorus. I have tried funny cakes before, but am I too old for all of this?

'Oh sod the olives, give me one of those' Kerry says grabbing a cake.

We all take one, Rachel a little dubious knowing she has the triplets with the shits to look after tomorrow, but we all go for it anyway.

After 30 minutes I think they are kicking in. We are all now currently dancing to the hockey cokey, which reminds me of Sam dressed up as the Easter bunny. Then we go for the Macarena finished with the Cha Cha slide before we all collapse, absolutely shattered and suddenly get the munches. I grab the crisps and we eat them like we haven't eaten for weeks. They soon disappear, so I start raiding my cupboards, and actually start making cheese toasties for everyone. They are literally the best thing we have ever eaten.

By the time the bread and cheese has ran out, and pretty much all the wine, the girls start organising taxis home. I hug them all and thank them for a great evening and for being supportive.

CHAPTER FORTY FOUR

Mid-30's lady looking for a relationship. Looking for the following;

1) *Loves socialising*
2) *Funny*
3) *Kind*
4) *Enjoys holidays*
5) *Enjoys dancing to the hockey-cokey*

The next morning I wake up feeling deflated again. Don't get me wrong, I had a great evening with the girls, but I was really warming to Aaron.

I can't even bare to look at the dating site again, even though I know I have some messages come through. I think part of me is worried I am going to see Aaron on there. Perhaps I rushed into opening up my account again.

I am that bored I even go food shopping, I try and pop in some healthy stuff, but when I am feeling low I tend to just target the chocolate isle and just want to eat junk food.

I message Rob asking if I can have Anna tonight as I am free but he is taking her to a family party. Oh well, it looks like a night in for me on my Bridget Jones then.

After shopping and cleaning the house from top to bottom I decide to go into work. There're a few conference bookings next week so I might as well sort that out. I could also do with having a chat with the chef as I'd like to discuss some vegan food options that I can add to our wedding meal choices.

Greg is there, working behind the bar on an afternoon shift.

'Hey Emily, are you ok? You look a little down' he says, looking concerned

I tell him all about Aaron.

'Oh Em, I am soooo sorry to hear that. Well girl, what are you doing tonight? Cus Simon has a family dinner, so you tell me you are free and we can go and hit the town'. He clicks his fingers and does a little hip wiggle.

I laugh 'Oh Greg, that would be great. We should definitely go out'.

We make plans for later which makes me feel a lot better, I finish off some work and head off home to get ready. I've decided I am going to go all out, paint my nails, spray tan my legs…..tonight, Matthew, Emily is going to get hammered.

Greg turns up at mine around 8.00pm. We start straight away on the cherry sourz shots and vodka and cokes. Greg is wearing his skinny black jeans, a tight black turtleneck top complimented with a shiny white belt and white cowboy boots. I am really surprised he hasn't finished it with a big white cowboy hat. This isn't his first Rodeo !!

I have decided to wear my favourite leather look skinny trousers, my black heels which I know will kill me later and I'll regret wearing them (but god, they look good and are so worth the pain) and a black short sleeved top which shows a little bit of cleavage. I also know I'll freeze to death, but hey, I don't think I look too shabby, and if I feel pretty good it'll boost my confidence which I so need right now.

After a few more drinks we hit the cocktail bar. We are both pretty drunk by now, so when we walk in the heat and atmosphere hits us straight away. There is a singer on, and we immediately go to the 'dance floor' to start drunken dancing. We don't even care we are the only ones on the dance floor. I am letting my hair down and I am having a great time.

After a few more dances, we go and have a seat down - after getting another drink of course. I must be drunk, as my feet aren't hurting yet.

Greg is busy chatting to someone over at the bar and he has left me for what seems like ages, so I go over to hurry him along. As I march over - well as much as I can march in these flipping shoes I playfully bump into Greg

'Hey, you're leaving me all on my own. My glass is all empty' I slur, checking out who Greg is speaking too

God damn. Its Sam. With a fit, leggy blonde on his arm.

'Hi Emily' smiles Sam, nodding over to me 'Sorry I took your friend away from you'

'Soz Em' says Greg, now turning to try and get the bar man's attention for another drink. 'We had a lot to catch up on, I owe Sam a drink after apparently he took my place as the Easter Bunny. AND according to Em, she said whoever the bunny was , was AMAZING'

Confidential

I blush a little but then start giggling as I am drunk.

'Well Sam' I say, starting to point my finger at him 'I forgive you as its you. And yes, for a bunny you knew all the dance moves'.

The three of us start laughing, then we realise we have forgotten about the leggy blonde.

'Excuse my ignorance' says Sam. 'Everyone this is Kimberley. Kimberley, this is Greg and Emily. They both work at the Elliott Manor, so they use Celebrations to buy party stuff'.

We all smile and say our hello's to Kimberley and exchange some pleasantries. She seems nice and really does have a great set of legs on her. I must admit, I am a little envious.

Greg and I chat for another 10 minutes before leaving them to it and find a table for 2 in the corner of the bar. We continue chatting, singing and have at least another 4 drinks. By now, I really am drunk, at least we are sitting down.

Greg decides we should hit Pop World and as we are leaving we pass Sam. I drunkenly prod Kimberley with my finger and say, 'You'd better treat him well, he's an angel'.

We say our goodbyes and then head to Pop world, arm in arm, singing away to Amy Winehouse 'F me pumps'.

Pop world is as cheesy as I remember. However, the clientele also seems 10 years younger and the floors definitely seem stickier.

I get chatted up a couple of times, but they don't really seem my type. One of them is far too drunk (not that I can talk).

He wouldn't remember what day it is, let alone remember talking to me. Another one just seems like a right prat, one of those blokes that are right about everything. Doesn't let you get you a word in edgeways, let alone allows you to have an opinion, where god forbid, you might actually be right !!

I decide not to bother talking to any other men that night and just have fun with Greg and we hit the dancefloor again. It's now the Dirty Dancing mega mix, my favourite so we both dance like no-one is watching.

At some point, Greg decides to attempt pole-dancing with the pole they have at the back of the club. He's not doing too shabby considering he is half-cut. Before he even tries to tempt me to join in I find a seat, I am more than happy to observe. A guy, a good 10 years younger comes and sits down next to me.

'Hey, I'm Mark. You not up for any pole dancing tonight?' he says, shouting loud over the music

'Hey Mark, I'm Emily. And no, definitely not into pole dancing. I take it you're not either?' I say, shouting equally as loud.

'Ha ha, narrr not for me. Are you having a good night?' he asks, attempting to sit closer to me.

'I'm drunk, so my night isn't too bad. That's my friend up there on the pole' I say pointing at Greg who now it appears has an audience clapping and encouraging him along as he attempts to spin around.

Confidential

It's quite entertaining to watch, Greg is just so confidence, and the more people who come and watch him the more he is encouraged.

Despite me saying no, Mark insists on going to the bar and getting me a vodka. I would say he is trying to get me drunk, but I am way past that by now.

Greg saunters over, laughing his head off, and a little sweaty. He brings over his newly found friends and introduces them to me. I haven't got a clue who they were as the music is far too loud, but I smile and wave. They all decide to hit the dance floor, and I tag along. Mark comes back with my drink and joins in too. I get a wink from Greg which makes me roll my head back in laugher.

We are so exhausted we go outside for a cool down. Its rammed outside in the smokers area, but I can finally hear myself, although my ears are ringing from all the music.

I nip to the toilet before I go to the bar, as the queue is absolutely massive. What is it with women's toilets and a queue ?? I am absolutely bursting and by the time I get in the cubicle I have practically wet myself. It's a good job I have no intentions of getting lucky tonight. I try and dry my trousers off as best I can under the drier, but it's not exactly working. Every time I try and hold my crutch up as high as I can to the drier it goes off. I give up in the end, especially because I am getting some looks from some younger ladies, who clearly haven't had kids and don't know how easy it is to dribble a little after kids. Geez, I cannot sneeze now for worrying I may have peed my pants.

Confidential

I join the others outside with a tray of drinks, I cannot believe I did not even spill a drop. Ok, well I may have done a little. I must have my beer coat on by now because I don't even feel the cold.

Mark has somehow managed to get his chair next to mine. Although secretly I don't mind, and I am flattered. He's nice enough, I just don't feel ready, and he does seem a little immature and young for me. He's wearing basketball trainers for god's sake.

Greg decides to go back to the dance floor, but my feet are absolutely killing by now. A few decide to join him, but the rest are going home. It sounds like it's the 5ive medley is playing and usually I am down with the dancing, but I am all danced out. I must be getting old. So it's just me and Mark left talking. He keeps asking me to go out on a date with him, but I am not interested and let him down gently. I know he won't probably remember any of this in the morning, and even if he does, he has his beer googles on and certainly will not be happy if his grandma turned up on a date with him.

Finally, I cave in and reluctantly give him my number. I really have had enough now, my feet are literally throbbing and feel like they have doubled in size. As I say my goodbyes to Mark he grabs me and pulls me in for a kiss. Now normally I would resist, but hey, we're both drunk, I have promised nothing in return and with the wet piss patch in my pants I will certainly be not taking this any further, so I return the kiss. Its very slobbery and I am so very wobbly on my feet. After the kiss, I head back in to find Greg.

Confidential

I find Greg on the dance floor, and by the look of him, he is ready to go home as well.

'Kebab?' I mouth at Greg

'Kebab' he mouths back. Greg kisses his newfound friends, and we head off out. Now normally at the thought of a greasy fat kebab I would be skipping to the kebab house, but these damn shoes mean I am not skipping anywhere. More wobbling. Every step I take (every move I make – sorry couldn't resist) feels painful.

We order our kebab and chips, get a taxi and Greg comes back to mine, where we eat our food in silence apart from the odd 'mmmmmsssss' here or there.

After our food I feel proper fat and disgusted with myself. I half-heartedly get ready for bed, think I brush my teeth for all of 20 seconds. Well its better than nothing. The make-up sort of comes off and I grab the spare quilt for Greg. I do manage to grab a pint of water to take to bed as I know I'll be thankful of that in the morning. I give Greg and big kiss and hug and head for bed.

My head is spinning, ears are ringing, feet feel like the size of elephants feet, but hey, it was a good night. And plus, I am a cougar !!!!

CHAPTER FORTY FIVE

Mid-30's lady looking for a relationship. Looking for the following;

1) *Loves socialising*
2) *Funny*
3) *Kind*
4) *Enjoys holidays*
5) *Enjoys dancing to the hockey-cokey*
6) *Doesn't mind if I don't pole-dance*

The next morning my head is absolutely banging. I am so thankful for the pint of water I brought to bed.

I drag myself out of bed and Greg seems to be the same state as me.

'Oh, dear lord Em. Why the shots?, why all the dancing? Why oh why?' he cries.

'Let me get you a coffee. I have even been food shopping so I can do you a bacon sandwich if you want?' I ask, heading to the kitchen to pop the kettle on

'I can't think of anything worse than eating at the minute. Give me coffee, give me water and give me paracetamol' he says in a sorrowful voice.

The rest of the morning Greg and I watch rubbish TV, laughing about our night out. I tell him about my sneaky kiss with Mark and bet him anything I will never hear from him again. I have a 'moment' when I suddenly remember prodding Sams date and warning her to be kind to Sam. Oh

Confidential

god, another embarrassing moment for me. Perhaps he will appreciate the fact there are people that have his back. Really, who am I kidding? I was a drunken state. Oh the shame !!

By lunch time Greg is finally ready to eat a bacon sandwich and we watch a David Attenborough wildlife programme. I don't know what it is about 'our David', but his voice is so soothing, and before I knew it, we had both fallen to sleep.

When we finally wake up we are both absolutely starving and I order a sneaky takeaway, which I know we will both love at the time, but equally regret the minute we have finished eating. I really need to do some workouts after this weekend binge. Far too much food and drink !!! And there's me wondering why I am not losing weight.

Evan messages me with really bad news that his mum has passed away. I feel so terrible and send him a sympathetic message. It must be really difficult, I cannot imagine what it would be like to lose your mum. I mean, we all know it will happen, but can you really prepare yourself for that? I know I certainly cannot. Although I don't seem my mum as much as I would like, I pretty much text her or ring her every day, and no-one can compare the love you have for your parents. That's if you are fortunate like me have good ones. It just makes me realise what a good mum I need to be for Anna.

I decide to video call my mum, and I am so delighted that she takes the call and actually gets it right. Her neighbour must have been round to show her. She updates me on Strictly last night and speaks to Greg for abit. She still makes me laugh in the fact she thinks Greg and I should be a couple. I don't

Confidential

think she has really understands the fact Greg is gay. But Greg takes it all in good nature and says if he batted for the other team I would certainly be in his top 3.

After a few good hours of doing absolutely nothing apart from watching rubbish TV and eating rubbish Greg goes home. It has been lovely spending so much time with him, as I appreciate I won't see him as much now he is dating Simon. I am a firm believer not to bum off your friends when you are dating, although I also know how difficult it is to do that. Especially at the early stages when you want to spend every possible moment with them. Oh god, I miss that feeling.

The rest of the week goes by really slow. I have some work conferences and meetings in place in the week and on Friday I have a big 30th to organise. When I say big, there are 150 expected guests to arrive. The family have spent a lot on this event, so I need to make it perfect.

The room is filled with 30th balloons everywhere, all white coloured. The tables and chairs are silver coloured, with glittery silver bows on the chairs. There is a lovely photo collage that I have used the blackboard stand to hang it on, covered with some fairy lights. All photos of the party girl from birth, growing up, holidays with her parents and grandparents, starting school. Then as she gets older seeing her with friends, finishing school and starting college. Then you see her on the dancefloor, drinking as she turns the legal drinking age. Or maybe a little younger, but who am I to judge, I was out nightclubbing at 16 – but that's before they took ID too seriously.

Confidential

The guests have also asked if they can use outside, so I add extra heaters so we can open up the patio doors. Outside we have fairy lights and white lanterns. I have also managed to get out the garden furniture which was in storage from the winter months and all cleaned it all up ready to use.

There is a disco playing and we have canapes and champagne/orange juice upon arrival for each guest. I have brought in extra waiters as they will walk round the party all night with trays of food or to top up wine/champagne. The parents have told me in under no circumstances must the champagne/wine run out, so we have ensured we have plenty in stock.

I have also booked a magician to visit each table to entertain the guests, plus a professional photographer who will take photos of each guest arriving and then during the party. I am using a wedding arch decorated in white and silver flowers that they can walk through and have their picture taken upon arrival. I am hoping not everyone turns up at once, so just in case they do I have one of the waiters there handing out the free drinks so they are not queuing for the arrival photo too long.

At 10.00pm, the parents have organised some professional dancers to come on the dance floor and do a disco medley. I really like this idea, and if it's a hit, I may book them for a future event.

Bob from Celebrations dropped off the balloons earlier, he said Sam was away on a 'dirty weekend' – alright for some I think, although I am just glad that my prodding didn't put Kimberley off.

Confidential

The party is amazing. I had to stay until pretty much the end to ensure everything ran smoothly. The professional dancers were out of this world. And we have certainly gone through many bottles of wine and champagne. On Sunday there is a big booking for Sunday dinner and they were planning on using this room, so I need to try and do some tidying up at least.

I get home around 1 in the morning. Absolutely exhausted. I had to swap to my flat shoes halfway through the evening. I have some great photos, and the dancers was definitely a success so I will be booking them again.

I notice I have a message from Aaron, asking if I am ok. It's probably too late to text, but I will message back. I do hope he doesn't continue messaging me, I don't want to keep getting my hopes up.

I really should message Evan as well, to see how he is coping after his terrible news.

Confidential

CHAPTER FORTY SIX

Mid-30's lady looking for a relationship. Looking for the following;

1) *Loves socialising*
2) *Funny*
3) *Kind*
4) *Enjoys holidays*
5) *Enjoys dancing to the hockey-cokey*
6) *Doesn't mind if I don't pole-dance*
7) *Can look after me when I am hungover*

I do message Aaron back, just being polite, wishing him and Grace well, and that Anna and I are doing ok. I end it with a 'thank you for messaging and take care'. I hope he doesn't text me back now. Not that I don't want to hear from him of course, its just too sad of what could have been.

Evan also messages me, asking if I would like to go out for a drink with him. I'm not really in the mood to be honest, I keep updating my dating profile, but not even looking at the messages I get. The mood I am in at the minute if I get one dick pic, or any of the usual prats I will end up telling them to f*ck off and then get banned off the site.

I agree to go out with Evan tonight. We have been talking for a very long time, and to be honest at first I even had doubts he was even single. But now I realise he was actually looking after his mum all this time, which indicates to me he is a lovely guy. I am not sure how many males I know that would do that.

Greg messages me to inform me that he has sorted the venue room and so there is no point going into work, so I work from home. I make a few enquiries about an Abba tribute night I am thinking of hosting. Plus taking some bookings for the bongo bingo night, updating our website with last night's event and responding to some event/conference enquiries. I had a few people come up to me at the party last night asking if I will hold some more parties, or enquiring what other events I have. Hopefully I will receive some further bookings, but who knows, as they were alcohol induced.

I make a cheese and mushroom omelette for dinner and start getting ready for my date. I decide on wearing a V-neck cream long sleeved dress with my brown flat boots. We are meeting at a pub about 20 minutes' drive from mine, so I am driving.

I arrive at the pub and recognise Evan straight away. He is shorter than I thought he would be, so I am glad I am in my flats or else I would be miles taller than him. That's not a problem for me, but I know some men are a little conscious of it. He has blonde curly hair and is wearing some navy jeans, smart shoes and a nice black shirt. Evan orders me a J20 and we go and sit down for a drink.

Our evening went fine, nothing amazing but equally nothing disastrous. I wouldn't say there were instant sparks, not like I had with Aaron, but there is definitely potential. He tells me about his work, about his hobby in rock-climbing. He also seemed really interested listening about what I do for work and me being a mum.

After a few more drinks we decide to call it a night. Evan is walking home, but as I am driving I be polite and offer him a lift home. Normally I wouldn't normally do this, but I just know he is no serial killer and doesn't have a hidden rope or knife hidden in his jeans pocket – so I am guessing I'll be ok.

As I drive him home he breaches the subject of his mum and tells me all about her illness and how she had deteriorated slowly. It was so sad to hear, and Evan starts crying. I really feel for him. As I pull up outside his house, he tells me this was his parents' house, that he has already lost his dad and that he sold his house to move in with his mum when she became poorly. At this point, he is really crying, and I give him a massive hug. I really don't know what else I can do.

I suggest going in for a cup of tea, I really don't feel comfortable leaving him like this. Evan agrees and I park up and go into the house.

The house is very old fashioned. The entrance is full of pictures of the family through the ages, it reminds me of the 30th party collage, but definitely a little sadder now his parents have passed.

I am presuming that's his mums shoes that are still in the hallway. No wonder he is so upset, it must be so hard having to live in a house that has constant reminders of his mum. I go into the living room where there are even more pictures of his parents and Evan as a kid. Lots of holiday pictures of them as a family at various beach destinations. It reminds me I really must print more photos of my parents and Anna and put them around the house. I am not really sure if I have any recent ones of my parents.

Evan makes me a cup of tea and brings in some biscuits. We continue talking about his mum and dad, and he cries even more. Bless him, he keeps apologising, saying he was really looking forward to our date but has ruined it with him being so upset. He obviously isn't ready for dating, which I completely understand.

As we sit talking more my stomach is in knots. I really need to let off some wind. I think it must have been that omelette I had for lunch.

I make my excuses and nip to the toilet. I let out the most massive fart, and really hope the TV is on loud enough to hide the noise. These damn tights are not helping as they are digging right into my belly.

After about an hour I really start yawning and my stomach is in absolute bits. Evan seems to be a little better now. I really think it was a case of having someone to talk too that wasn't his family.

'I am sorry to leave Evan, but it is getting late, and I think it is time for me to go home' I say yawning my head off by now.

'I had a lovely night Emily, and I cannot apologise enough for being so emotional. I think it was too soon to go out on a date. I feel so terrible'. Evan says

He looks so sad, I feel a little guilty leaving, but it really is getting late, and I am in agony.

'Please do not be sorry. I have had a lovely night, and it has been lovely finally meeting you in person' He seems so genuine but he is just not emotionally stable at the minute. It is not his fault; I am sure this is the last thing he wants and must be so embarrassed.

I give him a massive hug as I leave but being careful not to be touched by the stomach. As Evan closes the front door I cannot help but let out the biggest fart ever. It feels so good letting it out.

When I get into the car I am literally farting all the way home, my stomach easing at each release.

As I walk into the door I have a message from Evan

'Thank you so much for a lovely night. I cannot apologise enough for being so upset. I am so embarrassed. P.s. I hope you enjoyed your fart'.

I am a little confused, but then I realised there was a ring doorbell on Evan's front door. Damn it, he must have heard me letting one rip. I am so embarrassed; from memory it was a proper ripper, and I am not even sure if I lifted up my bum cheek as I was doing it. I so need to re-watch that, just for comedy purposes.

I message Evan back, explaining my trapped wind (well I might as well be honest), and reassure him that him being upset is more than natural.

CHAPTER FORTY SEVEN

Mid-30's lady looking for a relationship. Looking for the following;

1) Loves socialising
2) Funny
3) Kind
4) Enjoys holidays
5) Enjoys dancing to the hockey-cokey
6) Doesn't mind if I don't pole-dance
7) Has a good relationship with their parents
8) Can let you fart in their company

On Tuesday I pick Anna up from school. The sun is shining and she begs me to take her to the park. I am more than happy to go as it means her burning off some much-needed energy.

I thought when she started school this energy would lessen, especially with the reduced afternoon naps. But no, that doesn't seem to have happened and she has more energy than ever.

I decide to park up at home first, grab a flask of coffee and make some snacks before we go to the park. I can also change Anna into her scruffy outfit, save her ruining her school uniform as you can guarantee she'll snag her school cardigan, tights or something.

We dump our bags and I grab a few snacks and make my coffee whilst Anna puts on some leggings and a jumper. I insist she wears a coat although I know with all the running around she'll soon take it off.

As we walk to the park it is rammed, it seems everyone has the same idea as us, and everyone is making the most of the sunshine which is finally making an appearance. Summer is finally coming. I love the summer, although Summer isn't really coming at all. More like Spring, but the thought of sitting in a beer garden with the sun on my face is enough to lift anyone's sprits.

I head for a bench which is full of other mums whilst Anna runs to the slide. Oh great, it may mean I have to socialise and make some small talk, which as you are aware, is not one of my best qualities. I realise I have my book in my bag, so without being rude, I start reading my book.

Thank god for this book because these parents sitting on the bench are so dull. Honestly, they are so competitive with each other over who does the most with their children. Dear god, why do some of these mums realise that it's not a competition? That it doesn't matter how many clubs their children attend, how many holidays they go on, not all parents can afford that luxury. Honestly, these parents are so stuck up, I can take no more and I make my excuses and pretend I have to leave. But really I find another empty bench and get engrossed in my book, obviously whilst checking up on Anna from time to time.

'Hey you, can I join you?' I hear someone speaking.

Oh, for god's sake, just when I am really getting into my book and enjoying the peace and quiet. I look up, ready to give whoever it is a smile which means 'yeah ok to join' but secretly means 'you can sit here, but don't you dare try and make small talk to me', when I realise its Sam.

Shit shit shit. What the hell is he doing here? He doesn't even have kids !!

'Hey Sam, feel free to join me. How are you?' I say, closing my book. Honestly, how fake am I ?

'I am good thanks. I take it you were fed up with the competitive mums over there?' he says, pointing over at the bench I was previously sitting at.

'Yeah you could say that. Coffee?' I say, reaching for my flask.

I pour Sam a coffee and I cannot help thinking the last time I was here at the park was meeting Grace for the first time. That didn't go as well as planned.

'Thank you Emily. Before you ask, I have my niece for the week, her parents have gone away for as they are having a few marital problems, so I have offered to look after her whilst they go and sort their stuff out'.

'I am not a wierdo perv coming to the park with no kids'. He adds, taking a sip of my coffee

I start laughing 'Its ok, I wouldn't put you down as a park peedo. How is your week going with your niece?'

As we start catching up, Anna comes over, wanting some snacks. Although she has met Sam before, she still doesn't realise he was the Easter Bunny, and I don't want to ruin that fantasy for her, although she knows it was someone in a costume.

Anna sits making small talk with Sam and once the snacks have ran out she heads back off to the park to join some friends she has made.

I really need to apologise to Sam so finally I pluck up the courage, trying to gather what I am going to say in my head.

'How is the dating going? I want to apologise to you, not sure if you are aware but I think I actually warned your date not to mess you around!!!'

Sam really laughs and reassures me that him and Kimberley are still going well. He tells me about his weekend away with her, and I must admit I am pretty envious of him. Don't get me wrong, I am happy for him, but it seems like he's only been on the market recently and has already found someone.

I am obviously doing something totally wrong.

At this point a little girl with stunning dark brown eyes and long brown hair runs over to us, crying her eyes out, holding out her hand.

'Uncle Sam Sam, I have fallen over and I am bleeding' she says, showing Sam her cut finger.

She is inconsolable, despite Sam giving her a big hug and trying to console her. I even offer her some snacks, but she seems convinced her finger is going to drop off.

I search in my bag, but I don't appear to have a plaster.

Confidential

'If it helps, I literally live 5 minutes' walk from here, do you want to come back to mine? I have a first aid kit with some bandages/plasters' I say, searching helplessly in my bag for a plaster or something

'Would that be OK Amy? Do you want to go back to my friends Emily's to see what she has in her first aid kit to help stop your finger from dropping off'? he says, hugging Amy tightly.

Amy slightly nods and so I call for Anna to come back. Once i have explained to Anna what has happened, Anna seems to take over mother hen role and takes Amy by the hand, the good hand of course. ('here take my strong hand' – Scary Movie – love it) We start walking towards my house, Anna talking to Amy as we go, trying to take her mind off her poorly finger.

Mother Teresa would be so proud.

As we go into mine we head for the kitchen, where I am strangely conscious of the washing up I have failed to do this morning. There're also my sexy pants hanging on the clothes rail trying to dry. Not only are my sexy pants there, but equally my big fat Bridget pants on show for the whole world to see, I am just hoping Sam is not as nosey as I am and doesn't spot them.

I grab my first aid kit and start cleaning up Amy's finger wound and then give her a bandage. A plaster would be more than suitable, but as we have gone this length I might as well pretend it is worse than we thought and give her a full on first aid check.

Confidential

Anna insists on showing Amy her room, so I make Sam a cup of tea. Luckily it is not awkward at all. I tell him about the Evan date, and he reminds me of 'that prat Will' that kissed someone on our date. My god, I had completely forgotten about that.

Two cups of tea later, Amy and Anna come downstairs from playing. Amy has a teddy bear that she is 'borrowing' from Anna. I can see Anna doesn't mind, but she really does want it back at some point as I know its one of her favourite teddies.

'Perhaps Amy could borrow Mr Crocodile whilst she is staying with her Uncle Sam, but it's just a loan? Is that ok with you Amy? That you borrow it, but will give it back to Anna?' I say in my kindest voice

'Yes that is ok' Amy agrees. 'Thank you Anna and thank you Uncle Sam Sam for a lovely day'.

Anna and Amy give each other a hug, and they ask if they could play again soon. Sam and I give each other a look and agree that we will arrange another play date soon.

'Thank you so much Emily' says Sam, giving me a kiss on the cheek 'I'll speak to you soon'.

Anna and I wave them both off, I am happy Anna has made a new friend.

CHAPTER FORTY EIGHT

Mid-30's lady looking for a relationship. Looking for the following;

1) Loves socialising
2) Funny
3) Kind
4) Enjoys holidays
5) Enjoys dancing to the hockey-cokey
6) Doesn't mind if I don't pole-dance
7) Has a good relationship with their parents
8) Can let you fart in their company
9) Carries emergency kids plasters

The weekend soon comes round again. Anna did not stop talking about her new friend Amy. I may have to ask Sam if he wouldn't mind if next time he is babysitting whether she could come round to play.

The weather is certainly warming up now and it feels good to actually hang my washing out on the line (now that's a sign I am getting old).

My mum and dad are coming over for the weekend as its their friends birthday. They are staying in a local hotel for 2 nights. I did offer to have them here, but their isn't really much space and I think they prefer their own company.

Tonight, I have the bongo bingo event, Saturday a wedding and nothing planned for Sunday, so I am taking my parents out for Sunday dinner. They have also asked if they could take Anna out for the day on Saturday, so we have arranged that with Rob.

The bongo bingo is an over 18s event. There is a drag artist who will be entertaining the guests and being the bingo. They did warn me some of their jokes are not suitable for a younger audience.

Each guest pays an entrance fee which includes their bingo tickets and entertainment. I have taken 60 bookings so will arrange 6 tables of 10. Nice even numbers.

The event goes down a storm. The bar has made a fortune. The drag artist 'Rusty Crack' went down an absolute treat. I am going to book them again for sure, I was in stiches, and was fascinated at their costumes and make-up. It's a shame my friends didn't come, they would have loved it. I must remember to tell them about it next time I organise one.

Some of the guests were attempting to stand on the tables to dance, which I had to kindly tell them to get down (my risk assessment couldn't cope with that). But apart from that, everything went well. Oh, and perhaps I need to buy some dobbers as some guests didn't bring any and they had to scrounge off other guests and I was scrambling for some pens.

The following day was a wedding with around 50-day guests and a further 30 guests at night. They are getting married at the local church first and will arrive at the hotel for 2.00pm.

The room is the standard white and gold colours with a 3-course meal in the day followed by a hot buffet in the evening, so I can set this room up with ease.

My plan is to leave the wedding around 9.00pm and go and see my parents at their hotel bar. I would have got them in at the Elliott has I get a pretty good discount, but it was last minute, and we are fully booked all weekend, with guests staying over for the wedding.

At around 9.15pm I head over to see my parents. To my surprise Anna is also there at the bar. Apparently she had a lovely day at the cinema, bowling and out for dinner that she wanted to stay at the hotel overnight too. After about half hour Anna starts yawning, so dad goes up to the room to get Anna to bed, which gives me and mum a chance to have a catch up. She fills me in on her Bristol friends and the party Friday night. I cannot stop yawning and at 11, I decide I cannot stay awake any longer and so I head off home.

The next day I go back to the Elliott to tidy up and rearrange all the tables back to normal. The place is an absolute mess, it looks like a bomb has gone off. I also call mum to check on Anna. Apparently she was so excited to have a sleepover in a hotel and was bouncing on the beds at 8.00am this morning.

Evan has messaged me, to apologise again for getting so upset, but that he had a lovely night anyway. I message him back telling him to not worry at all and reassure him again. He asks if I am free tonight to go bowling, I don't even bother looking at my diary as I know I am free, and we make a date to meet at bowling for 7.30pm.

Confidential

My parents have checked out their hotel after breakfast and took Anna back to Robs. They've done abit of shopping in town and now they are at the Toby Carvery waiting patiently for me for me to arrive. When I say patiently, I know my dad will be pacing as he is missing his Sunday afternoon drinking session as he needs to drive home.

As soon as I have finished work I drive to the carvery, and I am right, dad is pacing. You can tell he wants his dinner very quickly and they'll head straight off home after so dad can meet his friends. I am glad they've made a great social life in their new town – even if their only child is blown out for them !!!

It's very busy at the carvery, but I am really starving and pile my plate as much as I can. I probably won't eat for the rest of the day, so I am making the most of it. And plus a Sunday dinner is healthy isn't it? Apart from the roast potatoes, yorkie puds, roasted parsnips and of course, my favourite cauliflower cheese. Whoever thought cauliflower and cheese would go together is a genius in my eyes. So, come to think of it the only healthy part of this dinner is some broccoli and peas I have begrudgingly put on my plate – well it was the thought that counts !!

There is definitely an art form to piling your plate on a carvery, and I seemed to have mastered this skill over the years. By putting some veg in your yorkie pud is one trick, and squashing down your mash ensures you can put a good few parsnips on the top – come back here for more of Emily's top tips !! Although trying not to spill the gravy when you

Confidential

walk back to your table is also a skill I have yet to master, even with my waitressing skills.

After dinner I literally cannot breath. I am so stuffed. I even had to admit defeat and leave some, which I really dislike doing, especially when it is a carvery as I feel like the waiters are judging me.

'Her eyes are bigger than her belly' I can hear them saying as they take my plate away.

Mum even manages an Ice-cream sundae, which I know annoys dad even more, I wouldn't be surprised if she did it on purpose.

After mum has finished her pudding, we say our goodbyes and head off home. Dad practically wheel spins out of the car park.

CHAPTER FORTY NINE

Mid-30's lady looking for a relationship. Looking for the following;

1) Loves socialising
2) Funny
3) Kind
4) Enjoys holidays
5) Enjoys dancing to the hockey-cokey
6) Doesn't mind if I don't pole-dance
7) Has a good relationship with their parents
8) Can let you fart in their company
9) Carries emergency kids plasters
10) Loves a good Carvery

I manage a sneaky afternoon nap when I got home as I got really sleepy after my massive Sunday dinner. I even manage a number two, so hopefully I won't be windy tonight for bowling.

I meet Evan at the bar at bowling alley. He has brought his own bowling ball and glove as apparently he is in the local bowling team. I keep calling him 'Kingpin' and he takes it in good faith. He is an absolute pro, and completely thrashes me, although he did give me some tips. At one point he was showing me how to bowl straighter and stood behind me holding his arms around me, unfortunately I didn't feel anything at all, no fanny flutters, nothing, but perhaps he's more of a grower (not in that way).

After bowling we grab another drink and have a game of pool. I am no better at that either, nor basketball. I feel Evan is a little sporty and I am far too competitive to keep losing. But I accept my lost gracefully, I really need to play a board game with Anna so I can regain my winning status.

Evan asks if he could book the wake at the Elliott for his mum and of course I agree.

'Will you be there in the day?' he also asks. 'I have so much to organise, and it would be great if you are there to help me'

'Yes of course I will be there, and I will there for as long as you want me to stay' I reply, holding his hand for comfort.

'Why don't you come to the Elliott sometime this week and I can show you around and show you what we can provide?' I offer.

Evan looks genuinely relieved. 'Yes please, I am currently off work on sick leave as I just cannot concentrate at work. My boss has been amazing and told me to come back when I am ready. It is so hard doing it all, I don't have many family members that are in a position to help me, and I am an only child'.

I feel so sorry for him and I will make it my mission to ensure not only will I try and make the arrangements as easy for Evan, but I also want to ensure his mum has a good send-off. She sounded like a remarkable woman. Was always doing charity work and raised thousands for children's charities. When she retired she also used to volunteer at a horse-riding centre that specialised in catering for disabled children. She also used to visit a care home weekly, just chatting to the elderly, generally keeping them company.

We agree for him to meet me on Wednesday, and I can see some weight lift off his shoulders.

Evan walks me to my car, and I can see he is a little nervous. I hate this bit, it's the 'is he going to kiss me or isn't he?'.

Evan gives me a big hug and then, he goes in for the kiss. I respond, but it's the worst kiss I have ever had (apart from my first ever kiss, but we won't even go there). It was honestly like kissing my brother.

Evan pulls away and starts laughing

'I am really sorry Emily, but that was terrible. I felt like I was kissing my sister, not that I have one' he looks distraught as he clearly does not want to upset me

I start laughing 'Oh my god, I feel exactly the same. That was one of the worst kisses I have ever had'

'That did zero for me. Absolutely no stirrings whatsoever, and it's been so long' he says, proper laughing by now.

We are laughing our heads off, and I am so glad he sees the funny side. He holds out his hand for me to shake.

'Friends?' he asks

I reciprocate and take his hand 'Friends' I agree.

Then I pull him in for another hug and promise him that I'll still help him with his mums wake and whatever else he needs.

Confidential

'Even though you're a sloppy kisser' I call as Evan is walking back to his car.

'I think it was your farting that put me off' he returns the joke.

We are both still laughing driving away and we wave frantically at each other. I am not disappointed in the slightest, if anything I feel like I have found a true friend for life. I can't wait for me to introduce him to Greg, I know with Evan's sense of humour they will get on like a house on fire.

By the time I get home I have already had a few jokey texts from Evan. He also thanks me again for my support. I am really honoured to be asked to help him.

Confidential

CHAPTER FIFTY

Mid-30's lady looking for a relationship. Looking for the following;

1) Loves socialising
2) Funny
3) Kind
4) Enjoys holidays
5) Enjoys dancing to the hockey-cokey
6) Doesn't mind if I don't pole-dance
7) Has a good relationship with their parents
8) Can let you fart in their company
9) Carries emergency kids plasters
10) Is a decent kisser (but not a first date)

The next week I am on a bit of a downer. All my friends are in relationships (apart from Evan of course, but he is not in the right mind-set for a partner). I start to question what is actually wrong with me.

I haven't even got the effort to check my messages on the dating website. I just think I don't want the disappointment of meeting more people that are wrong for me.

The girls have picked up on my mood and try and involve me in some activities. I have been dog walking with Becka and her beautiful dogs, Nat invited Anna and I for dinner which was lovely. But when I put Anna to bed, I find myself alone in the evenings.

Kerry dragged me to a gym boxing class one evening.

'To relieve the stress' she said.

Confidential

I was puffing and panting and that was only the warmup !!! Kerry didn't even break a sweat, and I walked out of that class bright red, hair all over the place and dripping with sweat. When I saw I walked out, or should I say more like wobbled out, my legs had literally turned to jelly

I couldn't actually walk properly for 2 days, and I couldn't even lift the kettle without winching.

I think power walking with Becka and her dogs is much more for me, less sweaty and apart from my calves, I do not ache.

I even looked after Rachel's triplets for a few hours whilst she went out for lunch with her husband. That was a mission in itself, they were so hard work. I couldn't even drink a cup of tea in peace without one of them crying or needing a nappy change or a bottle feed. I managed 3 hours and had to go for a lie-down when I got home. I honestly do not know how she does it, credit to her. I did smile though as when she came back from lunch she kissed her babies like she had been gone for weeks. It was so lovely to see.

Evan came to see me at the Elliott to organise the wake. He's expecting about 80 guests, but that is a guess and estimated based on the messages of condolences and people wanting to know the date of the funeral. He seems so stressed, and I try my best to organise as much as I can for him without bothering him.

The wake is on a Friday, which I am relieved as I do not have to arrange childcare for Anna as I want to ensure I am there until it finishes.

Confidential

I have been round Evan's house again, and we went through some old photographs of his mum through the ages. I loved looking at the different hair styles and fashion and hearing Evan's stories of his childhood. I have promised him that I will help sort his mums clothes out whenever he feels he is ready. He wants to give as much as he can too charity, as that is something his mum would have wanted, especially with all her charity work.

Evan has asked me to attend the funeral itself, which is being held at the local crematorium. Of course I agree and pull Greg in to help me with the preparations for the wake and to be there for when the guests arrive in case I cannot leave the crem after the ceremony and need to be with Evan.

The funeral and wake go as well as expected. The crematorium is packed, with people even standing outside. Lots of people from all the charities she supported came to pay their respect.

The wake itself was also very busy. Far more than the planned 80 guests, but luckily I did plan for extra guests just in case. The last thing you would want is to not have enough catering at a wake, so I always over-order. Evan has made a lovely collage of photos of his mum that I helped him do. I can see lots of people smiling at them and reminiscing.

Evan makes a beautiful speech. The lovely and thoughtful words he said I do not think there is a dry eye in the place. Evan seems to be coping really well, although I think he is putting on a brave face on. I plan on going to see him tomorrow when I finish work, as I think that might be when it really hits him.

Confidential

With all the sadness around me I do realise how lucky I really am. I have a beautiful, healthy daughter, a great job which I love, amazing parents and the best friends I could wish for. I really need to stop dwelling on the fact I do not have a partner, at least I have my health and deep-down I really am happy.

It might just take time; I am just not a very patient person – it suddenly dawns on me take I after my dad.

CHAPTER FIFTY ONE

Mid-30's lady looking for a relationship. Looking for the following;

1) Loves socialising
2) Funny
3) Kind
4) Enjoys holidays
5) Enjoys dancing to the hockey-cokey
6) Doesn't mind if I don't pole-dance
7) Has a good relationship with their parents
8) Can let you fart in their company
9) Carries emergency kids plasters
10) Is a decent kisser (but not a first date)
11) Doesn't take life for granted

On Saturday I have another afternoon tea. This time we have about 60ish guests attending, I am really pleased the last one was such a success. I practically repeat the last event, except this time I have added some vegan and gluten free options. Apparently the food options were the reason some of the guests booked on the tea, as not many cater for gluten free.

I make a mental note of this to talk to Alberto, as we really need to look at introducing more gluten free foods, not just a boring salad. I know Alberto will be straight onto the challenge, he loves creating new and exciting foods on the menu.

Once the afternoon tea has finished I head off home and start getting ready for my night out. I was going to nip and see Evan first but he has gone to see his friend. It's my birthday,

Confidential

so me and girls are going out for a blowout. I have already had my nails and hair done for the occasion and I cannot wait. I was debating having a bikini wax done, but I do not think I will be getting any action this year, let alone tonight, so I save my money, and of course the pain.

We were planning on going out for a meal first, but according to Nat 'eating is cheating' so everyone is coming to mine first for a few drinks – and no meal.

I did get Alberto to cook up some additional food that I can takeaway as I won't have time to have dinner (obviously I did pay).

I lay out the food on the dining room, get the glasses out and continue getting ready. I have brought a new dress, it is my birthday after-all. My dress is a little black number, V-neck, showing just enough cleavage without looking tarty, and lies just above the knees. It is a little tight fitting, so I have to wear my big fat pull-in pants which do wonders for tucking my belly in, but then I seem to have rolls just above the pants. So, I adjust the pants to literally go as high as my bra. I know it will be killing me later, but it will be worth it.

I decide not to wear tights, but realise my legs are lily white, so I attempt a quick fake tan fix. I wear my favourite black shoes, which have a bit of a heel to show off my calves and give me abit of height, but not too high so I know I will be able to dance for a good few hours.

I haven't managed to clean up the house, but I know my friends won't care. It's not like they will turn up in their white gloves, running their fingers along my skirting boards. I do a quick toilet bleach though and ensure there are no hidden surprises in the toilet, just in case.

The girls arrive, Nat, Becka, Rachel and Kerry. All looking stunning as usual in their own styles. Becka has an amazing long dark green skirt with a black short top revealing her beautiful flat stomach. I make a mental note that I have to borrow her skirt, even though its almost a guarantee it won't fit, it's worth a try.

Greg cannot come as he is working for me Sunday organising another Christening. And although he typically loves a night out with 'his girls', I think he is more than happy spending the night in with Simon watching some Netflix series whilst snacking on popcorn and crisps.

I stick on some tunes, and we immediately start getting in the mood for going out. It appears everyone wants to forget their 'mundane' home lives and just want to let their hair down tonight and 'dance like no one is watching'. I am so down for that !!

After an hour or so we order a taxi to the first bar. It is pretty quiet in there, but we take it as a warmup, take a seat and start chatting rubbish. We get a few looks from some old boys as we are clearly being loud, but we ignore them. We are here tonight to ppaarrrtttyyyy.

We head to the cocktail bar which is rammed again. The queue for the bar is horrendous so I order 2 bottles of wine to save the ball-ache of having to go to the bar again.

Confidential

I see a few people I know and exchange pleasantries. When I say pleasantries, it is more like big hugs like we are best friends and chatting absolute nonsense.

We end up going into pop-world, which I am more than happy to do as by now we all have our dancing shoes on. After ordering more drinks, we head straight to the dance floor where we really do dance like no-one is watching. A few blokes come over and attempt to make small talk with us, but we just shrug them off.

At one point we head to the pole, and we all take it in turns to attempt a sexy dance, filming each other on our phones and shouting words of encouragement. I am pleased to see that young lad isn't there, I think his name was Mark, but I will call him 'snogger'.

We dance non-stop for another 2 hours. Rachel and Kerry have decide to go home as they are absolutely bladdered. Becka starts talking about grabbing a kebab and I know the evening is coming to an end.

I start getting abit of a downer. I know that once we get in the taxi to go home, they'll be going home to their partners, and I will be going home to an empty house. Just me and my kebab as comfort. Although I am starting to get a little hungry and the thought of a kebab is making me salivate a little.

In the kebab house I do my regular order and as we are waiting I recognise a familiar face. Its Will (you remember, the one who not only stood me up on our first date, but then kissed someone on our second date).

Confidential

He recognises me immediately and staggers over to me.

'Hey Emily', he says, surprisingly not slurring. 'Fancy seeing you in here. How are you? Have you had a good night?'

'Yes I have a had a great night. It is my birthday' I reply, conscious I am slurring, not that I should even care.

'Oh Happy Birthday' he replies. 'Look, I am sorry for what I did. I realise I was out of order, but I did not think you was really interested in me, and this girl had been after me for months'.

I laugh 'It's no problem. Don't worry about it. You could have at least messaged me to apologise, but like I said, don't worry about it'.

'Look, I have been a dick. I know. I think with my trousers rather than my brain. You are looking terribly good tonight' he replies, sitting down next to me

Obviously I am flattered, it seems like a long time since someone has given me a compliment.

'Look Will, I do not want to date you, but do you want to come back to my house for some no-strings fun?'

I realise this is very forthcoming of me, but I feel like I deserve some pleasure. It has been far too long, and a woman has needs after all.

Obviously Will agrees, and we grab our food and head off to mine, saying my goodbyes to Nat and Becka who are also getting themselves into a taxi, reassuring them I am not going home with a serial killer and that I will text them later to let

Confidential

them know I am safe. Not that they will read the messages, they will be fast asleep as soon as they have finished their cheesy chips.

As soon as we walk into mine Will and I start kissing, we rip each other's clothes off like some frantic animals and do it right there, in the kitchen. I realise how much I needed that and wasn't even bothered it took me abit longer to get my bridget jones pants off.

We head off to the bedroom, leaving our uneaten food on the side, which secretly I am gutted as the last time I had a kebab it was dog shitt induced, but hey, I can always have it for breakfast. I may even be able to eat Will's – I hope he ordered something nice.

As we head off to my room, half-naked, we go again. This time a little slower. It is still amazing though, and it's clear Will has had lots of experience in the bedroom. After we finish we are both left panting, knackered.

Will attempts to stand up (perhaps he is more drunk than I thought) and as I thought he was heading to clean himself in the bathroom he takes off the condom, throws it on the floor and wipes his dick on my bedroom curtains.

I cannot get my breath. How disgusting is that??? Absolutely vile. Throwing the condom randomly on the floor was a deal-breaker, but the curtains is a sacrilege. Disgraceful. I would usually deal with this thing by ringing them a taxi, not that I have to do this often of course, but by the time I get back from the toilet myself Will is fast asleep.

Confidential

I will deal with this in the morning and I will throw him straight out as soon as we wake up, but by now all I can think about is sleep, which I do, amazingly so peacefully. I must really have needed than more than I would care to admit. Was it worth the fact I will have to replace my curtains? Probably not, and I really liked those curtains as well.

Oh well, we live and learn.

CHAPTER FIFTY TWO

Mid-30's lady looking for a relationship. Looking for the following;

1) Loves socialising
2) Funny
3) Kind
4) Enjoys holidays
5) Enjoys dancing to the hockey-cokey
6) Doesn't mind if I don't pole-dance
7) Has a good relationship with their parents
8) Can let you fart in their company
9) Carries emergency kids plasters
10) Is a decent kisser (but not a first date)
11) Does not take life for granted
12) Does not spunk on curtains (long story)

The next morning I wake up early, roll over in the bed, and yep, Will is still there. Snoring his head off. I cannot even bear to look at my curtains.

I get up and make some coffee. I start banging some kitchen cupboards in the hope it wakes him up, but nope, not a peep.

Suddenly there is a knock on the front door. Damn it, my hair is all over the place as I didn't get chance to brush it with my 'guest' in my room. Plus I have on my manky dressing gown with egg all down it. I cannot exactly go upstairs to change. Oh well, it is probably an amazon delivery or something, although I cannot remember ordering something. Perhaps I ordered something when I was drunk.

I open the door and there is no one there, apart from an arm holding out a toy Crocodile

'Hello Emily, remember me? Mr Croc, I have been on my holidays and now I want to come home' 'Croc says'

I realise its Sam returning Anna's Croc back

'Well Mr Croc, I hope you had a lovely time on your holidays. Welcome home'

The arm now extends, and Sam is standing there, grinning from ear to ear. I take Croc from him.

'Thank you for bringing him back. To be honest I think Anna has completely forgotten about lending him to Amy.'

I remember the actual state of me, my breath must be rank, and I am suddenly really conscious of my eggy manky dressing gown and the fact I have on no bra. I start trying to pull my dressing gown tighter round me.

I think Sam is itching for an invite to come in, I am just about to offer him a coffee when I realise I have dickhead upstairs.

And right on queue Will comes down the stairs right in full view of Sam. He is wearing nothing except for his boxers. He nods at Sam, lets out a fart, scratches his nuts and goes into the kitchen.

I am mortified, I mean, talk about bad timing. The look on Sam's face says it all. He must think I do this regularly, that I am a right tart.

'Sam' I say, trying to figure out what exactly I can say to him 'That was Will'

'Yeah, the guy who was kissing another woman when you were on a date' Sam interjects 'You told me about it, right before you started shouting at me for chatting you up when I was supposed to be married'.

Now I feel terrible. I literally have no words. I don't really think it's worth me trying to explain.

'Anyway, I was only popping Anna's toy back. See ya' Sam heads off, he sounds genuinely racked off.

'Thank you Sam. It was a one-off, I was drunk and feeling low' I shout. Great, now all the neighbours have probably heard what I got up too last night. I don't even know why I feel so guilty. I am single, I have done nothing wrong.

Right, now I need to sort out this disgusting guy in my kitchen.

It doesn't take long for Will to get the hint that I wasn't cooking him a fried breakfast, or even making him another coffee. He tried to make some small talk, but even then I wasn't interested.

'Will' I say, plucking up the courage to say what I really want to say

'Last night was fun. But it won't happen again. What you did to my curtains was disgusting. It really was a one-off. So if you wouldn't mind leaving I have work to do'

Confidential

Will doesn't even try and argue the case. He gets dressed and heads out of the door muttering a goodbye as he leaves.

What the hell was I thinking? I am far too old for one-night stands.

I take a very long, much-needed shower and reflect on my actions (ha ha, this is something a counsellor would make me do – not that I have one. I just thought it sounded good).

CHAPTER FIFTY THREE

Mid-30's lady looking for a relationship. Looking for the following;

1) *Loves socialising*
2) *Funny*
3) *Kind*
4) *Enjoys holidays*
5) *Enjoys dancing to the hockey-cokey*
6) *Doesn't mind if I don't pole-dance*
7) *Has a good relationship with their parents*
8) *Can let you fart in their company*
9) *Carries emergency kids plasters*
10) *Is a decent kisser (but not a first date)*
11) *Does not take life for granted*
12) *Does not s—k on curtains (long story)*
13) *Wants a relationship – not a one-night stand*

The next few weeks past by in a blur. I focus all my energy spending time with Anna or working.

I hold a Whitney Houston tribute night. My mates came along for moral support, and I was really envious I could not join in the dancing and singing with them. Next time I will definitely book a night off so I can enjoy the night with them.

Its nearing the summer now, my favourite time of year. Although it is my busiest with time with work, it is so nice to be able to sit in my garden at night, visit lots of parks, and even better sit in a beer garden.

Confidential

I finally go back onto the dating site, had a couple of dates but it didn't lead to anywhere. They were nice enough, just no spark or I wasn't feeling it.

I have met up with Evan a couple of times, just as friends of course. He is not dating anyone but is planning a sabbatical for 6-months travelling around Europe. I don't blame him at all. I helped him clean out his mums house which was very difficult for him. The house is now currently up for sale with a few potential buyers.

I am so busy with work, lot's of weddings to host and organise. I am also trying to plan the end of summer BBQ, with some live bands playing outside in the hotel's garden. My hope for next year is that we can have a proper outside stage area so we can do regularly gigs outside. We could utilise the stage for summer events as well, obviously weather dependent.

The girls have organised a night out so I have promised I will meet them after work. Its Friday evening and I have a low-key party booking so I can leave once I know all the preparations have been done and the guests have arrived. Alberto and the waiter staff have the rest on hand.

I head straight to Becka's as that's where the girls are, drinking wine and dancing round the kitchen to some cheesy pop tunes. I quickly get changed (don't have time for shower), Becka curls my hair, Rachel helps me with my make-up, Nat fills up my drink and Kerry lends me some of her amazing platform peach wedges that she has (they are so amazing I may even forget to ever give them back).

Confidential

I quickly catch up with the girls, we are having such a great time doing silly dances that we would be more than happy to just stop in. But as we are all dressed up, we thought we would make the effort. We are just going to go to the cocktail bar where they have a band on. Maybe we'll end up in pop world. But I do know that I will be having a kebab, this is without fail, especially after my last few kebab failings.

The band at the cocktail bar is great, playing ska music so we are dancing away to A Town Called Malice and Baggy Trousers. I definitely need to book this band at the summer BBQ. I smile to myself, every time I go out I cannot seem to switch off with work, always looking at what other venues do, food they serve, events they hold, bands they play. Technically I should really get paid for me going out, its research after all !!!

Nat, Kerry and I head to pop world. Rachel needs to go home as she has the triplets all day tomorrow and as quoted 'cannot do that with a hangover'. Becka also goes home as she has a family do the next day, although they are both grabbing some cheesy chips first before getting a taxi.

Pop world is horrendous. Full of 'kids'. Although they aren't really kids, we are just old. We order a few drinks and we pretend its Nats birthday so she gets a free bottle of champagne. Although when I say champagne, its that weak its practically alcohol-free. But we drink it anyway, it would be a shame to waste it.

After a few more dances, my feet are killing - damn Kerry's beautiful peach shoes, so I tell the girls I am going to the bar for a break and I will get the next round.

I stand at the bar people watching, but I seem to get approached by every single weirdo bloke in the pub. I am in no mood to make small conversation and I almost swat them off like flies. Don't get me wrong, it's not like I was surrounded by them, and bear in mind, the ones that did approach me were really drunk.

This one particularly guy just wouldn't leave me alone. I was polite at first, making small talk, but he wouldn't take the hint and leave me. I was getting abit freaked out by now and as I tried to leave to go back to my friends he blocked me between his arms and the bar. I was starting to panic a little.

'Excuse me' came a male voice from no-where. 'But I think you are annoying my wife and I would like you to leave'

I look over to who was talking and was so relieved to find it was Sam.

The bloke apologised to both of us and made a swift exit.

'Thank you Sam. You are a life-saver. He was really starting to creep me out' I say, heading over to where Sam is standing.

'You're more than welcome Emily. Now I have a question to ask' he says, moving closer to me 'Would you like to go out on a date with me?'

I laugh, smile and immediately respond 'I have a list'

CHAPTER FIFTY FOUR

A few months later we are celebrating my mums 70th birthday at the Elliott. I have the night off but have been busy all day organising the event to ensure the night is seamless.

All my friends are here, with their respective parents and kids. Rachel has her handful with 3 kids who have started to crawl, but somehow manages to always has a glass in her hand (credit to her).

Sam comes over and wraps his arms around me. I am so happy I could burst. Anna dances over to us and demands Sam takes her for a dance. He is so good with Anna and she adores him.

Greg has brought Simon along and they seem so in love. I wouldn't be surprised if an engagement is on the cards.

Evan is part way through his sabbattical. Sam, Anna and I have booked a week away in France where we are planning on meeting Evan whilst we are there. I cannot wait. I just know Sam will get on great with Evan.

Cha cha slides comes on and I join my mum, Nat, Becka, Rachel and Kerry. I could pinch myself, I really could. I am so grateful of my life.

Confidential